SPEAK NOW

or forever hold your peace

BECKY MONSON

This is a work of fiction. Names, characters, places, and incidents either are the product of the author's imagination or are used fictitiously, and any resemblance to actual persons, living or dead, business establishments, events, or locales is entirely coincidental.

To my mom and dad.
Thank you for teaching me to believe in myself and
that there really weren't monsters under my bed.

I love you both.

PRELUDE

Am I really going to do this? Breathe, Bridgette, just breathe. The butterflies in my stomach are making me antsy. I fidget in my seat, and the person to my left gives me a look that says, "Please stop."

I rest my hands in my lap and try to keep calm and still my shaking legs, but it's difficult. *Get to the part already.*

And then the preacher says it.

"If anyone knows of any reason why these two should not be married, speak now or forever hold your peace."

I have to do this now. Right now. If I don't, I will regret it for the rest of my life, and I'll never know what might have been.

"I object!" I say, standing up from my seat in the back of the room.

Suddenly, two hundred heads turn toward me.

CHAPTER 1

Tonight's the night.

Tonight Adam and I will finally get engaged. We've been together for two years, and it's finally happening.

Adam Dubois. I am going to be Mrs. Adam Dubois. Bridgette Dubois. It has a ring to it, doesn't it? And Dubois is French for . . . er . . . something. I should look that up, since it's going to be my last name and all.

I take a deep breath as I look myself over in the mirror. I left my dark blonde highlighted hair down and slightly curled, as Adam likes it. Just enough eye makeup to highlight my gray-blue eyes (he doesn't like a lot of makeup on me) and I'm wearing Adam's favorite color, red. It's a low-cut knee-length dress that hugs my curves perfectly. Just the cut of dress Adam likes.

I scored some fabulous nude patent leather Louboutin stilettos in a steal of a deal to go with it, and I wore them around Gram's apartment all evening yesterday to break them in. I don't want to get blisters on one of the most important nights of my life.

He's been telling me all week that he wants to have a special dinner with me, to discuss something important. Little, subtle hints here and there. He's invited me over to his place and said he will order in from our favorite Italian restaurant, the one with the amazing lasagna—the place where we had our first date. It truly is perfect.

I top off my look with MAC's Russian Red. It's my favorite lip color and compliments the look well.

"Well, I'm off, Grams," I say as I walk out of my room, stopping by the front door to grab my favorite Coach hobo bag and heavy coat. It's guaranteed to be a cold night, since we are smack-dab in the middle of February. Good thing there's a subway entrance right next to Gram's apartment, so I won't have to spend too much time in the cold. Then, it's only a two-block walk from the subway to Adam's apartment.

"Have a wonderful night, my dear," Gram says from her favorite chair, where she's reading a book. She puts her Kindle down in her lap and looks me over. "Well, don't you just look stunning," she beams at me.

I do a little turn for her, and she claps her hands, saying, "lovely, just lovely," as I spin around.

"Okay, I better go. Wish me luck." I put my coat on and grab a thick scarf, draping it around my neck.

"Go get 'em," Gram cheers me on. "I can't wait to hear all the details. Will I be seeing you tonight?" She tilts her head to the side inquisitively.

"Don't wait up," I wink at her and open the door. She gives me a little snort and shoos me off with her hand.

I take the elevator downstairs, walk the corridor to the front door, say a quick hello to the doorman as he opens the door for me, and step out into the frigid night air.

Down in the subway, I wait for the F Train which will take me from Carroll Gardens to the Lower East Side, where Adam lives. I wonder if we'll live in his current place once we're married. It would be fun for a little while, but the Lower East Side of Manhattan has a more single-lifestyle feel to it and might not be the best place to raise a family. Not that I want to rush into that. But I do think about it. I'm secretly hoping we get out of the city altogether. But if we had to stay—I know Adam loves it here—I guess we could end up in Tribeca or maybe Park Slope.

I know the subway ride is only fifteen minutes, but tonight it feels like hours. I just want to get to Adam's place. My feet feel jittery. I keep shifting in my seat.

When I finally walk up the stairs from the subway and start the two-block walk to Adam's place, the butterflies start. In fact, they are multiplying rapidly. I kind of feel like giggling, which is so not like me, and I try my best to stifle it. I'm pretty sure there's a big, goofy smile on my face at this moment. Anyone watching probably thinks I'm high.

I reach Adam's building and dial his apartment number from the call box outside.

"It's me," I say brightly as he answers. I hear the door unclick, and I open it and leave the icy night air for the warmth of Adam's building.

In the elevator on the way to the fifteenth floor, I'm doing the fidgety thing again. I'm starting to annoy myself.

I wonder what kind of ring he picked out. I hope it's the princess cut in platinum I hinted about. Whatever it is, I'm sure I'll love it. I'll wear it for years and maybe one day pass it down to our daughter to use as her wedding ring. It'll become a Dubois family heirloom.

Okay, I'm getting a little ahead of myself. But I get to be a part of the Dubois family, and that is most definitely a benefit. I love his family as if they were my own, and I know they feel the same. I will have the best in-laws ever.

I'm excited to start a life with Adam. I honestly never thought I would find love again. Not after college. Not after the man who I thought was the love of my life walked away from me. It's still hard to believe that was four years ago. It seems like a lifetime ago.

But I did find love again, with Adam. He's really been an amazing boyfriend. It's almost been two years ago exactly since we met at the deli near Gram's apartment. I just happened to stop by that day, to surprise Gram with her favorite sandwich, and there he was. It was love at first sight. Okay, it was more like lust at first sight. But there definitely was an instant attraction. He later told me he felt the same when he saw me. He struck up a conversation, asked for my number, and two nights later we had our first date at what became our favorite Italian restaurant on the Lower East Side. It's been pretty much bliss ever since.

I knock on the door to Adam's apartment, and I hear his footsteps as he saunters toward it. I had pictured him waiting for me by the door (with a red rose, no less), since he knew I was coming up. I think I need to reel it in. My brain is on romantic overdrive.

"Hi, sweetie," he says as soon as he opens the door. He reaches for me and pulls me into a tight hug. Pulling back, he leans down and gives me a quick kiss on the lips.

"Oh crap," I say as we both start to reach for his mouth. Adam hates it when he gets my lipstick on his lips. He says it never comes off. I try to wipe it off with my thumb but have no luck.

Well, that doesn't get us off to the right start. Fortunately, he doesn't seem as put out by it as he usually is. Thank goodness. He grabs a balled-up tissue from his pocket and wipes off the offending Russian Red.

I look him over. He's barefoot, wearing jeans and a ratty, old sweater. I've tried so many times to get rid of that thing, but he always seems to find it in my "discard" pile and puts it back in his "keep" pile when we're cleaning out his closet. I'm somewhat taken aback by his outfit. I mean, I had figured he'd be wearing something nicer. I'm feeling ridiculously overdressed now.

I guess it doesn't matter. What matters is this night and what's about to happen—not what he's wearing or the fact that his thick, brown hair is a little tousled, not that, from the looks of it, he probably hasn't shaved in about three days. Seriously?

I guess I won't actually remember what he was wearing when I look back at this night. And if I do, it will end up being one of those funny stories you tell your kids.

He takes off my jacket and looks me up and down. "Wow, Bridge, you look fantastic." He kisses me on the cheek, purposefully avoiding my lips this time.

"Well, you said you wanted to talk to me about something important, and so I thought I would get a little dolled up, just for fun." I'm feeling a little ludicrous. Why couldn't I go with a simpler look?

He looks down at his outfit and shrugs apologetically. "Sorry, I threw something on when I got home from work. It's been a long day."

"Poor boy," I rub his cheek lightly with the palm of my hand. He pulls my hand away from his face— dang, I forgot he hates it when I touch his face. I'm zero for two tonight. Did I completely forget our last two years together?

"How's business?" I say, trying to get some conversation going to cover up the fact that I've lost my mind and am dressed up like we're going to the prom.

"Fine." He shakes his head. "Just hard after losing Joey and Chuck."

"I bet," I say and grab his hand to comfort him. "You've had to do practically everything yourself."

He scoffs at that. "Yeah, at least I have my brother." We both laugh. Frank Junior is not much help with anything.

The export/import business Adam helps manage has been more than lucrative for his family. Fortunately, sporting goods and equipment don't seem to take a downfall when the economy plummets. I guess people don't give up their hobbies when things take a downturn.

Holding my hand in his, Adam guides me to the couch, and we take a seat. I angle my body toward him so I can see his face. I truly do love that face. Those high-arch brows and deep-set brown eyes. Adam is handsome—not model handsome—but handsome as in boy-next-door.

"You hungry?" he asks evenly, clearly not as unnerved as I am at this moment. How does he stay so calm all the time?

Just thinking about it makes all desire to eat go away. Even so, I nod my head yes, and we get up and move over to the table.

I had, of course, envisioned a table set with place settings and candles, but Adam throws down a couple of paper plates and some random nonmatching utensils. He then pulls out a brown paper bag from the oven (where he had apparently been keeping it warm) with Gaia Italian Café printed on the side of the bag.

"Bon appetit," he says as he sets the bag down on the table between us.

I really need to work on not being such a girl. Who cares about that stuff, anyway? And come to think of it, I don't think Adam even owns a candle. It truly doesn't matter that my engagement dinner is on paper plates, and my future husband is wearing a scruffy, old sweater (gosh, I hate that thing). It's all good.

We serve up our dinner, which consists of lasagna, salad, and garlic rolls. The exact meal we had on our very first date. This is, of course, the same meal we request anytime we order from Gaia. But it's still romantic and thoughtful of him.

"So, you wanted to talk to me about something important?" I say, pushing my salad around the plate. I'm still finding it hard, with all of the butterflies, to find room to eat. Adam, on the other hand, is scarfing down his food like a ravenous homeless man.

"Yes, yes," he says, wiping his mouth with his napkin.

He places the napkin next to his plate and reaches for my hand across the table. "Bridge, we have been together for two years, and these have been some of the best years of my life. You are an amazing person with the most wonderful qualities." He looks me directly in the eyes.

Okay, now we're talking.

"But," he looks down at his plate.

Wait . . . did he say "but?"

He looks up at me, staring into my eyes. "But, I just don't see a future for us."

"What?" I take my hand away from his and grab the sides of my chair firmly with both hands to steady myself. Did I hear him right?

"Bridge, don't be angry." He tries to soothe me, seeing the reaction on my face. "I've been thinking about this for a while now, and I just don't think we are . . . meant to be." He gives me a repentant look.

I sit there, holding myself steady on my chair, not moving. Not even blinking an eye. I think I might be in shock. Or maybe I'm having a nightmare. I close my eyes, willing myself to wake up. But I'm not asleep, and this is not a nightmare.

Adam is breaking up with me.

"I . . . I . . ." I don't even know what to say. "Why?" is all I can sputter out. My bottom lip begins to quiver, tears welling in my eyes.

"Bridge, don't cry. Please? I hate it when you cry." He reaches for my hand again, but I don't extend it to him.

"Then don't make me cry," I offer, hoping against hope he might realize he's making a mistake. Because he's making a huge one.

"I'm truly sorry. I wanted this to work. Believe me, I did. But it's just not in the cards for us."

"Not in the cards for us?" My voice rises, alarming Adam. This was definitely not the night I

9

had planned out in my head. Complete opposite, more like it. I hate my girly overly romantic brain so much right now.

Were there signs? How did I not see this coming?

I grab the napkin in my lap and ball it up, blotting my eyes as the tears begin to come quickly. "But . . . I thought we were going to get engaged tonight," I say through what has become something like sobbing.

He curses. "Bridge, I'm so sorry," he says with sincerity, running a hand through his hair, tousling it. "I thought you felt the same."

Is he kidding? "No. No, I didn't feel the same," I say, pounding the table with my fist, my voice rising. "Call me crazy, Adam. But I thought we had a future. I actually thought," I close my eyes and swallow, "I thought we were going to settle down and have a family." I open my eyes, feeling the anger stirring in my stomach. "If at any point in this relationship I wasn't feeling it, I would have ended it. But I've given you two years! Two years I can never get back."

There's a string of expletives going through my brain at this moment. But I hold myself back from rattling them off. Instead, I put my face in my hands and blubber as I realize what I've just said.

Two years, down the tube. Two whole years.

"Bridge . . ." I hear Adam's chair squeak as he pushes back from the table and the shuffle of his footsteps as he comes around to my side. He puts his arms around me from the back and holds me. I keep my face in my hands as I continue to blubber.

"Bridge, I will always care about you. You have to know that. And I hope we can still be friends, because—"

"What?" I interrupt, looking up at him with what I'm sure are mascara-stained, crazy eyes. "Did you say *friends*? Did you actually say that?" I push his arms off of me.

"Yes, I want you to be in my life. Of course I do, Bridge."

I stand up and turn my body around to look at him. "I have friends, Adam. I don't need any more *friends*." I practically spit out the word.

I look at him, his stupid deep-set eyes and his annoying thick, brown hair, and I decide right then and there that I'm much too proud to beg. So I stand up defiantly (albeit, totally acting), and without a word, I walk to the door, grabbing my coat, scarf, and bag. I swing the door open with full force and walk out.

"Bridge," I hear him call from his door, but I don't turn back. "Come back. Can't we talk about this?"

But there is nothing to talk about. So I don't say anything. I just keep walking.

~*~

I'm sure I look like a zombie on the subway with mascara running down my face. I don't have any

11

tissues, so I use my scarf to wipe my black tears. An old bum two seats down offers me his used handkerchief, which I politely decline and try not to gag visibly.

I'm not exactly sure how I ended up back at Gram's place. I was on autopilot, blinded with feelings of despair and foolishness. How could I be so clueless? I need time to think. I need to reach back into my brain and do some analyzing. But right now I only have the capacity to feel sad and disappointed. I'll do my overanalyzing later.

"Oh honey, what happened?" Gram says to me as I walk into the apartment.

"I . . . I . . . Adam . . . he broke up with me." Really, it is more like "meeeeeeeeeeeeeee" because I start blubbering again when I get to that point.

Through hiccups and snot and tears, I explain the whole crappy, sordid night to Gram as we sit on the couch. My coat is still on, my snot-filled scarf still around my neck. She rubs my arm and offers a sigh or a "hmph" or a "tsk" when it's appropriate.

"Oh, Bridgette, I'm so very sorry," Gram says, her eyes round with empathy. "You know, if he doesn't see all that you are, then he doesn't deserve you."

I let out a big breath and give her a look of defeat. She's going to pull out the sympathetic looks and words of comfort already? I really don't want to go there yet.

"Thanks, Grams. I know you mean well, but I'm not ready to hear how 'it's his loss,' or 'I could do better,' or 'you'll find someone better,'" I say and look down at my hands, twiddling the ends of my scarf.

"Well, all those things are true." She pats my shoulder. "But I'll hold off on all that until you're ready. How about a cup of hot chocolate to warm you up? I'll put marshmallows in it, just the way you like."

I actually stopped liking marshmallows in my hot chocolate when I was twelve, but I haven't had the heart to tell her. "I'll pass tonight, Gram. I think I'm going to go cry myself to sleep."

"Yes, yes. Cry it all out. I will be here if you need to talk," she says, sympathetically. It occurs to me that Gram has most likely been through breakups in her time. I seem to imagine the only person she ever dated was Pops, but I can tell by the look on her face she knows exactly what I'm going through.

I go into my room and shut the door. I take off my coat and dress, put on a tee shirt and sweats, and crawl into bed without brushing my teeth or washing my face.

I cry until I fall asleep.

CHAPTER 2

THREE MONTHS LATER

"Bridgette, this is an intervention," Ashley says to me in a very serious tone as we sit in our favorite café.

"Huh?" I look up from reading the most recent text from Adam on my phone to see her and Justin staring at me. "What are you going on about?"

"Justin and I have been talking, and I—er, we—think your relationship with Adam's family is unhealthy," she says, sitting across from me, cradling a paper cup full of steaming coffee in her hands.

"Oh geez, you guys," I say, giving them a look of complete annoyance. This is not the first time we've had this discussion. It's never gotten to an intervention level, though.

"Bridge, it's not normal," Ashley says, tossing her long, red hair off her shoulder.

"I don't know how I can keep explaining it to you. Just because Adam and I broke up, doesn't mean I had to break up with his family." I look from her to Justin. They're giving each other conspiratorial looks, and Justin nods his head, nudging Ashley to continue.

14

"I, well, Justin and I," she looks at Justin and then back to me, "We think that you spending so much time with Adam's family is a bit . . . well . . . stalker-ish." She says the last part quietly as if someone were listening to our conversation.

"I am not a stalker!" I say, slamming my phone down on the table, not caring who hears me. "And frankly, I find it offensive you guys would say that. I'm not stalking Adam."

Justin and Ashley look at each other, skepticism in their eyes. I'm trying to ooze disgust and outrage at their stalker comment, but the truth is, they are not far off. They know me well, my two best friends.

I haven't been stalking him, per se. Have I spent time with Adam's family because I want to be present in their lives so I'm vicariously present in Adam's? I suppose that's part of the reason. I'm not using them. I really do love his family, and they love me—in fact, I think his mom was more devastated than I was about the breakup. Okay, she couldn't have possibly been more devastated than I was, but she was very upset about it. She told me she was going to disown Adam. That hasn't happened yet, but I didn't honestly expect it to.

"Okay fine. What about Adam? When's the last time you talked to him?" Ashley asks, sitting up straight in her seat. Oh no, she's got the "lecture" look on. Here we go.

"He texted me this morning, actually." I click on the text and hold my phone up for them to see. They don't bother looking.

It wasn't like it was some poignant text. Just a simple, "How are you?" which I interpreted as, "How are you? I've been thinking about you. I miss you. Let's get back together." Although not said, those things were obviously implied.

"When's the last time you saw him?" She folds her arms, sitting back in her seat, taking on the look of a therapist. I'm anticipating an "and how do you feel about that?" at any moment.

"I don't know." I look around the room, thinking about the last time I saw him. Like, physically saw him. It's been a while. With work picking up and my taking all the shifts I can get, I guess I hadn't realized. Plus, we've talked on the phone and texted since then. Well, maybe we haven't talked on the phone as much as just texted.

"I think we met up for coffee a few weeks ago." I look back at Justin and Ashley, suddenly recalling that last, somewhat stilted, coffee date. I could tell his mind was elsewhere.

"Bridgette, can we be honest with you?" Her position now shifts to leaning forward on the table, on her elbows, her hands clasped together. This is getting super serious.

I don't say anything because she is going to be "honest" whether I like it or not.

"It's been three months, Bridge. We think you should move on," she says.

"Yes, you should move on. Like perhaps to someone who, while not as muscular and well-built as Adam, has a certain boyish charm and a stunning smile," Justin pipes in, showing off said stunning smile and winking at me.

Ashley whacks his arm with the back of her hand.

"What? You jealous?" Justin does a double eyebrow lift in Ashley's direction.

"Uh, hell no," Ashley says, her lips faintly curled into a smile.

I roll my eyes at the both of them.

"Well, what if I don't want to move on? What if I still hope something might happen?" I fold my arms and sit back in my chair, my pouting face on.

"Bridge, if it hasn't happened by now, it's not going to happen. Sorry to say," Ashley says, giving me a concerned look. "Didn't you read the book I loaned you?"

"You mean *He's Just Not That Into You*?" I scoff. "I read it. It's a bunch of bull."

"No, it's not. It's good advice." Her mouth drops open in awe of my blatant disregard for her "dating bible" as she has referred to it.

"Well, maybe I'm the exception to the rules." I shrug, hoping it's the truth.

"Exception?" She scrunches her face. It's not a pretty look on her. "That was from the movie! Did you even read it?" She stares me down intently, looking for an answer.

"Well, I skimmed it a little but then figured the movie would be more entertaining." I shrug and smile sheepishly.

"You're ridiculous, Bridgette." She gets up from the table, plodding angrily over to the counter to top off her coffee.

I sigh. "Justin, you don't honestly think I'm a stalker, do you? I mean, Ashley dragged you into this, didn't she?" I plead with him using my eyes, hoping he's on my side.

"Well . . ." he trails off, answering my question without any other words.

Ashley returns, plopping down in her seat. She opens her mouth to start her lecture again but stops herself.

"You know what?" she says, tilting her head slightly to the side, "I'm going to stop bothering you about this. You can make your own mistakes."

"Well, thank you ever-so-much for your vote of confidence," I say sardonically.

"I have confidence in you," Justin says, feigning seriousness.

"Oh shut up, Justin." Ashley slaps him on the arm again.

"For what it's worth, I do appreciate how much you both care about me," I say, reaching across the table, grabbing them each by a hand.

"Crap, what time is it?" I say, letting go of their hands as soon as I grab them so I can look at my phone. "Oh man, I'm gonna be late." I get up and grab my jacket from the back of my chair, putting it on quickly.

"It's only eleven thirty, where're you going?" Ashley asks, looking up at me strangely.

"Um . . ." I trail off, looking out the window so they can't see my eyes. "I'm, um, sort of having lunch with Carla," I say, the name barely audible to the human ear. Carla may or may not be Adam's Mom. More *may* than *may not* . . .

"Oh hell." Ashley collapses back in her chair, defeated. "Bridgette, you really need some therapy." She puts her porcelain-skin face in her hands.

"No, I don't. I'm in complete control and know exactly what I'm doing. Talk some sense into her, would you, Justin?" I gesture over to her. "Love you guys! See you tonight," I say as I grab my purse and head out the door.

~*~

"Carla!" I say, somewhat breathlessly as I walk into the restaurant. "I'm so sorry I'm late. I wasn't paying attention to the clock." I take off my white blazer and hang it on the back of the chair, and with my hand, I swipe off the various raindrops that have gathered on the shoulders. It's a rainy May day in the city. I managed to make it to the restaurant before it started raining too hard. The cuffs of my skinny jeans didn't get too wet, but I fear my favorite red Steve Madden platforms may have suffered the most.

I take a seat across from Adam's mom, my not-future mother-in-law. Not for now.

She smiles a warm smile. "Bridgette, my dear, wonderful to see you," she says in her thick New York accent.

"I love what you've done with your hair," I exclaim, noticing her new hairstyle.

"Do you?" She runs one hand through her salt-and-pepper hair that's been shaped into a lovely chin-length bob. Her other hand is holding a rather large glass of red wine.

"I do. I love it. You look ten years younger."

"Oh stop," she shoos a diamond-encrusted hand at me. "You know, I wanted to do something different for a while now, but Frank didn't want me to. So I finally says to him, I says 'Frank, I'll do what I want, it's my own damn hair.' But I have to tell you, Frank really liked the cut. A lot." She gives me an insinuating wink.

Gross.

"But enough about me and my hair. How have you been, my darling Bridgette? I love your jacket. You know I had a jacket like that once. I think I had it in the 70s. It's so funny how styles come back, isn't it? I swear, this one time . . ."

I tune out a tad. Carla can talk your ear off if you let her. Her mood can also turn on a dime. She's a bit of an "Italian hot head," as Adam's dad refers to her. In truth, her candor and lack of filter were a bit off-putting when I first met her, but soon became endearing to me. We bonded quickly, and she's like family to me now. Especially since my own parents moved from Goshen to Charlotte two years ago. I hate that they're no longer a train ride away.

". . .so then, he sees me, only in my undies and it was very embarrassing . . ." She keeps going.

I laugh when she laughs and add in a "you don't say" and "no way" when it's fitting to the story.

The server comes to the table, interrupting Carla, and we place our order. As soon as the waitress leaves, she picks right back up on her story, not missing a beat.

"Oh, would you listen to me go on and on." She stops, taking a sip of wine. "Tell me what you've been up to, my dear. I haven't seen you in nearly two weeks. What's kept you away from me?"

"Well, not much, really. I've just been working . . ."

"And dating?" she interjects.

"Oh, well, you know me." I smile self-consciously, insinuating there's more to the story than what is the truth—I stay home most nights with Gram, hang out with Ashley and Justin, or I'm working. Oh yes, and I'm still holding out for her son. I nibble my bottom lip, which I always do when I'm not being completely honest.

"Ooooh, anyone in particular?" She winks at me, clearly hoping for something juicy.

"Oh no, just, you know, different . . . er . . . men," I stutter, making myself sound a bit on the whore-ish side. What a lovely thing to say to the mother of your ex. The ex you still love and want to be with.

21

Perhaps, though, if I imply I'm dating someone, maybe it will get back to Adam somehow, and he might get jealous and come find me at the Eiffel Tower and declare his undying love to me. Or maybe something a little less dramatic. Clearly, I am still letting my brain go off on crazy romantic tangents.

Well it's already out there now, it's not like I can take it back. I have to roll with it at this point.

"Tell me about all these men!" Carla says, excited and possibly living vicariously through me. She married very young, and I've often wondered if she thinks she missed out on sewing her wild oats.

"Oh, it's not that interesting. Just some guys I've met at, um, bars."

Work! I meant to say work. Bars? I don't even hang out in bars. Oh hell, I'm digging myself a hole.

"Well . . . that's nice . . ." she trails off, looking to the side as if thinking to herself that her son dodged a bullet.

He might possibly have. Apparently post-Adam, I've become a slutty bar hopper.

I need to fix this. "Well, there's this one guy that I met," I say without thinking it through, and she looks up, her eyes brightening. "His name is . . . uh . . . " Of course now I can't think of his name—any name since he's not even real. Why would I go completely blank for a guy's name? How hard is it?

"Justin," I finally say and smile awkwardly. "Justin is his name."

"Justin? Well, I'm going to have to meet this Justin of yours. You know I once dated a guy named Justin . . . or was it James? I can't remember. I know it started with a J. Anyway, this one time we were out on a date . . ."

Well, at least the conversation has gone back to her. And at least Justin is a real, tangible person. And we do work together, so that was true. He took me on a date once. Well, it wasn't so much a date as a way to try to cheer me up after Adam and I broke up. And it truly didn't cheer me up, since Justin is about the least sympathetic person out there. But he paid, so I'm going to call it a date. See? I've been on one date since things ended with Adam.

". . . and her name is Serendipity. Who in the hell would name their kid that? She goes by Serene, which is worlds better. I don't know what he sees in her, with that ridiculously long dark hair and her huge dark eyes. If you ask me, she sort of looks like a witch! But I told him she ain't got nothing on you . . ."

Wait—what did I miss? Who is she talking about? My heart starts pounding loudly in my chest.

"I'm sorry, Carla," I interrupt her, "I think I missed something." I shake my head. This is awkward. How do I find out what she was talking about without letting on that my mind had wandered, and I missed what she was saying?

"Were you saying Frank Junior is dating someone?"

23

"Oh please." She bats a hand at me. "I don't know if we'll ever find a girl for F.J. I've given up hope on him, what with all the clubbing and fooling around he does. I told him the other day, I says, 'Frank Alan Dubois Junior, when are you gonna give me grandchildren?' and you wanna know what he said? 'I probably already have, Ma.' He thinks he's so funny—"

"So Adam's, um, dating someone?" I cut her off, trying with all my might not to sound like the girl who is freaking out inside my head. It's a difficult plight.

"Oh Bridgette, darling, I'm so sorry to tell you this, but yes. Her name is Serene. They've been dating for nearly three weeks now." She looks at me, obviously concerned about how I'm taking this.

Shocking news: I'm not taking this well. But I must do my best not to freak out in front of her. If that got back to Adam . . . well, I don't want it to for many reasons, mainly my pride.

"No . . . uh . . . that's great!" I paste on a fake bright smile, pushing back the tears that are ready to spill out of my eyes at any given second.

"It is?" She looks taken aback by my reaction.

"Sure! I'm glad he's moved on." I pause, swallowing the lie deeply. "I hope he's happy. I really do."

"Hmm. Well, Bridgette, I'm not going to lie. I wasn't sure how you would take it. Heaven knows, I didn't take it well. Told him he was a complete moron. Serendipity. What the hell kind of name is that?" She closes her eyes briefly, shaking her head in disgust. "But I have to say, I'm quite surprised." She gives me an approving grin.

"We've been broken up for three months." Three months and four days, to be precise. "Of course he'd move on. I've moved on," says the big-fat-practically-crying liar.

"Well, I'd always hoped things would work out with the two of you." She gives me a thin, sad smile.

You and me both, lady.

The server brings us our food. I'm not feeling so hungry at this moment.

"You know, you should meet her," Carla sputters out after the server leaves, her eyes widening as the thought dawns on her. "Why don't you come over for dinner and bring that guy you're dating—Justin was his name?"

"Sure," I say brightly, but add internally, *First, let me get a root canal. That sounds like more fun.*

"Then it's all settled." She pulls out her planner and starts flipping through it until she gets to the calendar. "How about next Friday?"

"I . . . er . . ." I forgot Carla is a planner. If you say you're going to do something, she takes it seriously. How could she even think I'd want to meet evil-witch-man-stealer-whatever-her-name-is? Oh, that's right, because I told her I was "happy" Adam's moved on and that I was dating Justin. What have I done?

"Oh, come on." She bats her hand at me. "It'll be fun! Do you think that Justin of yours can make it?"

"Well . . . I would have to ask him . . ."

"Great! Text him right now and see." She looks at me, and then with her eyes, gestures down at the phone sitting to my left.

Text him? Right now? Oh the tangled webs I have woven . . .

I pick up my phone, looking at it. What do I do? I look up at her and see her nod her head in approval. I let out a nervous laugh. I think the best thing to do would be to simply send out a fake text. So I type in a random number and start texting.

Justin, do you want to do dinner next Friday with my ex-boyfriend's family?

I press send and set the phone down. "There, it's all done. I'll let you know what he says when he texts back." He will say no, obviously, and I will come up with a reason to not go either. It'll all be fine.

My phone beeps. Random number has texted me back. Oh holy hell . . .

"Don't ya wanna see what he says?" Carla looks at me inquisitively, since I haven't picked up my phone.

"Um, I'll check it in a minute. I'm hungry! I think I'll eat my salad —"

"Oh, just give it to me." She reaches across the table, and before I'm able to stop her, she has the phone in her hand.

26

"Let's see what he had to say!" With lightning speed, she grabs her glasses out of her purse and puts them on so she can read the text.

"'Who the hell is this, and how did you get my number?'" she reads, furrowing her brow, confused.

The phone beeps again. She looks up at me and then down at the phone.

"'There ain't no Justin here, you mother—' Well, I'm not going to read that!" She holds the phone away from her face, repulsed. "Huh, that's strange. Did you get the wrong number?" She looks at me curiously.

"I guess I did." I shrug my shoulders. I start shoveling salad into my mouth like I haven't eaten in days. I'm still not hungry; I'm basically eating my stress.

"Well, I'll fix that," she says as she taps her finger on my phone screen.

I try to tell her no, but my mouth is full of salad.

It's silent while she works my phone. "There's his name right there! I'll just send him a message," she says, fingers tapping away. "Justin, dinner with Adam's family next Friday?" She dictates as she writes.

"There. It's all done." She smiles at me. I sheepishly smile back, ninety-nine percent sure there's spinach in my teeth. But I don't care.

Oh how I wish I could start this lunch over. Start it over and say these words: "I'm not dating anyone right now." Why did I have to open my big mouth? This is why your parents teach you not to lie.

Because someday you may be having lunch with your ex-boyfriend's mother, and you will stick your foot in your mouth so ridiculously far that it will actually come out your rear.

My phone beeps. Oh. Dear. Heaven.

Carla clicks on the screen. "'Are you ... high?'" she reads the text slowly.

"Oh, that silly Justin," I say, as I reach across the table and snatch my phone out of her hand. "That's a little game we like to play. He asks if I'm high, and I say 'high for you.' You know, romantic dating stuff like that." I laugh nervously, cheeks blazing from the ridiculousness of that last statement.

I quickly text Justin.

Just shut up and I'll explain later

I put my phone on silent and slide it into the pocket of my coat.

"It's all settled then?" Carla looks at me, inquisitively.

"What's all settled?" I say, trying desperately to recover from the absurdity of the last five minutes of my life.

"Dinner at my house, next Friday?" She looks at me, concerned that I've already forgotten.

"Dinner, right, you know I don't think —"

"Oh, come on now, Bridgette. You know I won't take no for an answer." Carla cuts me off before I can tell her what a bad idea the whole thing is.

"Well, let me talk to Justin in person, and I'll let you know, okay?" Maybe this answer will suffice for now, and then I can text later and tell her no. "Okay, well let me know soon. It'll be fun. You'll meet Serene the witch." She sighs dramatically. "And we can all meet Justin. I thought this breakup between you and Adam would ruin what we have. You are like a daughter to me, you know. I always wanted a daughter. I sometimes wish F.J. had been a girl. Maybe he wouldn't have been such a disappointment. But you know these things . . ."

She keeps talking, and I go back to my nodding and courtesy commenting. I did feel a twinge of guilt when she said she thinks of me as a daughter. She's like family to me, after all. I don't want to disappoint her, but I don't think I could handle dinner with Adam and this new, stupid woman in his life.

Of course, on second thought, maybe if I prance around with Justin and show Adam how happy I am—maybe he'll realize what he's lost. And since Justin is an actual, tangible person, and not some made-up guy, I might pull it off. Plus, I do want to see this Serendipity girl, so I can point out all her flaws and feel better about myself.

Maybe this isn't such a terrible idea after all.

CHAPTER 3

"Absolutely not," Justin says as he grabs a tray of bacon-wrapped scallops.

"Justin, please. I swear I'll do anything you want. Anything!" I beg him, as I grab a tray of crab-salad canapés. You would think he would take pity on me after seeing my blood-shot eyes and red-blotched face. I waited until after lunch, after I hugged Carla good-bye, to ball my eyes out. I was barely able to contain myself enough to come to work. I'm still hiccupping every now and then.

"I will not go to some dinner party with you just so you can parade me around and try to make Adam jealous." He gives me an appalled look.

"That's not why I want you to go!"

That's exactly why I want him to go.

"Bridgette, you're completely delusional." He looks away from me, annoyed.

"Stand down, everyone, the Sea Witch is coming!" Ashley announces as she walks into the staging area, carrying an empty tray. We all suddenly look lively. The chef starts calling out directions more rapidly, while the prep cook vigorously starts handing out prepared trays to the servers. There are eight servers on tonight, so with the chef and the prep cook, it's been a little crowded back here, to say the least.

Justin and I each quickly grab a stack of cocktail napkins and head out into the dimly lit venue where we're working tonight.

"I'm not done begging," I whisper loudly to Justin as we walk out the door. He feigns ignorance.

Justin is my only hope. I could beg someone else to do it and convince him to change his name for the evening, but I want Justin to come with me. I need support, and I will take it where I can get it. Even from Justin. Besides, it's not like he has anything to do with his extra time. We're not even sure what he does. He's with us a lot, and obviously he works, but he often has "something to do," and neither Ashley nor I have a clue what that is. We've asked, of course, but he's very vague and changes the subject. We stopped trying a while ago. It wasn't getting us anywhere, anyway. Now it's become more of a fun game for Ashley and me. We've come up with ideas (some ridiculous, some gross, some illegal), for what he might be up to. I'm not even sure we want to know the truth, at this point. It might be dull and ruin the guessing game.

Ursula stalks by us as we leave, looking slightly rageful. Ursula, whom we lovingly refer to as "The Sea Witch" (as in Ursula—the witch from *The Little Mermaid*), is our boss and the owner of the catering company we work for, Edelweiss Catering. She's tall, thick, and very German. She's mostly scary, with a dash of frightening.

I start offering people the canapés. Everyone is talking and laughing over the music in the background, drinking their alcohol and eating the hors d'oeuvres we're passing around. Tonight's party is hors d'oeuvres only, thank goodness. The full-service meals are the harder ones. More prep and more cleanup. As it stands, this black-tie event is set to end at midnight, which means we won't be done until nearly two in the morning by the time we clean and I take the subway home, that is.

I nod pleasantly as people take a canapé off my tray. We are told not to fraternize with the attendees, which is fine by me. I have no interest in finding out what's going on — unless famous people are involved — which happens sometimes. One of the perks of this job. The biggest one, actually. That, and the leftovers.

I like this job a lot, even with Ursula and all her scariness. This was the first job I got after applying for a ton after I moved in with Gram. My goal is to eventually get into event planning, and I thought catering would be a good way to get started. I didn't expect to be working here as long as I have, though. I've applied to so many places, with no response. I'm kind of hoping one day Ursula will see me as Catering Assistant material. No such luck, yet.

Unlike me, most of the people who work for Ursula are only working here to keep money coming in while they land their dream jobs. So most of them are actors. Or wannabe actors. That's why Ashley is working here and also how we met. It's how we found Justin, too. Unlike most of the other servers, though, Ashley has real talent. She just hasn't found the right part yet. Justin, I'm not really sure about. We've asked; he's been very vague. I suspect he's in the not-sure-what-I-want-to-be-when-I-grow-up category, or he's too busy playing video games, or whatever he does, to make up his mind.

"How you holding up?" Ashley says, out of the side of her mouth as she sidles up next to me. Talking to each other in front of the attendees is also forbidden, so we've learned ways to be discreet.

"Meh," I say through fake-smiling teeth. I shrug my shoulders, and she gives me a sympathetic look.

We move away from each other so as not to get caught by Ursula. The last of the canapés is taken off my tray, so I head back to the staging area to get another tray full of hors d'oeuvres.

"Bridgette?" I hear a male voice say my name as I near the staging door. An extremely familiar voice.

I turn around. "Yes?" I ask, searching through the crowd for the person who's calling my name. Thinking it couldn't possibly be him. Not after all this time.

"Bridgette Reynolds?" The voice gets closer. A face comes into focus. My blood starts pumping through my veins at a ridiculous pace.

"Ian?" I say, my eyes bugging out of my head and my stomach twisting into knots instantly. "Ian Davies?" It can't possibly be him. But, on closer inspection, it is him.

I swallow hard to push back tears that are already on the surface because of Adam. But seeing

Ian after all this time pushes those tears to the very edge.

"Bridgette? Oh wow." He wraps his arms around me, lifting me up and spinning me long enough for me to gather my tears and force them back.

"What are you doing here?" he asks, as he puts me down, gesturing to the catering uniform I'm wearing, which, thank goodness, is a black skirt and a white dress shirt, paired with lovely black no-slip shoes. And by lovely, I mean they are hideous. I can handle this ensemble, though. There are other, much-less-attractive uniforms I've had to wear.

"I work for the catering company. What are you doing here?" I gesture to his black suit, white shirt, and black tie. Armani, no doubt.

"I work for the brokerage." He nods his head toward the party going on behind him. "I can't believe I'm seeing you. Here, in New York. What're you doing here? Do you live in the city?" Ian asks.

"I moved in with Gram in Carroll Gardens," I say, shaking my head. "I can't believe it's you."

This is all incredibly hard for me to wrap my brain around. I had honestly given up hope that I would ever see or hear from Ian again. Of course, I had envisioned running into him—many, many times—but it wasn't like this. Most of the time, I was in a tight dress, wind in my hair . . . not at a party I'm working, in a not-so-flattering uniform, smelling of onion.

Four years. It's been four years since I've seen the likes of Ian Davies. Four years since he ran off with my heart to London for an internship, and I went back to live with my parents to figure out what I wanted to do with my life. Four years since things ended so badly.

I hear a throat clear behind me, and my eyebrows shoot up, my eyes wide.

I lean my head slightly in toward Ian, whispering, "There's a very large German woman standing behind me, isn't there?" I look to his face for an answer.

He nods, looking slightly stunned at the site of Ursula.

Oh no. I'm fraternizing. This is bad.

Taking a cue from my pained look of helplessness, Ian opens his mouth. "I was just telling—I'm sorry, what was your name?" He gestures toward me. My, his acting is good. I don't remember that.

"Bridgette," I squeak out, my back still turned to Ursula. I envision her looking Frankenstein-like, with steam coming out of her ears.

"Yes, thank you. I was telling Bridgette here that the food has been spectacular tonight," he says, seamlessly oozing charm and confidence.

"Vell, I zank you fery much," Ursula says, still behind me. I turn to see her nodding her head approvingly, looking slightly—what is this exactly? Nervous? And is she batting her eyes a little extra? Oh heavens, is she trying to flirt?

Ah yes. Ian's still got it. That understated charm, which woman of all ages—and apparently all sizes and nationalities—find so alluring. I know I fell for it once upon a time. It's kind of hard not to fall for it even now.

"I'll just be getting back to work." I smile at Ursula and quickly turn away from her, mouthing a "thank you" to Ian as I head back into the staging area.

I walk in and set my tray on the counter, still reeling from seeing Ian again and then having my boss catch me chatting with the guests. That is a huge no-no. She has fired for less.

"What was that all about?" Ashley asks as she comes in with an empty tray.

"Yah, who was that guy?" Justin says, coming in practically on her heels.

"Do you remember Ian? I told you about him a while ago." I turn to Ashley, because Justin will assuredly not remember.

"Do you mean Ian from college, 'the one that got away,' the one who took off for London and you've never heard from since?" Ashley counts off the facts with her fingers.

"Yes, that one." I give her an odd look. "I can't believe you remember. You have the memory of eagle."

"I believe you mean an elephant." She shakes her head at me, a tendril of red hair falls out of her tight bun, and she tucks it back in.

Ian was more than "the one that got away." At least until Adam came along.

"Whatever. Anyway, so he's out there, at this party. Do you know how long I tried to find him? And now he's here. " I still can't believe it. I truly never thought I'd see him again.

"I saw Ursula catch you fraternizing," Justin says, shaking his head in disapproval. "How did you get out of that one?

I open my mouth to respond, at the same time the door swings open and in walks Ursula. We quickly go over to the food prep table and grab trays filled with hors d'oeuvres and shuffle back into the party. This discussion will have to wait until later.

The rest of the night goes quickly and fairly smoothly, minus the near calamity Justin caused when he dropped a tray of ham and gruyere palmiers. Luckily it was in the staging area. Dropping trays in front of guests is grounds for firing according to The Sea Witch.

I catch Ian's eyes every now and then as I serve, and he always smiles at me. I still can't believe he's here. I'm dying to talk to him again, but for fear of being caught by Ursula, I restrain myself.

At the end of the night, the party goers say their good-byes with handshakes and the occasional hug or fist bump. I begin clearing plates and napkins from tall cocktail tables with the rest of the servers. I happen to look up at the main entrance to the ballroom and spy Ian there, trying to get my attention. He nods his head toward the doors, silently inviting me to meet him outside the ballroom. I make a quick scan of the room, looking for Ursula. With no visual of her, I make a beeline to the tall, ornate ballroom doors and make a quick exit.

"Hey," I hear Ian say to my right. I turn my head to see him standing there, left hand in his pants pocket, right hand hanging casually at his side. The light is much brighter out here, and the sight of him standing there brings back instant memories, and with them, old feelings. My heart speeds up. That dark, thick head of hair, those stunning green eyes . . .

"Hey," I say, smiling brightly. He smiles brightly back. Oh wow, I've missed that smile.

"I won't keep you long. I just wanted to say good-bye." He studies my face, now seeing me in the full light.

"Oh," I say, trying not to sound as disappointed as I feel. How will I ever see him again?

"And I wanted to give you this." He hands me a business card. I take it from him and look at the small black card with his name and information in tiny silver-blue print. "Sorry. It's all I've got." His hand motions toward the card. "Let's have lunch this week. Catch up."

"Yeah . . ." I trail off, looking down at the card, "I mean, yes. Definitely. Lunch would be great." I look up at him and smile brightly.

"Great. Call me early next week, and we'll figure something out." He grabs my hand and pulls me toward him into a tight hug. "It's so great to see you," he says in my ear.

"And you," I hug him tightly back, feeling a tingle go down my back with his lips so close to my ear.

After we say our good-byes, I walk back into the ballroom feeling somewhat elated, which is a feeling I haven't felt in quite some time. Three months and four days, to be exact.

"Where were you?" Justin asks, as I walk into the back. He's wiping down trays and stacking them on carts to be wheeled out to the catering truck.

"Saying good-bye to Ian." I grab a tray and follow suit.

Justin gives me a disapproving click of his tongue and mutters "fraternizer" under his breath. I ignore him.

"By the way, I've changed my mind," he says as we work side by side.

"Changed your mind about what?" I shoot him a curious look.

"I'll go with you to Adam's thing on Friday," he says without looking up at me.

"You will?" My eyes widen with skepticism. This is Justin. He only says truths about fifty percent of the time. "Why? What made you change your mind?"

"Well, I thought about it," he says, putting down the tray he's finished cleaning, "and I thought—my friend Bridgette needs me. How could I let her down in her time of need?"

"Really?" I look at him, disbelieving.

"Nah, I think it's gonna be a total train wreck, and why should I miss out on that?" He winks at me, and I give him my best dirty look in return. "Plus, I get to pretend to be your boyfriend for the night. We can ogle at each other and give each other cheesy nicknames. It'll be fun."

"And what nickname will you be giving me?" I question him hesitantly.

"I think I'll surprise you." He smiles a big mischievous grin.

"I think I'm worried."

"No worries, Snookems," he smiles, giving me a quick hip check.

"Oh geez," I roll my eyes, but giggle a little, despite not wanting to encourage him.

CHAPTER 4

University of Connecticut, freshman year

"Bridge, huh?" I looked up to find a pair of striking green eyes staring down at my chest. His hand reached out for mine.

"Uh," my eyes moved to the chest area of my charcoal-gray tee shirt, and I realized he wasn't a total perv. My nametag.

Yes, this was perfect. Obviously, the first person to help me would be a hot guy. Strike that, one of the hottest guys I'd had the pleasure to lay my eyes on. I looked down at my current situation, on the floor with both knees scraped and bloodied. This was not good.

Why had I thought this "fresh start" at college would be a chance to reinvent myself? Tripping and falling just before walking into freshman orientation was not the kickoff I was hoping for.

"So your name is . . . Bridge?" he asked, as I gave him my hand and he helped me stand up.

"Bridgette," I said, finding my balance. "I get lazy sometimes. Poor penmanship."

He was taller than me but not by a ridiculous amount. My guess would put him around six feet. Nice build. Solid, strong shoulders. He wore jeans, a white tee, and flip-flops. Very surfer meets preppy. He had dark brown hair with a bit of a cowlick in

41

the back that was both endearing and frustrating at the same time. And his eyes. Holy crap. I don't think I'd ever seen green eyes like that. His face was boyish, with a bit of scruff. I instantly wanted to rub my hand on his face, but I stopped myself. No need to add to the crazy.

I looked down to find his nametag, which wasn't there.

"Oh," he said, noticing the trail my eyes had made. He held up the rectangular figure, pulled the backing off the sticky paper, and slapped it on the left side of his chest. "Ian," he declared, pointing to the tag.

"You okay?" he asked, looking down at my legs, and my eyes followed his. Luckily, my jean shorts were not hurt by the fall, since they ended well above my knees. I feared for my favorite pair of black sandals as the blood was now dripping down, headed that way. How lovely.

"Um, I guess not," I said, opening my bag to try and find a tissue or anything to clean myself up with. It was a brand new bag for school, so I knew my search was in vain. But I said a silent prayer that something would magically appear.

"Come here," he said, pointing to a bench only a few feet from us.

He helped me walk over to the bench and, putting a hand on my lower back, helped me sit. I tugged nervously on my dark blonde side braid as he reached in his bag and pulled out a little red container.

"You carry a first aid kit? A boy scout?" I asked, eyeing him dubiously.

"Let's just say I have a mom who's a little over-the-top," Ian said, a slight grin appearing on his face.

"I guess I should be thankful for that," I said, as I watched him open the first aid kit and dig around.

He pulled out the supplies he needed and then, putting his arm underneath my knees, he lifted my legs and placed them in his lap.

"This might sting," he said, after he opened up an antiseptic wipe. He carefully started to clean one of the injured knees.

He wasn't kidding. I squirmed in my seat and took a deep breath.

"Sorry," he said, with an intonation that indicated he was, in fact, sorry, and not just saying it.

"It's okay," I whimpered as he moved to the other knee.

He was very gentle, to say the least. And with his eyes downward, working on my knees, I could stare at him without getting caught. He had a nice head of hair, nice and thick. Also, a fantastic jawline. It was a good view.

"There you go, good as new," he said, gesturing toward my newly bandaged knees.

"Thank you," I said, looking down at them. "And thank your mom as well."

He smiled at me. "I would pass on that message, except it would only feed her need to keep smothering me with this crap." He tapped the kit with his finger.

"You from around here?" he asked, leaning back in his seat.

I was well aware that my legs were still propped in his lap, and for some strange reason, I didn't want to move them. It was comfortable there. I also noticed he took no action to move them himself. Sitting with Ian like this was strangely nice. I don't think I'd ever experienced instant comfort with a stranger like that.

"I'm from Goshen," I said.

"Goshen?" he asked, as all people not from Goshen usually did.

"Small town. About an hour and a half west of here," I said. "You?" I asked, remembering my manners.

"New Haven," he said simply. No explanation there, everyone knew where New Haven was.

"So, what brings you to UConn?" he asked.

"Uh, school?" I scrunched my eyes at him. "Isn't that why everyone comes here?"

"Yes, obviously." He oozed sarcasm. "I meant, what are you studying?"

"Studying . . ." I said slowly, realizing something was missing.

"My classes!" I quickly removed my legs from his lap and started looking around frantically, trying to find the single piece of paper that had my schedule on it.

"You mean this?" Ian held up the wrinkled paper. I think it might have taken the brunt of my fall. Well, along with my knees.

"Oh, thank goodness." My eyes closed for more seconds than the normal blink. I breathed a sigh of relief. I reached out my hand to grab my blessed schedule, but Ian quickly swiped it away.

"Let's see what we've got here," he said, studying the paper.

"Give it back," I said, trying to grab it from him, but he kept moving the paper away every time I came close to reaching it. He was being almost as annoying as my sister. But being a pest was her job.

He finally relinquished my schedule after a few moments.

"So tell me, Bridge from Goshen, what do you want to be when you grow up?"

"I can't really say," I told him, after agonizing for a few seconds about how to answer that. "I'm still trying to figure it out."

"Well, don't go into dance," he said, pointing to my knees. I could feel heat instantly on my face.

"Yes, thanks for that," I said and rolled my eyes.

"So, what do you want to be when you grow up?" I asked him, now curious.

"Rich," he said simply. "Not exactly sure how I'll get there, but that would be the end result."

I nodded my head. This would likely be the answer from about ninety percent of the student body. The rest would probably be of the save-the-world variety.

"I have a proposition for you," Ian said, mischief in his eyes.

Oh no. Whatever he had to say, I prayed it wouldn't ruin what I've thought of him so far.

"A proposition?" I asked, eyeing him with suspicion.

"Not that kind of proposition." He scowled after reading my face.

I stifled a laugh. The look on his face was too funny.

"Okay, what do you propose?" I asked, folding my arms and sitting back.

"Do you know anyone on campus?" he asked, scratching his jaw while he talked. It was sexy.

"No, you?" I asked, when my brain finally registered that he had asked me a question. I was lost for a moment. That jaw. Damn.

"No one," he stated. "So, Bridge from Goshen, I say we should be friends," he said, tapping me on the knee with one quick touch. It left a non-visible imprint.

I scoffed at him. "You can't just say 'let's be friends,' I hardly know you. It doesn't work like that." I won't lie, the word "friends" did make my stomach sink in a stupid girlish way.

"Doesn't it?" Ian asked, a single eyebrow raised in my direction.

"No, it doesn't," I said.

"Well, I think it does. And I think you and I should be friends."

I eyed him suspiciously. He looked innocent enough, but what if he was a wolf in sheep's clothing? Gram had warned me about those kinds of people.

"I promise I don't bite," Ian said, as if reading my mind. He held up his hands in surrender.

"Okay," I finally said. Even if he eventually turned out to be a creeper or a weirdo, it would be nice to have a friend for now. I was feeling slightly homesick, and I had only been here for less than twenty-four hours.

He rubbed his hands together, like we'd just made a deal of sorts.

"But," I said, holding a pointer finger up, "our friendship is on a trial basis for now."

"A trial basis?" He furrowed his brow.

"Yes, a trial basis. Let's give it two weeks and reassess," I said, the corner of my mouth turning up slightly.

"Sounds like a good business deal," he said, reaching out to shake my hand.

"Yes," I said, shaking his. I liked how his hand felt in mine, and apparently my heart did too, as it was pounding furiously in my chest.

"Friends," he said, still shaking my hand.

"Friends," I echoed.

CHAPTER 5

The sound of my phone vibrating against the nightstand next to my bed wakes me up. I blink my eyes hard trying to clear them of sleep so I can see the screen on my phone. It's a text . . . from Adam! I sit up and click on the message.

Heard my mom is making you come to dinner to meet Serene. :)

I quickly text back:

Not making me. I want to come.

I lie. I don't want to have dinner with him and his new girlfriend. Well, actually I do in a sick sort of way, so it's not entirely a lie after all. I hit send, and not long after, my phone vibrates in my hand.

Means a lot to me that you are still part of the family.

Me too.

So is the Justin you're bringing your friend from work? Are you dating now?

Oh gosh. Oh crap. I suppose I'm in too deep now. I've got to keep up pretenses. Plus, if he's asking, does that mean it bothers him?

Yes. :)

Is all I text back.

I sit there tapping my finger nails on the back of my phone, waiting for a response. My phone vibrates. All he sends back is a smiley face. Not sure what to make of that.

I fall back down on the bed, thinking about yesterday. About Adam . . . dating someone. I probably should have expected this to happen at some point. But I didn't. I've been hoping against all hope he would figure out it's me he should be with. Although, sometimes dating someone else can help you realize that as well. I'll just have to hope that this is the case. Also, seeing me with Justin might speed up the process too. Well that is the hope, at least. Thank goodness Justin agreed to go. I don't know what I would have done if he hadn't. I couldn't have gone by myself. The image of me going there alone makes me quiver slightly with embarrassment. What a pathetic sight that would be.

Without warning, Ian appears in my head, and I smile to myself, thinking about how amazing it was to run into him last night. It wasn't how I'd dreamt it would be, but these things never go as planned, do they? Well, they never do for me, at least.

I decide it's time to get up. Taking my phone with me, I open my door and walk out of my room.

"You here, Grams?" I ask fairly loudly. I look down at my phone and see it's nearly 11 a.m. At this time of the morning, I can usually find Gram sitting in her favorite chair watching *The Price is Right* or reading a book on her Kindle. But sometimes she goes out for a walk or plays bridge with some of the other ladies in our building.

"In here, Bridgette," I hear her say. I go around the corner to find her in the living room, reading. "Just give me a second." She holds out a long, slightly wrinkled finger, "I need to finish this chapter. I'm almost done."

I plop down on the couch nearest her, and while I wait, I look around the bright room. I do love it here, although I wish Gram would update it a little. The décor is very 1980s. I've tried to drop hints, but she's not catching them. I may have to come right out and say it. Heaven knows she's got the money for an update. Not that I should ever complain. I get to live in an upscale neighborhood, in a beautiful apartment building, rent free. I'm the envy of all my city friends with their stuff-everyone-into-a-studio-to-save-money type of living.

My grandpa, whom I called Pops, and she used to fight over this place—whether to get rid of it, or whether to keep it. Pops hated the city, but Gram loved it. She still does. When Pops passed away three years ago, Gram sold their large four-bedroom, three-bath home in Goshen (for a mint, I might add) and moved her life into the city. Her children (mostly my dad) protested, but she said there were too many memories in that house, and she wanted to live someplace where there weren't so many reminders of Pops. Plus, she always liked to wind Pops up by saying things just to say them ("I've decided to be a Republican!" or "I'm going to get my navel pierced!"). Living in the city was one more jab aimed at him, even though he was in his grave.

Gram shuts the case to her Kindle and places it in her lap. "How are you doing this morning, my dear?" She smiles pleasantly.

"Eh, not as horrible as yesterday," I shrug. Gram was here to witness the blubbering fool who came back to the apartment after the lunch I had with Carla.

"Give it time. You'll get better." She nods her head positively.

"You act like you know from first-hand experience," I raise my eyebrows, inquisitively.

"I'm not free of heartbreak, my dear. I've had my fare share." She winks at me. "I did lose your grandfather, after all."

Oh right, stupid, inconsiderate me.

"Oh Grams, I'm so sorry. I didn't mean—"

"No apologies," she cuts me off. "Enough with the serious tone. I've got to tell you what happened on *The Young and the Restless* yesterday." Her eyes brighten.

"Oh yes, fill me in." I haven't been able to see it for the last few days, and heaven knows, if you miss an episode you may miss a huge plot turn.

She fills me in on what happened, and I listen intently. I love that we can spend time together like this. What grandmother out there still likes to watch soap operas, and with her granddaughter no less? I'm pretty sure most grandmothers would find the sleeping-around shenanigans in soap operas to be revolting. But not Grams. She loves it all. Well, she acts like she doesn't approve, but I think that's only for show.

". . . oh and then I have to tell you what happened to Ian and Jessica —"

"Oh! Speaking of Ian," I interrupt, remembering I haven't told Gram about seeing Ian last night.

"Sorry to cut you off, but you're never going to believe who I ran into last night," I smile, thinking about seeing those beautiful, green eyes again.

"Well, don't leave me wondering. Who?"

"Ian Davies! Remember from college?"

"Well, isn't that interesting," she says, cocking her head thoughtfully to the side.

"You don't have a clue who I'm talking about, do you Gram," I know the look on her face well.

"I think I just need a little reminder. The mind isn't so stable these days." She taps the side of her head with her index finger.

I guess I shouldn't find it incredibly disconcerting that she doesn't remember. She only met him once or twice. Although, all I talked about for the first year I lived with her was Ian. But then Adam came along, and he's pretty much all I was able to talk about after that. Poor Gram. Who wouldn't want to repress all this boy crap I spew? I need to work on finding other things to discuss besides men. But not now.

"Ian was the guy who was my best friend in college." I look to see if her memory has been jogged. Apparently not sufficiently.

"Remember, we were friends freshman through junior year, and then it turned into something more when we were seniors? I brought him to Goshen a few times."

"Okay, yes, yes I do remember now. Handsome fellow, with the green eyes." Her face lights up as she remembers. I think as you get older, your mind starts to pick and choose what information can stay in and what needs to go to make room for more. For her, Ian was just a blip in my life, a memory that could be easily replaced. For me, Ian is one of those people who will be burned in my brain forever. Just like Adam. You never forget the people you love. Especially the ones you give your heart to.

"Well, what a small world." She nods her head.

"I know. I couldn't believe it."

"Now, remind me, why is this the first time you've seen or heard from him?"

I sigh. "Well, things ended pretty badly." I stare down at the shaggy carpet, as thoughts and feelings from that time swirl in my brain.

"Remind me."

"He was going to London for an internship and wanted me to come with him. I didn't think I should go; it was bad timing for me. He took that to mean I wasn't as into our relationship as he was—"

"Were you?" she interrupts.

"I was. I think I didn't do a good job of showing it at the time, though. I could have been better." Way better, to say the least. I twiddle my hands in my lap remembering the rest of the story, not feeling like telling Gram all of it.

"So, what has he been up to?" she asks, tapping her fingers on her pink kindle cover.

"I'm not sure. We weren't able to catch up. Ursula caught me talking to him."

"You were fraternizing?" She clicks her tongue, disapproving.

I give her a sarcastic glare. "Anyway, he wants to meet for lunch next week."

"Well, that'll be good for you to catch up." She nods her head once.

"Yes, it will be. I can finally get the chance to apologize for everything." I look down at my hands still twiddling in my lap.

"Hmm," she says thoughtfully, tapping the Kindle case. "It's always been my opinion that things like this happen for a reason." She gives me a patronizing look.

I shoo her with my hand and say, "Oh Gram." She's always going on and on about how there are no coincidences and everything happens for a reason. I'm not too sure I agree. Although, I suppose this is sort of kismet. I've been wanting to find Ian for so many reasons, most importantly so I could apologize for how things ended, but I could never find him. I looked off and on (more on, really), but then Adam came along, and I stopped. Even still, I thought of him often and hoped I would one day get the chance to see him again. I'd given up a long time ago that it would actually happen, though.

"What are you reading?" I gesture toward the Kindle still sitting in her lap.

"Oh you know, just the odd historical piece," she says with a wink.

The "odd historical piece" usually means some type of smut romance. Before the Kindle was invented, Gram used to crochet book covers so she could hide what she was reading. She wasn't fooling anyone. My sister and I used to sneak peeks at the books she read. All were filled with throbbing members and heaving bosoms. It was a little much, knowing your grandma read that kind of stuff. At least with the Kindle I don't have to know exactly what she's reading. I can pretend in my head that it's the *Little House on The Prairie* series.

"Fancy some cocoa?" She pushes aside the foot rest with her house-slipper-clad foot and stands up from her chair.

"Sure," I answer, thinking coffee sounds like a better idea. But Gram doesn't keep coffee in the house. She's been cut off by her doctor. I wouldn't ask her to keep it around just for me. That wouldn't be very kind, seeing as she fought with the doctor tooth and nail over the loss. It was one of her favorite vices, if coffee could be considered a vice.

I slouch back into the couch thinking about the events of yesterday. Crying over Adam, seeing Ian. On second thought, I need to be comforted. Cocoa actually sounds pretty good. Maybe Gram will have some marshmallows.

CHAPTER 6

Mondays are the pits for any employment, but especially if you work for Edelweiss Catering. Mondays are deemed "marketing days" by Ursula. Since catering can be rather slow on the first day of the week, except for the odd luncheon every now and then, we are asked to trade off doing street marketing. Today it happens to be my turn. Lucky me.

Street marketing consists of holding a sign on the street and passing out flyers to drum up business — in a German dirndl, no less. With my dark blonde hair in two braids, I basically look like Heidi. Well, a slightly slutty Heidi, as the top of this dress really emphasizes my chest area. Poor Justin is working with me today in lederhosen. His costume is worse than mine, by far.

Adam used to love it when I wore this outfit for work, the few times he saw me in it, at least. I tried to hide it from him for as long as possible, but it was inevitable he would see me in it someday. I had expected a horrified look, but instead he looked turned on by the getup and asked me if I would wear it for him later. I agreed at the time but never followed through.

Justin and I paste on fake smiles as we stand out on the corner of Wall and Broad Streets, Justin twirling the fairly large rectangular sign and me passing out quarter-sheet-size flyers.

"This is degrading," Justin says through smiling, gritted teeth.

"You say that every time," I say, keeping my smile intact as well. "If you hate it so much, then why not find another job?" I try to hand out a flyer to a passerby who completely ignores me.

"And miss seeing Ursula? What would my life be worth then?" he says with a cheeky grin.

I hold out a flyer, and a middle-aged woman dressed in all black grabs it, glances at it briefly, and then balls it up and throws it on the ground. New Yorkers do not do subtle. I had to learn that one the hard way — and also learn to not take it personally.

"How does Ashley always get out of doing this?" Justin asks as he spins his sign.

"She has an audition today, that's how."

Hopefully, this will be the part she gets. But it's a long shot. Watching Ashley try out for all of these parts makes me anxious. I don't know how she does it. So much scrutiny, so much rejection. I don't know how she handles it all. I couldn't.

"Besides, I think she tries to avoid working with you." I give him a cunning smile.

"Why?" Justin stops spinning his sign, a serious expression on his face. "Did she say something about me?"

"No," I say, scrunching my face at him for taking me so seriously. That wasn't like him.

"Bridgette?" I hear a voice to my right. A voice I recognize. *Oh please, no.*

I close my eyes, wishing him away, but then slowly turn to my right, and there's Ian. Looking dashing in a suit and tie, holding a fountain drink in his hand. I cringe at my slutty Heidi outfit. *Curse you, Ursula.*

"Ian," I say, with what probably looks like a pained expression. I'm feeling quite pained at the moment, for so many reasons. My heart has also decided to speed up and skip around like a silly, little school girl.

"What are you doing out here?" he asks, not taken aback at all by my trampy German attire.

"Just some marketing." I hand him a flyer, which he takes eagerly and scans.

"So we meet again," he says, looking up at me after he tucks the flyer into his pocket.

"Yes, so we do," I say, gesturing toward my outfit, saying without words that I know I look like an idiot.

"It's hard to believe that I haven't seen you or spoken to you in four years, and now I've run into you twice within the span of three days," he says with a quizzical expression.

"It must be meant to be, I guess." Or karma hates me and thinks this is the funniest thing ever.

"Must be." He takes a sip of his soda.

"Ahem." Justin clears his throat behind me. I quickly turn to him, telling him to shut up with my eyes.

"You're busy." Ian motions to Justin, who is now twirling his sign with more gusto than is necessary. "Can you do lunch tomorrow?"

"Um, yes. Yes, lunch tomorrow would be great." I smile at the notion and also feel grateful that he will get to see me in normal clothing, for once, after seeing me in my work uniform and then in this hussy getup.

"Great. How about twelve thirty? You still like Japanese?"

"Yes, I do," I say, surprised. "You remember?"

"Of course I do." He gives me a wicked, little grin that makes my spine tingle.

I give him my cell number, so he can text me an address, and we say quick good-byes. I watch him walk away, and he turns around and catches me.

"I will try my best not to report to The Sea Witch your continuous need to fraternize," Justin says as Ian walks away.

"It's not fraternizing. He's not the client," I say, pasting the phony marketing smile on my face, as I go back to passing out flyers to the passersby.

"Yes, but he could be a potential client," Justin says, having to always have the last word. I don't really care about having the last word, so I let him.

"Me thinks he likes you," Justin stage whispers to me, going back to his sign spinning and fixed fake grin.

"Did you really just say 'me thinks?'" I turn my head toward him.

"I did." He stares straight ahead not making eye contact with me.

"Well, he doesn't. Not like that. Not anymore, at least. Anyway, Ian is a long story," I say, my mind racing back to the time I spent with him: the place we first met, the friendship that kindled immediately, the night it changed to something more, and then the night it all ended.

Justin doesn't ask about the story, and I don't offer. We go back to our flyer handing and sign spinning. It doesn't matter anyway. It's in the past. And although seeing Ian has brought back feelings I had buried long ago, all I want to do is clear things up with him. I'm not looking for anything more than that.

We'll have lunch, clear the air, and then I can get back to focusing on this weekend and how I'm going to get Adam back.

CHAPTER 7

"I can't believe you remember that," I exclaim over sushi in Midtown.

"Well, I don't mean to brag, but I do have a pretty good memory," Ian says, grabbing a piece of eel roll with his chopsticks. He's got the sleeves of his white shirt rolled up and his tie flipped over his left shoulder to keep it safe. I actually hate it when Wall Street types do that, but on him . . . well . . . I don't hate it.

"You have an amazing memory. I wish mine were better." I swirl a piece of spicy tuna roll in some soy sauce with my chopsticks.

"Probably the tightness of that getup you were wearing yesterday. It's cutting off the circulation to your head." He winks at me.

So he did notice after all. *Men.*

Luckily, today he got to see me in normal clothing. I agonized over what to wear but finally settled on a pair of dark, slim jeans, a cream-colored top with lace details on the back that I found in Soho a couple of weeks ago, and my favorite pair of dark brown ankle boots.

"Do you remember the time you got us kicked out of the library?" I ask, changing the subject away from that obnoxious dirndl.

Ian throws his head back, laughing. "Oh wow, yeah I remember. And it wasn't me who got us kicked out, it was you." He gives me a snide look.

"What? No way. It was totally you." I eye him, not sure I'm right. Did I get us kicked out?

"Yeah, it was me," he says, smiling slyly. "Well, it was mostly me," he adds with a wink.

"How dare you use my poor memory against me." I feign disgust. Ian laughs loudly.

My gosh, it feels good to hear him genuinely laugh. Adam is not a laugher. Not a boisterous one, at least. He mostly just nods his head and smiles.

Besides the laughing, there are a lot of things I've missed about Ian that I hadn't realized. How he is so methodical about everything. Even sushi. He has a method to it. He mixes just enough wasabi in his soy sauce, and he always tops each piece with a slice of ginger. I also forgot what a gentleman he is. Opening the door for me when we walked into the restaurant, pulling my seat back for me at the table. I want to say Adam did those things at first, but now I can't remember if he ever did them at all. It was never a big deal to me. I don't need those things. I'm a big girl. I can take care of myself. It's a nice gesture though, isn't it? I guess I'd forgotten.

He's also so complimentary. He even mentioned my Russian Red lips. Well, he didn't know the brand, but he noticed the red and said he liked it. I have to admit, it's been pretty freeing to be able to wear lipstick again, without getting a scoff from Adam.

"So, how did you end up in New York?" I ask, after eating some edamame.

"Work. You?" He mixes some more wasabi with soy sauce.

"I needed a change, and Gram was lonely, so I moved in with her." I grab a little bit of ginger and put it on a piece of spicy tuna roll.

"So I take it Pops passed away?" he asks.

"Yeah," I say, feeling instantly sad. I miss him.

"I'm really sorry to hear that," he says, his eyes full of empathy.

"Yes, well, life goes on," I shrug. It's a stupid thing to say, so clichéd. But it's the truth.

"And Gram?" he asks.

"Spry as ever. Maybe a little worse, actually," I say and roll my eyes just thinking about how crazy that woman is.

"I bet," he chuckles. "What about your parents? Your sister?" He cocks his head to the side, inquisitively.

"All good. My parents moved down to North Carolina—Charleston area—about the same time I moved in with Gram. Ally went with them." Ian closed-mouth smiles at that.

"So, how long have you been here?" I ask, wanting to get back to him.

"I moved here not long after London," he says, looking down at his plate.

And there it is. A segue toward the elephant in the room.

"Ian," I put my chopsticks down and place my hands in my lap. "I need to explain to—"

"Don't. Really," he cuts me off. "You don't need to. It was four years ago." He looks me in the eyes.

"No, but I need you to know I feel horrible about how everything . . . happened," I say, woefully.

"Bridgette, please." He shakes his head. "Water under the bridge, okay?" A faint smile plays on his lips. "Anyway, you got on with your life, I got on with mine—"

"And now we're here," I interject.

"Yes. And now we're here." He looks at me in a nostalgic kind of way.

Butterflies in my stomach start to rumble. Oh no, this was not part of the plan today. I was supposed to apologize to Ian, get the gnawing guilty feeling that has haunted me for the past four years off my back, and then get back to fixing things with Adam.

But suddenly, sitting here, I'm feeling all sorts of things I was not planning on feeling. It's like all of a sudden, we're back in college, settling back into our old Bridgette and Ian ways.

"You okay?" Ian asks. Apparently my inner struggle was outwardly playing on my face.

"Yes." I shake my head, blinking longer than necessary, trying to bring myself back. "Yes . . . sorry, I'm fine." I take a deep breath. "I do need to ask you something, though." I purse my lips together, slightly nervous to ask the question I've wondered about for some time now.

He puts his chopsticks down on his plate, giving me his full attention.

"How come you never called me, never tried to make contact?" I look to his face for an answer.

He looks away from me and then down at the table. "I don't know . . ." he trails off, probably looking for the right words to say. "I guess I was hurt a little . . . or maybe a lot," he says, looking up at me and giving a small, awkward smile. My heart sinks. I hate that I hurt him.

"I tried to find you, you know. I looked on Facebook. I basically scoured all social media." I smile slightly, hoping he doesn't see me as a stalker, but rather a concerned friend.

"Oh, I don't do any of that. Don't have time for it. But thanks for letting me know you were stalking me." He smiles mockingly.

Damn.

"I wasn't stalking you. I was just trying to see what you were up to, what you were doing. You know, making-sure-you-were-alive type of stuff." Oh yes, perfect explanation. That didn't sound like stalking at all. *Way to go, Bridgette.*

"Ah Bridge, I should have called you." He looks directly at me. "Sorry. I'm a prideful idiot." He runs a hand through his dark hair, tousling it slightly.

We sit there in silence for a moment, looking at each other, not knowing what to say.

"So, we're good?" he finally interjects, giving me a small smile.

"Sure, we're good." I reach across the table to shake his hand to show how good we are, but he doesn't know what I'm doing and ends up giving me an awkward high five.

Okay, so we're not exactly settling back into our old Bridgette and Ian ways.

"Now," he says, picking up his chopsticks, eyeing the salmon roll. "Let's be done with all this in-the-past junk."

"Sounds good to me." I pick up my chopsticks and grab another piece of the eel roll.

For the rest of the lunch, the conversation is more lighthearted. We both seem to relax, and old Bridgette and Ian make small reappearances as we reminisce more about college, avoiding topics that fall into the "in-the-past junk" category.

I don't bring Adam up. I almost do, but then I decide it's best not to. It's probably not appropriate. And anyway, I don't really want to talk about my current ex-boyfriend with my past ex-boyfriend. Relationships have not been discussed, except our own, and that was barely a discussion.

"It was really good to catch up," Ian says, pulling me into a hug outside the restaurant. He instantly nuzzles his chin in my neck, just like he always used to. It feels so good, so comfortable. I've missed him.

"It was so great," I say.

"Let's not lose touch again," he says as we pull out of the hug.

"Yes, let's not," I agree.

"I'll call you," he says, as we start to walk away from each other, heading to our destinations in opposite parts of town.

I don't say anything. I just smile and wave at him. I do turn to look back at him as I get a few feet away, and I catch him doing the same thing. It's kind of cute, like something from a movie, and we both smile at each other, knowing we were thinking the same thing. I find myself missing the days back in college when life was simpler. I miss having a simpler life.

CHAPTER 8

University of Connecticut, freshman year, winter

"You wanna know what I think, Bridge?" Ian asked as we sat at a small, round table, chairs side by side in the Dairy Bar eating ice cream. Actually, he had finished his and had moved on to mine.

"What do you think?" I asked, not truly wanting his opinion on the subject.

"I think you're jealous." He cocked his head to the side, his mouth turned up in a typical Ian smirk. His insanely green eyes were penetrating mine. I looked away.

I slapped him on the arm. "I'm not jealous," I exclaimed. "You're an idiot."

"Come on," he said, tapping his spoon against the side of the cup of ice cream. *My* ice cream, which I had wanted to finish, but somehow he was eating it. Typical.

"Why would you think I was jealous?" I asked, starting to feel annoyed.

"Because of the way you're acting right now," he said, pointing at me with the spoon.

"I'm not jealous," I said with finality. He had some nerve. "And how am I 'acting?'" I used air quotes, sarcasm oozing from my voice.

"I don't know. There's just something different this time," he said, lifting one eyebrow as he looked my face over.

"You're an idiot," I said, once again.

"So if you're not jealous, then why do you care if he's going out with someone tonight?" He looked out the window at the snow-covered ground, and my eyes followed. The powder was fresh, and it twinkled from the night lights.

"Huh?" He pestered me for an answer, poking me in the arm.

"I don't care!" I exclaimed a little too loudly. Glances shot at me from around the room.

"Okay, fine," he said, relenting, both hands up in the air as if I had a gun on him. His right hand still held the spoon.

"What about you, anyway?" I said, punching him lightly on the arm as he went back to finishing off *my* cookies and cream.

"What do you mean?" he asked.

"I mean, didn't you call dibs on her?" I asked. I tried to raise one of my eyebrows, but I could never do it like he could. I'm pretty sure I looked like I had some sort of eye twitch problem.

He lifted one perfect eyebrow to mock me, knowing exactly what I was trying to do.

"Yah, so." He shrugged his shoulders.

"Doesn't that go against the bro-code, or whatever?" I asked.

"Nah, it's all good. He can have her," he said, polishing off the last of my ice cream.

I rolled my eyes. Typical Ian. He never wanted to ruffle feathers, always keeping the peace. Especially with his roommate, Brandon, who could be so infuriating. Brandon was a typical male of the species. Ian was not. I wasn't used to someone like Ian.

Of course, I wasn't of the mind to ruffle feathers either. Jenna was my roommate, after all. Who knew Ian's roommate and mine would hit it off so well? I sure didn't. Huh. Maybe I was a little jealous. Of what, I wasn't sure. I liked Brandon, and I didn't know why. He was tall and doughy—but not fat, just not fit. I liked that when he hugged me I felt so feminine. He was like a big teddy bear. He was also funny as hell. Jenna was not the smartest cookie in the jar. I doubt she would ever get his jokes.

Oh gosh, I was jealous.

"Aha!" Ian exclaimed. "I saw that look. I was right."

"What did you see?" I looked away from him. Ian was a master at reading people's faces. Well, really, my face. He could tell exactly what I was thinking just by looking at me. Damn him.

"Okay, fine," I said, folding my arms and sitting back in my chair. "Maybe I'm a little jealous. But it only just dawned on me. I hate that you know me so well."

He put an arm around me. "But then who would be there to call you out on your crap?" he asked with a smirk.

71

"Yes." I puckered my lips in full pout. "It's so much fun being called out on my crap," I mocked.

His smirk turned into a smile, and he pulled me in for a side hug.

"Well, I guess if Jenna and Brandon are out tonight, then you and I are stuck together."

"I knew you liked her," I said, shaking my head slightly, and also not liking it at the same time. He could do so much better than her. Oddly, I felt that way about all of the girls Ian had dated or shown interest in. I was protective of him, so that must have been the reason. I got the idea he was protective of me as well. Without him saying it, I knew he didn't approve of my interest in Brandon either.

"I never said that." He shook his head, but I could tell by his face he liked Jenna. He wasn't the only one who could read faces.

"Movie?" he asked as we stood up to go.

"Yep," I said, and then smiled to myself.

I had Ian. And right now, that was enough.

CHAPTER 9

"Oh Ash, I'm so sorry," I hug her at the door of Gram's apartment. She's just shown up, red-faced from crying, after being rejected yet again for another part.

"I just don't get it," she says, coming in and taking off her light-weight jacket. We were headed toward warmer weather, but the evenings could still be fairly chilly. "They told me I was what they were looking for, asked me for callbacks three times, even told my agent I was who they wanted. I thought this was it. This was finally it." She hangs her head in defeat.

I don't get it either. Ashley is practically oozing with talent. She's the whole package. She can sing, dance, and act. Plus, with her stunning red hair and her amazing skin, which I covet, I have no idea why she hasn't been snatched up yet. It makes no sense. Sadly, this isn't the first time she has made it so far, only to be dropped at the end.

I guide her into the living room and grab a box of tissues that's sitting on an antique end table, pulling out a few to hand her.

"Thank you," she says, taking the tissues and blowing her nose loudly into them. "I'm so glad we didn't have to work tonight," she says after she finishes trumpeting with her nose. "I don't think I would have been able to be cheery and customer service-y tonight."

"Ash, I don't know what to say. What can I do to cheer you up?" I grab her hand and hold it, trying to give her some comfort.

"Oh nothing, really. I mean . . . chocolate would help." She sniffles, dropping my hand and falling gracelessly onto the couch.

I go into the kitchen, searching for chocolate. There's a bit of a lack these days. Gram and I decided we needed to eat better, so we threw a bunch away. Knowing Gram, though, she probably has some stashed, just in case.

I grab a chair and stand on it, reaching up into the cabinet above the refrigerator—the place that has always been Gram's not-so-secret, secret hiding spot. She's been hiding things in the cabinet above the refrigerator since my sister and I were kids. We always knew where to find the good stuff.

I feel around blindly with my hand, because I'm not tall enough to see directly into the cabinet. I land on something that seems bar-like and could possibly be chocolate. Bingo. A large Symphony bar. Perfect for Ashley to eat her feelings with.

"Where's Gram?" Ashley asks as I walk back in the room, carrying the extra-large chocolate bar.

"She's out seeing a movie with her bridge club ladies tonight." I sit down next to Ashley and begin unwrapping the chocolate.

"How come you didn't go?" she asks as I hand her a large chunk of chocolate, which she immediately starts eating.

"Didn't feel like it." I break off a chunk of the chocolate bar and nibble on it.

"Well, I'm glad you didn't. I didn't want to go home to my roommates. They'd pretend to be sympathetic, but would really be happy I didn't get it. And Justin would have been no help." She sniffles and takes another bite of chocolate.

"Yeah, Justin isn't exactly the sympathetic type." I smile to myself, thinking about Justin and his lack of emotional intelligence.

One time when Adam and I had gotten into a huge fight, I somehow ended up seeking some comfort from Justin, and all I got was a couple of impersonal pats on the shoulder and then a "you cool now?" Super helpful.

"He's probably too busy running his underground drug ring anyway," Ashley throws out, apathetic.

"Or doing some live action role playing," I say, and she gives me a small laugh.

"I don't know," Ashley says after she swallows some chocolate. "Maybe I should just give up. Call it good and go start my career in a job where wannabe actors go after too much rejection. Any idea what that might be?" She looks up at me.

"Working for Ursula?" I give her a wry smile. "And no, you're not giving up. Come on, I'm sure all of the super famous got lots of rejection to get where they are now. The part—*the* part—will come along. I know it." I pat her on the knee.

Ashley sighs, her eyes crestfallen. "I guess if I give up now, then my parents would be right, and I would hate for that to happen." She gives me a weak smile.

"Yes, and we wouldn't want them to ever be right, so you just need to keep working at it." I give her a confident expression.

"I'm tired of thinking about it. Let's talk about something else." She brightens up slightly. "How was your lunch date with Ian?"

"Oh right. It was good, I think."

"What do you mean, you 'think?'" She asks, an inquisitive look on her face.

"Well, I never really got to apologize. He wouldn't let me. Said it was 'water under the bridge' or something like that," I grab a piece of my hair and start twirling it, contemplating.

"Let me see a picture of him," she says, nudging me with her hand. "I didn't get to see him up close at the event. I need a visual."

I go to my room and grab my old scrapbook from college.

"Damn, he's hot," Ashley declares, after looking through all the pictures of Ian and me together.

"Yea, he still is," I say and then sigh. These pictures carry so many good memories of my time with Ian. I can even remember how I felt when we took some of them. Happy. Elated. I just wish I had been able to express myself better back then.

"So, will you see him again?" Ashley asks, reaching for what's left of the chocolate bar sitting between us. My, how quickly it's disappearing.

I shrug my shoulders. "Don't know? He said he would call me, so we'll see."

"Do you want to see him again?"

"Yeah, of course. I mean, I think I do." I look downward, pensive.

"Why wouldn't you?" Ashley asks, taking a bite of chocolate.

"I don't know. I mean, yes, it was great to see him, and yes, old feelings did resurface—for me at least. It seemed like they did for him too. But I don't know if we can get past everything. He said it was in the past, but is it truly? Plus, and I know you don't want to hear this, I still can't help but hope things will work out with Adam."

"Bridge . . ." she trails off, the disapproving tone of her voice saying it all.

"I know, Ash. You don't need to say how you feel. I already know."

"And by the way, Justin told me about this whole ridiculous charade you have planned for Friday night. Bridgette, that's a recipe for disaster." She gives me a reproving look.

Sometimes, I really do hate it that Ashley knows me so well. I've only known her for just over two years, and she knows me better than my own sister. Better than Gram, even. I also hate it that when it comes to Adam, she has been pretty much on the nose. We even stopped speaking for two weeks, because she told me Adam was all wrong for me and would eventually break my heart. I don't know about the all-wrong part, but the heartbroken part was right on the money.

"You're probably right. But I have to see this chick Adam's dating. And I want to see his family, too." The family part was interjected as an afterthought, although true.

"And you also hope him seeing you with Justin might make him jealous," she adds, cocking her head to the side knowingly.

"Maybe that's part of it, too." I smile sheepishly. It sucks to be called out on all your crap, even though, in hindsight, I do usually appreciate it. It's in the here and now that I hate it.

"Okay, well, you know how I feel," Ashley reprimands, and I nod and roll my eyes. "That being said, you're gonna have to look extra hot if you're going to meet this tramp. So, let's go figure out what you're going to wear." She gives me a conniving, little smile and then stands up, grabbing me by the hand and dragging me up with her.

I do love that even if she hates my choices, Ashley still has my back. That is a true best friend right there.

CHAPTER 10

"Come in, come in," Carla says from the doorway of the Dubois family condo on the Upper East Side. Calling it a condo is an understatement, really. "Have a seat in the sitting room, I'll just be right back." She ushers us toward the sitting room.

Justin and I walk into the sprawling residence, and I see Justin go bug-eyed at the sight before him. I've been around the Dubois Family and their money for a while now. I'm used to it, and I never really cared about it. Don't get me wrong, I appreciated it. When Adam and I were in the good part of our relationship, I got to go with them on some fantastic family trips. The money, while nice, did not define them to me, though.

Now, seeing the condo through Justin's eyes, well, it truly is a sight to behold. Everything is white with subtle gold accents. The carpets are plush and white, the couches, end tables, lamps, counters, cabinets—all white. It was a little nerve-racking when I first saw this place. I felt like I was in a museum. I was so anxious I was going to spill something. But Carla is always walking around carrying a large glass of red wine, which at any second could splash (and has on several occasions), so I stopped being so uptight about it.

"Holy sh—,"

"Justin!" I exclaim in a stage whisper, whacking him slightly on the arm with the back of my hand.

"Sorry," he says, now taking his voice to a whisper. "You never told me Adam was loaded."

"Well, he's not. His family is," I say quietly as we sit on the couch. I don't mention that when Adam's dad retires, he will be in charge of the company, so then he *will* be loaded.

"Something to drink?" Carla asks as she enters the living room, carrying a monster-size glass of red wine for herself.

"I think I'm good for now," I say, and Justin nods his head, agreeing.

I couldn't drink or eat anything at this moment. There wouldn't be much room with all the butterflies fluttering in my stomach. I look around the room, expecting Adam and this witch he's dating to appear at any second.

"Adam should be here any minute," Carla says, as if reading my mind.

"Is that Bridge I hear?" F.J. says as he walks into the living room, breaking out in a loud and very off-key version of "Like a Bridge Over Troubled Water"—something he always does when he sees me. He's gangly with a bit of a beer gut. He looks a lot like Adam, but with tacky taste. Unbuttoned shirts displaying chest hair and gold chains and bracelets abound.

"Who's that geek?" he asks, nodding his head toward Justin.

"F.J.!" Carla exclaims, exasperated. "This is Justin, Bridgette's boyfriend."

"Really?" he asks, not convinced.

"Yes. Really." Carla rolls her eyes at him. "Justin, please forgive my son. He has about as much class as a goat. F.J., go call your brother and find out where he is." She gives him a dirty look.

"What? What did I say?" F.J. asks, shrugging his shoulders in innocence.

"Would you just shut up, and go call your brother?" Carla practically spits the question at him. "I have no patience for that kid. None." She mutters "disappointment" under her breath while adjusting her ornate diamond-encrusted watch, looking at the time.

"I'm going to check on dinner. You sure you don't want a drink?" Carla looks to Justin. We both politely decline, and she walks out of the room and into the kitchen.

"What's up with that F.J. guy?" Justin asks once Carla is out of hearing distance.

"Oh, he's harmless. He's a bit spoiled. Doesn't want to work. I think he would rather live off his parents. He's a good guy, though."

"Good guy?" he asks, not believing me. "How come he was so shocked that you and I would be together?" he asks, bemused.

"Don't know," I shrug.

"I still can't believe you never mentioned that Adam's family is loaded," Justin says, apparently already recovered from F.J.'s comments and clearly still in awe of his surroundings.

"It's not something that's important to me, so why would I?" I shrug.

"Well, it's important to me. Does Adam have a sister?"

"No. He doesn't." I whack him lightly on the arm once more.

"What? It's a valid question. I think I just found my new goal in life. To marry a rich girl," he nods his head, liking his idea.

"What a respectful idea," I scoff.

The front door opens, and my heart starts to speed up. In walks Frank Dubois. He puts his keys on the console table near the door.

"Bridgette!" he exclaims, as he comes into the living room. I stand up, and he gives me a big hug.

"It's great to see you, Frank," I say.

"You too. When was the last time I saw you? When Carla and I took you to dinner last month?" He cocks his head to the side, pondering.

"Yes, I think that was it." I smile warmly at him, feeling relieved it was him and not Adam. I don't think I'm ready to see Adam and this girl yet. I may never be ready, and it's about to happen.

"How ya been?" he asks, taking a seat in the plush white chair next to the couch Justin and I are on.

Frank Dubois is tall, thin, and balding. F.J. gets his body from him, for sure. Everything except the balding part. F.J. and Adam will never have that problem.

"I'm good." I nod my head, smiling.

"And who do you have with you?" He gestures toward Justin.

"Oh, sorry. Yes." I shake my head slightly, remembering my charade. "This is Justin." I can't seem to add "my boyfriend" to that. Not to Frank.

Suddenly this farce is making me feel thoughtless and cheap. I adore this family too much to lie to them. I'm going to figure out a way to tell them the truth. I have to. This whole thing is not me.

The front door opens and in walks Adam. My stomach sinks.

Following right behind him, her hand in his, is Serendipity—or Serene. Whatever they call her. Carla was right; she does look like a witch. If witches are gorgeous supermodels.

Seriously, this girl looks like she stepped straight out of a magazine. Her long, dark hair, smooth and silky, shines in the light of the Tiffany fixture hanging above her, which also adds a glow to her flawless, porcelain skin. She has a prefect, tiny little nose and luxurious pouty lips. And her legs . . . they just keep going. She's dressed in a very tight, little black dress that only goes to her mid-thigh.

Suddenly, I feel quite dumpy in the red, crewneck cashmere sweater, skinny jeans, and peep-toe, black stiletto booties that Ashley and I worked so hard to put together for tonight. This is definitely not going as planned. So much for finding flaws with her to make myself feel better.

Adam smiles at me when he sees me. He guides Serene over to where I'm sitting with Justin, and we both stand up.

"Bridgette." He wraps his free arm around me, half-hugging me, still holding hands with the supermodel witch. "It's great to see you."

"Serene, this is Bridgette." He gestures to me once we've pulled out of the hug.

"Lovely to meet you," she says, smiling politely, her eyes showing no delight in the introduction. Her voice is sultry, eluding supermodel-ness. Very whore-like, in my just-formed opinion.

"Justin, good to see you again," Adam says, extending his hand out.

When Justin lets go of Adam's grip, he uses the same hand to grab mine, intertwining our fingers. Yes, okay, this is good. Good job, Justin. Wait, wasn't I going to tell them that Justin and I aren't actually together? I'm thinking that idea may have gone out the door when Serene waltzed in, with her stupid, painted-on black dress and endless legs. I thought I hated her when I found out she was dating Adam. Now that I've seen her, I more than hate her. I loathe her.

"Adam," Carla says, coming back into the room from the kitchen, "you're finally here." She gives him a little peck on the cheek. "And Serene, lovely to see you as always." She gives her a little air kiss. Serene gives her a thin smile.

"I can't get a hold of him, Ma," F.J. says loudly as he comes down the hall from one of the back bedrooms. "Oh, hey bro, there you are." He holds his phone up to show he just tried calling him and then slides it into his pants pocket.

"Let's eat before everything gets cold." Carla nods toward the dining room.

We all start to move to the dining room, Justin and I following behind Adam and Serene. I see Adam whisper something to Serene, and she nods her head and walks ahead of him as he slows down, allowing Justin and me to catch up with him.

"Justin, mind if I have a minute with Bridge?" he asks politely.

Justin looks to me, and I smile, letting him know it's okay. He saunters off toward the dining room.

"This is weird, right?" Adam asks, grabbing my hand. His hand feels strange, foreign even. I expected something different.

I let out a small relieving laugh. "Totally," I nod my head, agreeing.

"I want to stay friends, Bridge. I don't want it to be weird. My family loves you like you're their own." He smiles. I simply nod my head, not sure what to say.

He kisses me on the cheek and then drops my hand and starts walking into the dining room. I follow behind.

The dining room is set up for a lovely dinner party. Carla has always been the best hostess. I wish

I could fully appreciate it right now, but I'm feeling a little like I'm in a dream sequence.

That short exchange with Adam, seeing him and Serene together . . . I've been a blind fool. This was a mistake. Adam is no longer mine and seeing what he's got now . . . well, I don't think he will ever come running back to me. Ever.

I'm such an idiot. Adam was never going to wake up and suddenly realize he loves me. That stuff only happens in the movies.

I take a seat next to Justin, my eyes tearing up as it all dawns on me, and I'm considering making a run for it, and then Justin puts an arm around me, steadying me. I look at his face, meeting his eyes and he smiles.

"You got this." He leans in and says softly into my ear, and then kisses me on the cheek.

Okay, so maybe Justin has more emotional intelligence than I'd thought.

Well, I don't "got" this, but I can fake it. I set my shoulders back and sit up a little straighter, swallowing the lump in my throat and the near-burgeoning tears. I can play nice, and then I can go home and cry about this later. I'm a grown-up for hell's sake.

We all sit down at the table, and Justin keeps up our dating hoax even when no one can see it, holding my hand under the table. It's comforting and helps my waning confidence.

Carla brings out the dinner, an Italian feast as always. An antipasto platter to start, both chicken and eggplant parmesans, baked ziti, salad, and garlic rolls. It looks amazing. I wish I felt like eating it.

Everyone starts to dig in. I get a plate of food, but instead of eating, I just push it around with my fork. Justin is practically shoving the food in his mouth. It dawns on me that he probably hasn't had a good home-cooked meal in a long time.

The conversation between bites is fairly pleasant. It's mostly Carla trying to tell a story about how she got pulled over by a policeman earlier today. F.J. interjects comments every now and then. The rest of us listen and eat.

I, of course, can't help but peek over at Adam and Serene, sitting across from us. She's barely eating either and seems blasé about the conversation. She rarely interjects a smile, or even a nod, to communicate she's listening. Carla doesn't seem to notice her aloofness. She barely looks at Serene, actually. It's almost as if she would rather her not be there.

Watching Adam with Serene, I notice he's kinder with her than he was with me. Not that he was mean to me, just not as thoughtful. He dishes up food for her, and when she asks for a drink, he quickly grabs her glass and fills it. Maybe I never gave off the vibe that I wanted him to do that stuff for me, so that's why he never did.

"So Justin." Carla, finally done with her story, turns her attention to us. "What do you do for work?" she asks, and then takes a large gulp of wine. She's had quite a bit of wine, come to think of it.

"Bridgette and I work together. That's how we met," he says, putting his arm around the back of my chair, doing an impressive job of keeping up the façade.

"That's nice. Isn't that nice, Frank?" She nods at her husband sitting at the other end of the table. "It's also quite a coincidence. That's how Adam and Serene met." She nods over to Adam and Serene who are sitting directly across from Justin and me. "Serene here works as a receptionist, don't you Serene? You know, I always warn my boys not to fish off their own dock. It's quite unprofessional." She nods, agreeing with herself.

"But—" Adam says, looking appalled. Serene seems unaffected.

"But what? It's unprofessional." She looks back and forth between the two of them.

Well, this just got awkward. Everyone shifts uncomfortably in their seats. Everyone but Carla, Adam, and Serene, that is. Justin looks over at me, his eyes wide with amusement. He's quite enjoying this. I'm not going to lie; I'm not hating it.

"Are you really going to bring this up again, Ma?" Adam leans in, looking ready to pounce. So this wasn't the first time?

"Well, forgive me for worrying about my boys," she says loudly, heated.

"Oh please. That's not worry. That's you being controlling." Adam's face is getting red. I don't know if I've ever seen him this mad before. It's not pretty. "I can't believe you're going there. Right now, with everyone around."

"Enough," interjects Frank, his voice demanding.

"Oh Frank." Carla rolls her eyes at him. "You tell them what you said to me this morning. Go on. Tell Adam what you said," she demands.

"Carla, this isn't the time or place —"

"He said that he thinks this is a mistake," she interrupts, pointing her finger back and forth between Adam and Serene.

Adam's face is so red I think steam might actually start to rise from his forehead. Serene still doesn't looked phased at all. I'm feeling jittery, like I feel when I'm over-caffeinated.

"Well if you ask me, I think it's a great idea," F.J. offers, reaching across the table to grab a roll.

"No one asked you, F.J.," Carla snaps, disdainfully.

"You think this is a mistake?" Adam looks to his dad, who doesn't meet his eyes. We all momentarily sit in awkward silence, avoiding eye contact. Justin has grabbed my hand under the table and is squeezing it off and on, as if to communicate through our hands how crazy this all is.

"Well, let me tell you what kind of 'mistake' this is," Adam says, ending the odd silence. He backs his chair up and stands. He grabs the back of Serene's chair and spins it around effortlessly, so she is facing him. He gets down on one knee.

Oh no. Oh please no.

"Serendipity Jones, I know we haven't been together very long, but I don't care. I want to spend the rest of my life with you. I knew from the minute I saw you. You're the one." He reaches in his pocket and pulls out a ring. A huge diamond solitaire on a platinum band. "Will you marry me?" He holds the ring out for her to see. I let go of Justin's hand, grabbing the sides of my seat with both hands, steadying myself.

Serene looks at the ring and then looks at Adam, and suddenly a huge smile spreads across her face. "Yes!" she exclaims. "Yes, I'll marry you!" He puts the ring on her finger, and they both stand up and begin to kiss and then end with a big, grand hug.

"No!" Carla exclaims, and then puts both her hands to her mouth, covering it in shock. Her eyes well with tears.

"I'm sorry to tell you, Ma, but this is happening," Adam says, as he pulls out of the hug with Serene, keeping a hand around her waist.

And then all hell breaks loose. All at once, the entire Dubois family starts yelling and screaming at each other. It's loud and heated, and I'm expecting at any moment that Carla will rent her clothing in protest.

I'm frozen to my seat, and my breathing is thick and slow. This is something like a nightmare. To be present when your ex-boyfriend—one that you dated for two years and thought you would marry—proposes to someone else, the same person he's only been dating for four weeks . . . well, I'm no expert, but I'm pretty sure this is what hell must be like. I'm in hell.

I unfreeze enough to look over at Justin, who is sitting there, slack-jawed. He's frozen to his seat, barely blinking. I nudge him with my hand, giving him a questioning look that asks, *What should I do?*

Justin shakes his head, as if to bring himself back from a trance. He leans over to me and whispers in my ear, "I think it's time we made an Irish good-bye." He nods his head toward the front door. Meanwhile, everyone is still screaming at each other, not paying any attention to us.

"Irish good-bye?" I ask, confused.

"It's where you duck out of a party without saying anything." He grabs my hand, and we stand up at the same time. We start to walk out of the room.

Feeling awkward for just up and leaving, I turn back to the rest of the party and say, "We'll . . . be right back."

But no one's listening. They don't even hear the front door open as we leave, and we can still hear them fighting as we walk down the hall toward the elevators.

"Okay, I thought that was going to be a disaster, but I had no idea," Justin says once we're inside the elevator. He seems elated by that fact, which is super annoying.

I don't say anything, and as soon as the elevator doors open up to the lobby, I walk as fast as my legs can carry me, past the concierge and doorman, and out of the building into the lukewarm evening air.

"Bridgette?" Justin follows behind me, trying to catch up, but I start moving at a speed-walker's pace, not caring what an idiot I probably look like. I get far enough away from the Dubois's residence, plop down on the first bench I see, and put my face in my hands. I begin to blubber. I feel Justin take a seat next to me.

"Bridge." He pats my back impersonally. But he stops after a few times, and then I feel his arm wrap around me from the back. I sit up, tears streaming down my face, and he pulls me into a hug, and I wrap my arms around him, crying on his shoulder.

I'm sure people are watching this scene unfold, tourists mostly. New Yorkers, for the most part, don't people watch. They're too caught up in their busy lives to pay attention. But a dramatic scene, such as this, would catch the eye of a few people for sure. They probably imagine I just found out someone died, or I've got a deathly disease. The truth would most likely be disappointing: I've just witnessed my ex-boyfriend, the man I thought I was still in love with and was meant to be with, propose to another woman. In front of my eyes.

I'm sure if the onlookers heard the truth, most would give a "pshh" and walk away. Some might give me an understanding expression and then move along. I wish I thought so little of what just happened. I wish I could fast forward and get to the part where I'm totally fine with it all. Or rewind and not go to dinner at all.

Ashley is *so* going to gloat about this one.

I slow down the crying and sniffling and pull back from Justin's grasp, wiping my nose with the back of my hand. I really wish I had a tissue.

"Here." Justin reaches into his pocket, pulls out a half-filled travel-size pack of tissues, and hands them to me. "Ashley told me to bring some, just in case." I start blubbering again. I'm not sure whether to be grateful Ashley knows me so well or ticked because she predicted the night would go this horribly.

"Sorry, Bridge. That had to be rough." He pats me on the shoulder a couple of times, awkwardly.

"Yeah," I sniffle. "I'm not sure what I was expecting, obviously not that." My eyes well up again, threatening a waterfall, but I push it back.

"Come on, I'll treat you to a latte." He grabs my hand, pulling me up with him as he stands.

"Okay," I sniffle.

He doesn't let go of my hand as we walk down the sidewalk. The gesture is sweet and so needed. I never thought I would think this, but thank goodness for Justin.

CHAPTER 11

"Mom, I've gotta go. I need to get ready for work," I say over the phone. I've got it balanced on one shoulder, holding it with the side of my head, my neck rapidly developing a cramp, while I organize Gram's living room, which desperately needed to be done.

We say quick good-byes and hang up. I've just been telling her about the soap opera that is my life and Adam getting engaged. And, of course, she gave me the same Gram speech about how there will be someone else out there for me and all of that other junk people say to try to make you feel better.

What a difference a week can make. Well, okay, ten days. What a difference ten days can make. I was a bit of a wreck for a while. Off and on, at least. But this morning when I woke up, I felt better. Good, even. I hope it lasts. Of course, rehashing the whole story with my mom may have set me back a little. But overall, I'm much better than I was ten days ago. I hate when I do such pathetic, girly things. I annoy even myself. I'm quite sure Justin and Ashley are over it, and Gram too.

I haven't heard from Adam, and I honestly didn't expect to. What could he say? *"Gee, Bridgette, I'm sorry I got engaged to my hot new girlfriend in front of you. That was weird, right?"*

Carla called me that night after Justin and I made our getaway. I didn't answer. I did call her back the next day, and she was overly apologetic and sounded completely heartbroken about the whole evening. She asked me to go to lunch, and we agreed to meet up soon. I need a little more time before I have to hear more details about Adam and the model-witch.

"Gram, what's this?" I ask as she walks back into the living room, a cup of tea in her hands. I'm sitting on the floor going through the DVDs, trying to find ones to get rid of. I have to go to Manhattan today for work, so I'm going to bring a box of things to drop off at one of the donation bins on the way to the subway.

"Oh that." She bats a hand at the DVD I'm holding. "I saw it in a magazine and thought it would be a cute movie to watch with the girls, but I was wrong."

"It's called *The Bridge Club Girls*," I say, holding it up for her to see.

"Yes, you know, we play bridge. I thought it would be a fun movie about ladies who play bridge," she sits down in her chair, propping her feet up on the foot rest.

"Gram, it's a porn." I stifle a giggle, not wanting to embarrass her.

"Well, yes, I figured that out." She sets the teacup on the side table next to her chair. "It didn't take long to figure out. They just jump right into, don't they?"

"You *watched* it?" My eyebrows shoot up, eyes widening as far as they can go. I drop the DVD on the floor, as if her watching has contaminated it.

"Well, yes. Not all of it, mind you, just a bit. Horrible acting. Just awful."

"Gross," I say, scrunching my face in disgust, "I can't believe you watched any of it." I pick up the DVD and drop it in the donation box.

"Well, I'm only seventy-five. I'm not dead yet." Grams shrugs her shoulders.

Ew. This discussion quickly changed from funny and lighthearted to gag-worthy. And this coming from someone who never would allow me to swear past a damn or a hell. She has such a double standard. I've known her my whole life, and the woman never fails to shock me.

My phone chimes, telling me I have a text.

Want to meet up for coffee?

It's from Ian. I haven't heard from him since the last lunch we had together. I quickly text back.

Sure, when?

My phone vibrates almost immediately.

Tonight? Around 8?

I text back a yes, and he sends me an address.
"Who was that?" Gram asks.

96

"Ian. We're having coffee tonight." I smile as I think about seeing him again.

"Well, good for you. Getting yourself back out there." She smiles, nodding her head only once.

"Okay, Gram, don't get ahead of yourself. It's just coffee." I roll my eyes.

"Oh yes, of course, dear. It's just coffee. Sorry to jump to conclusions." She patronizes me with her tone.

"Do you know," she puts a finger up to her chin, "that reminds me. Yesterday on *The Young and the Restless*, Jessica declared her feelings for Ian."

"No way," I say, totally interested. I didn't get a chance to watch yesterday's episode.

Gram fills me in since I most likely won't have a chance to catch up. The fact that I watch a soap opera with my grandma is probably not normal, but I love it.

"Oh crap," I say when I look at my phone and see the time. "I better get going. We're short a server today, so we need to step it up. We lost another one to the bright lights of Broadway." I shake my head, feigning shame.

"Such a pity, someone following their dreams." She winks at me.

"Indeed." I wink back. I pick up the box of things to donate. "Gram, are you sure you don't want me to leave *The Bridge Club Girls* here so you can share it with your friends?"

She bats a hand at me. "Oh, stop. Just get out of here." She gives me a reproving look.

I give her my best sarcastic smile before I walk out of the room.

CHAPTER 12

University of Connecticut, sophomore year, fall

"Thank you," Ian said, leaning in and whispering across the table to me. The library was unsurprisingly cold, and I was annoyed with myself for, once again, forgetting my sweatshirt. My thin, moss-green tee shirt and black mid-thigh shorts were not doing much to protect me from the cold. I should have known better by now and layered.

"No problem," I whispered back. "You're better off without her anyway," I said, folding my arms across myself and rubbing them with my hands to try to create some friction, anything to feel warm. It's like a meat locker in here. I swear they do it on purpose to keep us awake.

"Yeah, well," he looked off into the distance, his face contemplative. "You're better off, too," he said, turning his face back to mine.

"I think we are both better off having Jenna Anderson out of our lives," I said, still rubbing my arms. Ian nodded in agreement.

It was going to be weird having to get used to a new roommate. I'd decided Jenna and I could no longer live together. I had to kick her to the curb. She'd broken my best friend's heart, after all. Plus, she stole my clothes. Particularly my underwear. Which was weird, and also creepy. My new roommate, Amy, seemed pretty benign. At least she didn't give off an underwear-stealing vibe, but time would tell.

"You cold?" he asked, eyeing my arm rubbing. Without prodding further, he stood up and walked over to my side of the table. He pulled a chair up close to mine and pulled me into him.

Jenna was an idiot. How could she have let this guy go? He was intuitive, smart, funny . . . so many things going for him. And he was my best friend. Probably the closest friend I'd ever had in my entire life.

"Brandon coming?" he asked me as he held me close.

"Yea," I said, thinking that if I were dating anyone else and he caught me and Ian sitting like this in the library, he probably wouldn't take it so well. But Brandon was used to Ian and me. He never seemed to care or get jealous of our friendship. It was one of the things that I appreciated about him. Maybe even loved. The jury was still out, but I suspected I was headed that way.

"It's seriously so cold in here," I complained. Ian still had his arms around me, but it was only barely helping. There was a time when this gesture would have made my heart race and my skin heat, but since we've settled into our friend zone, the effect died down. There are remnants there. I won't lie. But it's not enough to keep me warm.

Ian's hand moved down to my side, and with a light touch, he tickled me.

100

"Stop it," I demanded, but in hushed, library-appropriate tones.

"What?" He feigned innocence, but I could see something devilish in his eyes.

He sat still for a moment, and I figured the temptation had passed.

I was wrong.

Next thing I knew, he was tickling me all over, relentlessly. I tried to keep the laughter in but was unable to stifle it completely.

"SHHHHH!" One of the librarians working nearby reprimanded us with a stern look.

"Sorry," I said quickly. Ian echoed.

"You idiot," I said, punching him in the arm.

"You're warm now though, aren't you?" He gave me a double eyebrow raise.

"Not really. I'm mostly embarrassed." I whacked him in the gut with the back of my hand, giving a sheepish grin to the librarian when I noticed that she saw me do it. I did take note that Ian's gut was not a gut at all, but basically a stone-hard brick that could be felt even through the white, graphic tee shirt he was wearing. Not like I had never noticed before. I suppose I had forgotten since Brandon's gut was, well, like a gut.

The librarian stepped away from her perch, thank goodness, and we went back to studying, or whatever Ian was doing. I had no idea why he was even here, except to pester me. He didn't even have his laptop. Just a book open to something random.

I rubbed my arms again. I was going to have to find an alternative heat source.

"Still cold?" A mischievous grin took over his face.

"No," I lied.

"Liar," he said, and before I could stop him, his hands were all over me, tickling me on my sides and under my arms.

I was unable to hold it in at all this time. I might even have screamed. The fact that I was in the library was a minor consideration in the back of my mind. Ian and I were in our little cocoon we often went to, and the main thing on my brain at that moment was to retaliate. He was relentless, and it took me a minute to find a breath so I could get him back, but once I found it, I took it and ran. I knew exactly where Ian was ticklish, and I went right for it. I reached for his neck and tickled him behind the ear, and he flinched long enough for me to get him on his sides.

That's when it all got a little crazy. It turned from fun tickling into a full-blown tickling fight, and it wasn't until Ian's chair fell back with him in it, making a loud thud when it hit the floor, that I jerked out of retaliation mode and back into reality.

Of course, along with reality, it also dawned on me that the librarian had come back and was standing not far behind the fallen chair. My eyes went wide, and I threw out a "sorry" while I tried to help Ian right himself. Ian was laughing, so apparently not sorry at all.

"Please gather your things and leave," the librarian said, a look of fierce PMS on her face.

"Really?" Ian protested. I did my best to say "shut up" with my eyes and then turned toward the librarian. Taking notice that her nametag said Karen, I gave her my best please-forgive-me smile.

"I'm so sorry. It won't happen again." I said. Karen the librarian's face didn't budge.

"You're right, it won't. Not tonight at least," she said, a smug smile on her face. "Please gather your things and leave," she repeated.

I could see Ian beginning to protest, but I stopped him with a shake of my head. We started grabbing our stuff. Well, Ian didn't have anything, so I packed all of my stuff in my bag, giving Ian a death stare.

"You mad?" Ian asked, as we walked toward the steps that exited the library.

I didn't say anything. I just kept my head forward as I walked down the steps of the library out into the night air, which under normal circumstances would have felt nice compared to the library. But my face was heated from embarrassment, so it just felt warm.

Ian picked up his pace so he could get ahead of me and turn around to face me. He grabbed my shoulders.

"Bridge, you can't be mad," he said, trying to meet my eyes.

"I'm not mad." I looked up at him, keeping my face serious. "I'm glad we got kicked out."

"You are?" he asked, scrunching his face, confused.

"Yes. Because I wouldn't be able to do this if we were in there."

Before it could register on his face, I dropped my school bag on the floor and pounced on him like a tiger on its prey. Tickling with no mercy, I knew I could only get in a few good moves before he would strike back. He was stronger than me, after all.

I made the mistake of relenting, just slightly, and he took full advantage of it. Grabbing me, he pushed me toward the grassy area only a foot or so away from us. We were both laughing so hard we couldn't breathe. I was able to get away from his grasp for a moment, and I tried to take off running, but he was too fast. He grabbed me and tackled me to the ground. I fought back, kicking and laughing, but it wasn't enough to keep him from pinning me under him. He was leaning over me and had both of my wrists pinned above my head, my legs locked underneath his. He was a master, probably from practice with his older brother. My sister and I only got into fights that were more like cats—scratching and screaming in a rage, most likely over clothes or makeup.

"You moron," I said through heavy breaths while I tried to figure out my next plan of attack. "How're you supposed to get me now?" I questioned him, motioning with my head to our hands intertwined above my head.

"You underestimate me." His eyebrows raised once, quickly.

Oh crap.

Before I could gather enough strength to push him off with my feet, his chin was on my neck, tickling with his shadow of a beard, and this was worse torture than any of the other ways he had tried to tickle me. I was laughing so hard my sides hurt and my face ached.

"Okay!" I screamed when I couldn't take it anymore. "Okay, you win."

He lifted his face so it was inches away from mine. "That was too easy," he said, and I held back wanting to headbutt him, annoyed that he thought the task was so simple. I thought I put up a good fight.

"Get off me," I said, trying to wriggle my legs out from underneath him. But he wasn't budging.

I looked into his eyes, pleading with him to move. Our breathing was rapid from all the exertion. He stared at me and I stared back. Then the victorious smile that was on his face slowly morphed into something more serious. My breath hitched in my chest as the air immediately, and without warning, changed between us. Our eyes were locked, and slowly he lowered his face toward mine. My heart raced faster and faster.

His face moved even closer to mine, our eyes still locked. It wasn't like we'd never been in this position before. Ian and I were known to wrestle and play-fight more often than not. But this time there was something different. My brain was screaming in my head for him to stop, but for some reason, I didn't want to. In that moment, I wanted it.

"What are you two freaks doing?"

"Brandon!" I said, pushing Ian off of me, the trance ended immediately.

"Hey, man," Ian said, his butt on the grass, leaning back on his hands. I looked at him, searching his face, and he locked eyes with me, his annoyance apparent on his face. We both started to move to standing, trying to find our balance.

I felt something along the lines of nervousness but also mixed with confusion. What had just transpired between Ian and me? And what did Brandon see?

"Why aren't you in the library?" Brandon asked as I walked toward him.

"This jackass got me kicked out," I said, pointing a thumb behind me at Ian.

"Figures," Brandon said, and I caught an eye roll as I neared him.

As I got closer, I definitely was feeling nervousness, like I'd been caught. But two things worked in Ian's and my favor that night. It was dark, so Brandon wouldn't have been able to see our faces locked like they were. And also, this was not an abnormal thing for Ian and me to be doing. Brandon was used to it. If it bothered him, he never let on.

"Wanna go get something to eat?" Brandon looked from me to Ian.

I looked back at Ian, and our eyes connected for a moment before he looked away.

"I think I better head back," Ian said, shaking his head briefly.

I felt a mixture of relief and sadness that he didn't want to go. Whatever just happened was weird, and I knew I needed time to think about it, but I also wanted Ian with me. I felt like only part of myself when he wasn't there.

Brandon looked to me, wordlessly seeking my answer about grabbing some food.

"Yeah, sure. Sounds good," I said, leaning down to grab my bag.

"You sure you don't want to come?" I said, turning toward Ian, my best friend—the man who knew me better than I knew myself, but, right now, sort of felt like a stranger.

"Yeah, I'm sure. I've got stuff to do." He gave me a warm-eyed smile, and I instantly felt better. But his smile quickly morphed into something else as Brandon pulled me into him and leaned down to kiss the top of my head.

"See you later," Ian said, his voice and face full of irritation.

"See ya," Brandon said, not noticing a thing. But I noticed. Of course I did. I knew Ian better than anyone else did, after all.

Without a word, Ian turned and walked away.

CHAPTER 13

"Would you shut up, Justin?" Ashley whacks his arm with the back of her hand.

We're sitting in our favorite café after working a luncheon. We spend more time together here than any other place. It's simple, nothing fancy, has pretty decent food, and open late, which is perfect for our work schedules. We're not on a first-name basis with the staff, but they recognize us.

"It's fine." I let out a sigh. "We can talk about it. I'm good." I swirl a french fry in some ketchup and shove it in my mouth.

I look up to see Ashley giving me a look that says she doesn't believe I'm fine. I honestly am. I didn't even nibble on my bottom lip when I said it, so it has to be true.

"No, but seriously, Ash, you should have seen that place. It was like something out of a magazine," Justin continues, obviously not caring whether it bothers me or not.

The Dubois family condo was featured in *New York Spaces* a while back, but I'm not going to tell them that.

"I've gotta find myself a rich girl." Justin leans his head back against the booth.

"Oh geez," Ashley says, rolling her eyes at him. "And why would a rich girl want you?"

"Hey, I've got a lot to offer." He holds up a skinny arm, flexing it to show off his muscles, which, in-fact, are quite toned, but definitely lacking in girth.

Ashley and I look at each other and then burst out laughing.

"Whatever, you guys. You'll see; I'll show you."

"Yes, you just showed us, and we were not so impressed." Ashley smirks at him.

"Well, maybe I have more going on than meets the eye." He smirks back and adds a wink.

"Ew." Ashley scrunches her face, looking repulsed.

"Enough, you two," I say, trying to end the banter. Those two can go on and on. If I didn't know them better, I would think it was flirting. "Tell me what I should wear tonight." I turn toward Ashley, since Justin couldn't care less about clothes or fashion.

"Where're you going tonight?" he asks, curious.

"She has a coffee date with Ian, which she's already told you about. Do you listen to anything?" Ashley gives him a disapproving look.

"Only things that aren't boring," he scoffs. "What are you going out with that guy for?"

"We're not going out. It's only coffee. And anyway, I'm glad to have Ian back in my life." I smile slightly.

"Oh, I know," Ashley says, "you should wear that shirt we got at H&M. The one with the flower on it."

"Ooh yes." I nod my head, remembering the shirt. "Good choice . . . but wait." I look at the time on my phone, realizing that I haven't checked in a while. "Crap, it's nearly six! There's no way I'm going to have time to get home and back to meet up with Ian. What do I do?" I say, panic rising in my voice. I'm wearing my work uniform, and I smell like food, and not in a good way. I'm not a pleasant sight or smell.

"Bridge," Ashley says calmly, seeing my panicked look, "I'm walking distance from here. Just come back to my place and get ready."

I feel instant relief wash over me. "Right. Good plan, Ash."

"We'd better get going now. It's going to take us a while to get the food smell off you." She smiles slightly. "You coming, Justin?" She looks over to him for an answer.

"Oh, totally, for sure," he says, taking on a girly voice.

"Fine. Whatever." Ashley rolls her eyes at him. "I'll see you later?"

"Yep," is all he says.

"What're you and Justin doing later?" I ask a bit after we part ways with Justin. It's always been the three of us since Adam and I broke up, so to hear that the two of them have plans is slightly off-putting. Not in a bad way, though. In a confusing way.

"Oh, we're going to see a movie," Ashley says breezily. "Justin picked out something."

"Oh, fun," I say, suddenly very glad I have plans with Ian.

If I never have to sit through another movie that Justin picks out, it'll be too soon. He has this weird taste for the artsy and strange ones. They don't even show them in mainstream movie theaters. We have to go to smaller theaters that are so pretentious that everyone looks appalled when I call them theaters. It's "cinema," apparently. Most of the movies are so dreadfully slow, or have horrible endings, or both. I don't know what he sees in them.

We get to Ashley's apartment after climbing six flights of stairs, which makes me realize I definitely take the elevator in Gram's building for granted.

Ashley is packed into a two-bedroom apartment with four other girls. All of them looking to find their way into show business. The bedrooms are stuffed with twin beds and rolling wardrobe racks because the lack of closets in these old high-rises is ludicrous. It reminds me of college, only more crowded. Much more.

All of the roommates are gone tonight, leaving the apartment to just Ashley and me, which is a first I think. Usually one of them is here.

Ashley starts rummaging through her clothes, trying to find me something to wear. After about a half hour of putting outfits together, we decide on a pair of distressed jeans (that I may never return — they're fabulous), with a champagne-colored silk blouse and a black blazer. Feeling good about the outfit, I hit the shower to get the food smell off.

111

Thirty minutes later, I stand in front of the mirror, scrutinizing my makeup as Ashley curls my dark blonde locks with a curling iron.

"So, have you talked to Adam?" she asks, her eyes concentrating on my hair.

"No," I say, wiping the side of my mouth where a little of my signature Russian Red lipstick had spread. "I don't know if I will. Not for a while, at least."

We are silent for a moment as Ashley continues to work on my hair.

"Thanks, by the way," I say, breaking the silence.

"For what?"

"For not gloating about the dinner with Adam's family. And how you were right."

"Bridge, I wouldn't gloat about that."

"I know, but thanks anyway." I smile in the mirror at her. Finished with the curling, she starts separating the curls with her fingers.

"So you and Justin going out, huh?" I raise my eyebrows, insinuatingly.

"Oh please." I see her rolling her eyes in the mirror. "It's Justin. We're hanging out. Nothing more than that. Besides . . ." she trails off.

"Besides, what?"

"It's nothing." She shakes her head.

"Nope, too late," I say, turning around to face her. "Tell me."

"Oh fine," she sighs. "I was going to say: besides, even if I did like him, it doesn't matter."

"Why?" I ask, confused.

112

"Because, Bridgette, you blind idiot." She rolls her eyes.

"What? What do you mean?"

"Isn't it obvious that he's got a thing for you?" She looks at me as if I should know this, but I have no idea what she's talking about.

"Justin?" I say, totally taken aback by this information.

"Yes, Bridgette. Justin. How can you not see it?" She shakes her head, disbelieving my ignorance.

"Because I don't. At all," I say, fervently. "Justin and I are nothing but friends." Ashley shakes her head, rolling her eyes at the same time.

"Did he say something to you?"

"No, he didn't. I can just tell." She folds her arms.

I close my eyes briefly, trying to rack my brain for clues. Remembering back to college and Ian and . . . maybe I'm not very good at recognizing that. There were clues with Ian, though. But with Justin, there's nothing there. I just know it.

I shake my head. "He doesn't, Ash."

"How do you know? Has he said something to you?" she asks, a little heated.

"No, why would he need to? Are you mad?" I take a step back from her, seeing her face get red with heat, something Ashley does when she's angry. It's not hard for her skin to turn red, but I can tell by the tone of red what she's feeling. Right now, it's anger.

"It's nothing." She turns her head to the side, looking away.

I look at the clock on the wall behind her. It's seven thirty. "Crap, Ash. I have to go." I start walking toward the front door to grab my jacket and put my shoes on. Ashley follows me.

"This conversation is not over," I say, leaning against the wall by the front door to balance myself so I can slide a black ballet flat on my foot. Thank goodness I brought these with me. I'm always dying to get out of my work shoes as fast as possible, so I usually bring a spare pair.

Ashley shakes her head, her skin starting to turn back to its normal shade. "Never mind. Maybe I'm wrong. Just forget it."

I can tell by the look on her face that she doesn't think she's wrong, but I don't have time to point it out. We say quick good-byes, and I run swiftly down the stairs, careful not to trip.

Stepping out the front door of Ashley's building into the remnants of dusk, I take a deep breath. I shake off the conversation I just had with Ashley. That will have to wait. Time to go meet Ian.

CHAPTER 14

University of Connecticut, sophomore year, winter

"Oh, Ian," the buxom blonde hanging off Ian's arm said for, like, the gajillionth time. This time it wasn't even over a joke. I was so over her.

From across the booth, I watched them ogle each other, and I internally gagged. I needed to stop letting Ian convince me that double dates were fun. Don't get me wrong, sometimes they were, when I actually liked the girl he brought with him. There had been a string of morons lately (don't get me started on Sarah the Stalker), and Kenzie was no exception. I don't know why she bothered me so much, but she did. Maybe it was her name. So perky and cute, just like her, well, everything. It wasn't so much her as it was her and Ian. She was not who I imagined Ian with. I would just have to deal with it for now. Ian never stuck around with anyone for too long.

"Babe," Brandon leaned over to my ear, speaking softly. "If you're going to keep putting your hand on my leg, could you please stop knocking off my napkin?"

"Sorry," I muttered. So much for romance. Brandon and I had been together for nearly eight months now. We were past the romance stage. Which was kind of weird because it hadn't been that long. I thought that didn't happen until at least a year. But it was comfortable with Brandon, and there was something to say about comfort.

I pulled my menu up to my face to hide the two love birds across from me, who were currently nuzzling noses (who does that?). I felt like I was in my own little cocoon behind my menu, and it kept my hand from traveling down to Brandon's thigh, where I might accidently knock his napkin off. Heaven forbid.

"Bridge," Ian called, pulling me away from my bubble.

I peeked over the top. "Yeah?"

"Watcha eating?" He cocked a lone eyebrow at me.

"I don't know yet," I said, void of inflection, and went back to my menu.

"Wanna split nachos? Kenzie here doesn't eat meat."

I peered over the top again, a questioning look on my face. Ian doesn't get bothered by much, but vegetarians drive him insane.

This was an interesting development. I shut my menu and placed it in front of me. A quick glance at Brandon found him texting busily on his phone. Typical.

"So, you're a vegetarian, Kenzie?" I said, knowing fully well that this was the first time I had given her my full attention.

"Vegan, actually," she said.

I smiled. It was a mischievous smile, but only Ian would know that. Vegetarians drove him insane, but vegans made him down-right incensed. He and my vegan roommate Amy had gotten into it more than once. Oh, this was going to be fun.

"So, what made you want to be a vegan?" I asked.

"Bridge," Ian chided, knowing where I was going.

"Well, I just think it's how God intended," she said, peering at me through her long eyelashes.

Oh dear heavens, she's brought God into it. Ian hated it when vegetarians used God as their excuse. He'd usually say something about how if God had intended for us to be vegetarians, then explain the cow. They are massive, slow, and delicious. Clearly meant for human consumption.

"So you think God intended for us to be vegan," I said, nodding my head, prodding her further.

"Yes. You know, the whole 'thou shall not kill' thing." She bobbed her head.

"So, you think that extends to animals then," I said, looking from her to Ian. I could see a vein tense in his neck, his jaw firm. I knew Ian, and I sensed that this had not been discussed previously, and he was not liking the answers. At all.

I'm not a betting gal, but if I were, I would put a million dollars down on this not lasting past next week.

I take back what I previously thought. This might be the best double date ever.

"Yes, Ian," I turned to him. "I'll split nachos with you. Get extra beef this time." I didn't look directly at Kenzie, but from the corner of my eye, I could see her look at Ian with pouting lips.

"Sounds good," was all he said. A humph came out of Kenzie's mouth, but he didn't concede in any way.

I reached over and put my hand on Brandon's leg, out of sheer habit.

"Babe," he reproved with his tone, as the napkin slid off his lap and onto the floor.

"Sorry," I said, but I wasn't really sorry.

All felt right in the world, actually.

CHAPTER 15

"No, she did not." Ian shakes his head at me, disbelieving. The dim lighting of the café playing nicely on his face.

"I'm not kidding! She freaking stole my underwear. Who does that?" I scrunch my face, still not truly believing it myself, after all these years. I saw it with my own eyes, so I know it happened.

"I dated that girl. She didn't seem like an underwear stealer," he says, still not convinced.

"Well, obviously you didn't know her that well. I mean, I was her roommate, and I didn't even get the 'underwear-stealing' vibe from her, but I'm here to tell you she did."

Ian laughs loudly at that. "Wow, I had no idea." He reaches up and scratches his jaw, a rather handsome five o'clock shadow on his face. I love his laugh. I don't miss that about Adam. He never laughed like Ian does. I often wondered if he just didn't get the jokes, but now sitting here with Ian, I'm starting to wonder if maybe he didn't get me.

Reminiscing with Ian is so fun. There are so many things about college that he remembers that I don't and vise versa. There's never a dull moment in our conversations. It was always that way. With Adam and me, sometimes it felt like I had to work at it, but never with Ian.

"Do you remember that girl, Sarah, who stalked me for a while?" Ian asks, and then takes a sip of his coffee.

"Oh, yeah, I remember her. She was scary."

"I ran into her not long after I moved into the city."

"No way. Here?"

"Yeah, not far from my building."

"Did you get a restraining order?"

"Nah, I took her out on a date."

"You did? Why would you do that?"

"You know . . . people change . . . wanted to give her a second chance . . . she was hot."

"So, had she changed?"

"No."

We instantly stop the conversation and stare at each other, a game we used to play back in college. It's like the blinking game, only instead of not blinking, we're not allowed to laugh or smile. We called it "laughing chicken," which is not a very original name now that I think of it.

It's very difficult to play, and I would seldom win. The game always began after witty banter, when we should be laughing. Somehow we both just knew by the tone of our conversation that the game was on. There was never a "let's play laughing chicken."

I tried to play it with Adam once. He didn't get it.

I freeze my face in a serious expression, trying to think of something sad to keep me from laughing. When you really want to laugh, it's nearly impossible to do. The trick is to move your mouth around trying to keep it from turning into a smile. The problem is that you're staring at someone using the same strategy, and they look like a complete idiot. It makes it quite difficult.

I do this duck mouth that used to always get Ian, and I see the side of his mouth twitch. And then the other side twitches, and then, not being able to help himself, he breaks out into a huge smile and starts laughing.

"Yes!" I throw fists in the air. "I win!"

"That was a low blow with the duck lips," he says, still chuckling.

"Well, you know me." I wink at him.

"I do know you," he says, his smiling face slowly morphing into a more serious expression.

And there are the butterflies.

We look at each other, my fingers twiddling with the straps of my black hobo bag sitting in my lap. Ian's tapping his fingers on his cup. There is an intensity in the air. I can tell just by looking at him that he is thinking the same thing I am, which is how much I've missed this.

"Well," Ian breaks the stare, looking to his watch. I know what's coming next, and I don't want to hear it. "I guess I better get going."

Damn.

"Yeah, me, too." I look at my phone and it's nearly ten. I had no idea we'd been sitting here for two hours. It felt more like twenty minutes. I wish it wouldn't end.

We walk out of the coffee shop together, not saying anything.

"Walk me to my stop?" I ask, hoping he will say yes, wanting to spend a little more time with him.

"Sure," he says.

We start walking toward the subway. I can see the bright entrance sign not far from us, maybe a half block away.

"It was great to see you again." I look over at him as we walk.

"It really was. I didn't realize—"

He cuts himself off, shaking his head.

"You didn't realize what?"

"I just didn't realize how much I've missed you." He smiles to himself, looking down at the street as we walk.

"Me, too," is all I can say. I want to say something profound but I've got nothing.

We reach the top of the stairs to the subway entrance quicker than I wanted.

"Lunch next week?" I turn my body to face him.

"Yeah, that sounds good," he says, nodding his head.

"Well, thanks again," I say, starting to move in for a hug.

Instead though, Ian grabs my face with his hands suddenly, pulling me into him and, he kisses me softly and gently. Then, letting go of my face, wrapping his arms around my back, he pulls me in even closer, and we kiss with more intensity.

Oh my gosh, this. This is what kissing should feel like. I know I shouldn't compare, even though I've been doing it all night, but I never had this with Adam. Kissing him never felt like this.

I'm instantly transported back to the first time Ian and I kissed. That time in my apartment when Ian told me how he felt, and I knew I felt the same. This feels so right. So amazing. So perfect.

I wrap my arms tighter around Ian as the kiss deepens even further. I want this. I want more of this.

Just before I completely lose myself in this moment, Ian pulls away abruptly. He lightly pushes me away from him and curses under his breath.

"I can't do this." He shakes his head as if to bring himself back from a trance. Then he turns around and starts walking away, running a hand through his hair in frustration.

"Ian?" I start to follow him, but he's walking too fast. I hear him whistle loudly, trying to hail a taxi, and I see one pull over and watch as he quickly jumps in, shutting the door behind him. He doesn't look back. And I'm left there, standing on the sidewalk, wondering what the hell just happened.

CHAPTER 16

"What do you think it all means, Gram?"

We are sitting by the window at a deli, eating sandwiches. Outside, the gray sky and random sputters of rain mock my mood.

"I'm not sure. On the one hand, he did kiss you, which should be a pretty big deal. Well, it was in my day, at least. You young kids are kissing everyone nowadays. If you ask me, it's quite unsanitary." She clicks her tongue, disapproving.

"Gram, focus."

"Yes, my apologies. I don't know why he kissed you and then walked away."

"He practically ran, Gram." I slump back in my seat, picturing the scene in my head, like I've done nearly a thousand times. Well, maybe it's been hundreds.

"So why do you think he did?" she asks, and then takes a bite of her pastrami on rye.

"Well, isn't it obvious? He still hasn't forgiven me for college." I look down at my plate, feeling defeated. My turkey croissant is not exactly what I need for the emotional eating I want to do right now. What I need is that big, fat slice of chocolate cake eyeing me from the counter display case.

"Yes, you know I still don't understand exactly what happened. You've been very vague," she says, and then takes a sip of her soda.

"I know. I don't really like talking about it. It's kind of a black mark in my past." I eye the chocolate cake again.

"Did you cheat on him or something?" she asks, curiosity obviously taking over.

"No. Yes . . . sort of." I exhale loudly.

"Well, which one is it?" Gram looks taken aback by my answer. I don't think she was expecting that.

"All of it. You know, I don't really want to talk about it." I look out the window at the dreary weather.

"Yes, of course. Sorry to pry." There's a slight look of hurt on her face that she tries to cover up.

"Oh Gram, you aren't prying. I'll tell you. I just don't feel like talking about it right now."

We sit there in silence, Gram eating her sandwich and me staring at mine.

"I guess there's one silver lining, tiny as it is," I say, picking up my sandwich but still not taking a bite.

"And that is?" Gram looks at me inquisitively.

"It's definitely helped me get my mind off Adam." I take a bite of my sandwich, hoping the saltiness will help me get over my chocolate craving. It's not working.

Oddly, when I think about it, I don't know if I've thought of Adam much at all since I met up with Ian. Granted, it's only been a day, but still . . . that's got to be a step in the right direction. At least the signs are pointing toward the fact that I'm starting to move on from the whole Adam situation. Of course, I'm having lunch with Carla tomorrow, so who knows where I'll be after that.

"Well, that's good then, don't you think?" She eyes me, searching my face.

"Yes, but now my mind is completely on Ian. Like I can't think of anything else," I say, still ogling the chocolate cake, dreaming of its sugary deliciousness. My mouth salivates just thinking about it. Yes, I think chocolate cake is definitely happening.

"Well, give him time then," Gram says. She reaches for the sugar packet container, opens her purse, and dumps all of the pink, yellow, blue, and white packets into it.

"Gram!" I say, looking around wildly. Someone had to see that. I mean, she's not even trying to hide it.

"What?" she looks up at me after she returns the empty container to its regular spot on the table.

"I thought we discussed this. That's stealing." I point to her stolen-goods-carrying purse.

"Oh, nonsense. I do it all the time. No one cares. Besides, they have tons of these. I'm simply helping them with the rotation so they don't get stale," she says, going back to her sandwich.

"Gram, I seriously can't go out with you anymore if you keep doing that," I say, pointing my finger at her in full lecture mode. This is not her first offense.

"Stop being such a goody-goody, Bridgette. You really need to loosen up," she says like some marijuana-hocking junky.

I start to say more but then stop myself. There's no use in trying to talk her out of it. We've had this discussion plenty of times. I silently scold myself for not remembering to hide the container when we sat down. The crazy part is Gram has money and lots of it. She doesn't need to steal the sugar packets, but now it's like a habit or something and she can't stop. Maybe it gives her a little rush.

I shake my head at her, puckering my lips into my best duckface. "Gram, what am I going to do with you?"

She looks up from her sandwich. "Well, you can start by buying that chocolate cake you've been eyeing." She nods her head toward the counter display case where the lone piece of chocolate cake has been beckoning me. "Go get it," she says. "We can share."

I give her a small smile. Chocolate cake it is.

CHAPTER 17

"Oh, Bridgette, what am I going to dooooooooooooo?" Carla blubbers as we sit in a corner table at her favorite restaurant.

People are staring. Actually, it's more than staring. It's outright judging at this point. I'm trying desperately to soothe her, but nothing is working. I signal the server to bring more wine. It's my only hope at this point.

"She's a gold digger. I know she is," she says through sniffles.

"Well . . ." I taper off. I don't know what to say here. Is this even appropriate? My ex-boyfriend's mother—an ex whom, until very (very) recently, I was pining over—is now venting to me about his new fiancée. Awkward is probably the most appropriate word to describe it.

"You know she doesn't love him. You saw her! Why would that pencil-thin witch be interested in my son? I mean, don't get me wrong, I think Adam is handsome, of course. But not handsome enough for that slut-looking-supermodel. I pictured my Adam with someone more plain, you know? Like you." She gestures over to me.

Ouch. And here I was thinking my tailored, black shorts, paired with a white button-down shirt, and the most amazing Kenneth Cole platform sandals, looked more than plain. Silly me.

She shakes her head, "I can't let him marry her; I just can't."

We sit in silence. I'm trying to think of something to say, but what is there really? I don't know Serene personally. I have no idea if she's marrying Adam for his money . . . money that he doesn't have just yet. Perhaps she is, or maybe she truly loves him. That thought stings still, to be honest. I spent so much time thinking my future was with Adam. Even if my heart is feeling less broken, I still feel the need to hate her.

Carla grabs her purse and starts fishing around until she pulls out a packet of tissues, and taking one from the packet, blows her nose loudly and obnoxiously. The staring, which had tapered off for a bit, commences yet again.

"Anyway, enough about Adam and that tramp. What's new with you? How are things?" she says, as she wipes her nose aggressively with the tissue.

"Pretty good, I guess. Just working. Nothing exciting." I shrug my shoulders. Wow, my life sounds dull. I guess I could go into the whole Ian drama, but I don't feel like it. Plus, I would have to give the whole backstory for any of it to seem like a drama to Carla.

"And how is Justin?" She winks when she says his name.

Oh dang it, Justin. I totally forgot about that whole ruse. I've yet to come clean.

"He's fine," is all I say. I'm not in the mood to confess right now, plus it probably wouldn't help the situation much.

"Well, I hope things work out with you two." She grabs her wine and takes a rather large swig. I just nod my head. "He's really into you, that one," she says after she swallows.

"Really? How so?" That was a knee-jerk reaction. Obviously, I already know it was all acting on his part. Mine, too.

"I could tell by the look in his eyes when he watched you." She nods her head.

Well, that was not what I was expecting. Did Justin do that great an acting job?

"Heaven knows, I've never seen that look in Serene's eyes when she looks at my Adam." Her eyes well up with tears again, and she grabs her wine glass and gulps more down, probably trying to squelch them. "They've already set a date, you know," she says with a frog-like voice, as she chokes back the tears.

"What? They've set a date . . . already?" My stomach sinks. I guess I wasn't expecting them to actually set a date. But, of course, that's what you do when you get engaged. I already knew Adam wasn't mine anymore, and I was coming to grips with that. But for some reason this piece of info sets me back just slightly. It seems so final.

"Yes, September twenty-first." Carla taps the side of the wine glass with a long manicured nail.

"Well, that's far enough away that maybe things will change," I say, trying to give her some hope. It also helps my spirits lift a little. Not that I want to be with Adam again . . . or do I? I'm so confused at all the feelings going through my mind right now. I think I might need therapy.

"No, Bridgette." She leans toward me and looks me directly in the eyes, "September twenty-first of *this year*." She practically spits the words out as she says them.

"This year? But that's only three months away!" I say louder than I intended.

"That's what I said to them. But they seem set on it. Oh, what am I going to do?" She starts blubbering again, and the staring starts up as well.

Three months? Who gets married in only three months' time? I don't even think you can book a venue in that amount of time in this city. Not a decent one, at least.

The server brings our food to the table. Both of us just stare at it. I know I don't really feel like eating, and I'm pretty sure Carla feels the same.

My phone beeps.

Sorry.

Ian. Thank goodness. I wasn't sure I would hear from him after we met up the other night. He didn't reply to any of the texts I sent him. I will not admit to how many I sent, but I will say it was more than four and less than twenty . . . or so. I don't know. My shame kept me from counting.

"Who was that?" I look up to see Carla looking inquisitively at my phone. I better grab on tight in case she feels the need to rip it out of my hands. That's not happening again, not if I can help it, at least.

"Just someone from college," I say, hoping to divert her from the questioning game she so loves to play. "Let me reply really quickly." I start typing rapidly after she nods an approval of sorts, half occupied with her wine.

What happened?

My phone beeps again, not too long after I hit send.

Don't want to explain over text. Coffee Monday night?

I text him back a "sure" and then put my phone in my purse. A sudden feeling of relief lands on my shoulders. I was carrying more tension there than I thought. Obviously, Ian and I have more to discuss about our past. Clearly it was not just "water under the bridge."

The rest of the lunch is somewhat strained. I don't have much to offer Carla in the way of sympathy or good advice. I don't feel like it's my place. The only thing I can offer is a listening ear, and I think Carla might be drained, because she doesn't have much to say. Not as much as she usually does, at least. Poor Carla. This is so hard for her.

"Sorry to go on like I did," Carla says as we walk out of the restaurant.

"Why are you sorry? I'm here to listen," I say, and I truly mean it. Even given how awkward the whole situation is.

She gives me a hug, and we say good-bye.

Thank goodness I got the text from Ian. At least I have that to hold onto. Having Ian around took off some of the burn from the breakup with Adam. I was beginning to wonder if I would have gone back to my old stalking-Adam ways without Ian in my life. I doubt it, but I guess I won't have to find out.

CHAPTER 18

University of Connecticut, junior year, winter

"Want me to punch him?" Ian asked, his arms around me as we sat on the couch in my apartment living room. I was looking glamorous in a graphic tee shirt and cutoff sweats.

"Yes," I sniffled.

"Seriously, Bridge, I never liked him for you," he said, leaning his head against mine.

"I know," I said through the balled-up tissue I was holding up to my ever-running nose. I was finally over the hiccupping, thank goodness. He never came out and said it until right now, but I could always tell that Ian was not Team Brandon.

"You could have said something sooner, though," I said, feeling defeated and heartbroken.

"Would you have listened if I did?" he asked, pulling me tighter into him.

I sighed. "Probably not."

We sat there in silence for a bit, Ian rubbing my arm with his hand, holding me tight.

"Now that it's out, what didn't you like about him?" I asked through my sniffling.

"I don't know," he said. But I could tell by his tone that he was just buying time to figure out how to articulate what he really wanted to say. "I guess it wasn't him so much. It was more the fact that you weren't totally yourself around him."

"How so?" That caught me off guard. I felt like I had been myself around Brandon.

"You just—I don't know how to explain it," he said, still not coming clean. "I guess . . . I guess you just seemed to conform to what Brandon wanted and not really what you wanted."

"I did?"

He only nodded his head. I felt like there was more there, but I wasn't sure I wanted to prod further. Was I really that big of a doormat?

"Anyway, it doesn't matter now, does it?" he asked. I shrugged my shoulders, conceding. No point in rehashing it all now. Brandon and I were done.

"I guess not," I said, the tears starting up again.

"I will seriously punch him if you want me to," Ian said. I actually believed he would if I asked. Part of me wanted him to, of course. But what good would it do? Plus, like it or not, Brandon and Ian were still roommates.

"I guess I won't be spending much time at your apartment anymore," I said. Pulling out of his grasp, I sat back on the couch. I pulled my knees into my chest and wrapped my arms around them like a cocoon.

"That's cool. We can hang out here." Ian said. Leaning back against the couch, he placed his hands in his lap.

"I'm sure *Brittany* would love that." Brittany was Ian's flavor of the month. In truth, I didn't mind Brittany, but I liked to say her name with as much snobbery as I could. It's a snobby name, after all. *Brit-knee. Brit-nay.* Any way you sliced it, really.

"Don't worry about her," Ian said, his head falling back against the couch.

"I'm not," I said, and I truly wasn't. Ian and I were a package deal. The women in Ian's life who protested were quickly kicked to the curb. Brandon never seemed to mind Ian and me. That was another reason it would be hard to start over. Who knew if the next guy would be so understanding? If there would be another guy. I couldn't even think about that at the moment.

"So, how long does this last?" Ian asked, turning his head toward me.

"How long does what last?" I asked, scrunching up my face at him.

"This." He made an imaginary circle around my face with his pointer finger. "This whole, woe-is-me-Bridgette thing you've got going on here."

"You jerk. We just broke up today," I said, as I unwrapped a hand from the cocoon I had put myself in and slapped him on the arm.

"Couple days? Week? Two weeks?" He kept going, searching my face to see if he'd even come within the ballpark of the end date for my mourning.

"Are you serious?" My mouth fell open in complete shock at his lack of any emotional intelligence. Ian was better at that than most men.

"Yes, I've never been around brokenhearted Bridgette. I'm just wondering how long I will have to listen to it." His lip twitched as he held back a grin.

I called him a not-so-nice word and pushed him with both of my hands. He dramatically toppled over to the side.

"I'll get over it when I'm over it. I'm not like you," I said, pushing him again. This time I used more strength.

"What's that supposed to mean?" Ian asked as he righted himself, his brow furrowed in my direction.

"It means you can just move on without even a thought. It takes us girls longer than that." I wrapped my arms around my knees, cocooning myself once again.

Ian feigned exasperation. "I don't just move on without a thought. It can take me a while, too. I just don't make it worse by watching sappy movies and listening to breakup music."

"I don't do that," I said, protesting. Although I probably would do both of those things eventually.

"You'd be surprised how long it takes me to get over someone," he said, his head looking forward.

"Yah, sure," I said, with an eye roll that he couldn't see.

"Some people you never get over," he said quietly.

"Why, Ian Davies, that was probably the cheesiest thing that's ever come out of your mouth," I said, teasing, but also feeling somewhat shocked by his admission.

"Well," he shrugged, "it's true."

"So, who is it?" I nudged him with my elbow.

"Who's what?" He scrunched his face at me.

"This girl you never got over," I asked, digging my elbow into his arm further.

He shook his head, looking away from me. "No one."

I didn't press further, because I could tell he wasn't going to tell me even if I tried.

"Give me a week," I said, knowing it would take longer than that to get over Brandon, but that I would most likely stop sulking by then.

"That, I can do," he said, reaching his arm over. He pulled me toward him, and I nuzzled my head into his neck.

I could totally handle this, as long as I had Ian.

CHAPTER 19

"BRIDGETTE!" Ursula yells as she walks into the staging area.

Crap, what did I do now? We're cleaning up from our latest catering job. One of my favorite kind of parties. Famous people. I can't say who was in attendance but their names rhyme with Drad Bitt and Banjolina Holie. Quite exciting.

"Yes?" I say somewhat timidly. Seriously, I'm wracking my brain here. I don't think I did anything wrong. But you never know with The Sea Witch. I could glance in the wrong direction for one second, and she would catch it. She has eyes in the back of her head and on pretty much every other part of her body. She can just "sense" when something is amiss.

"Vee need to talk." She gestures for me to come over to where she is.

I look back at Ashley and Justin who are both staring. Their expressions look as if I am facing my impending death. I just might be.

Ursula turns around and walks out the door, and I follow her. My heart rate is picking up by the second.

"Bridgette, I have been vatchink you tonight," she says in her thick German accent.

Oh crap.

"Yes, I'm really sorry about that," I say, not entirely sure what I'm apologizing for.

"Vat are you sorry about?" She furrows her brow.

"Um, nothing. Never mind. Vat . . . er . . . I mean *what* were you saying?" Oh that was brilliant. I blame Justin. He was making me do my Ursula impression before she came in the room yelling my name. Not one of my smartest moves.

She shakes her head as if she's begun to doubt what she intended to say.

"Business is pickink up, and I need a new caterink manager," she finally says, and rather flatly.

I stand there, gaping at her. She needs a new catering manager? What does that have to do with me?

"You vant zee job, don't you?" She gives me a confused look.

Catering manager? Me? Uh, yeah, since the day I started working for her. Is she really saying what I think she's saying? It can't be. It's been so long that I've wanted this job, but then months passed (years, actually) and it never happened . . . I guess I thought it never would.

"Bridgette?"

"Yes! Sorry! Yes, I would love to be a catering manager." I can barely contain my excitement, but I must in front of this stoic woman. Jumping up and down and squealing would probably not go over well. "Thank you so much for this opportunity," I say.

"Oh no. Zee job is not yours. Not yet, at least," she shakes her head.

"What do you mean?" Did she not just say the job was mine?

"Vat I'm saying is zat I am vatchink you. If you keep up vat you are doink, the job could be yours."

Okay, so not quite as exciting as I had previously thought. I still have to prove myself? Doesn't three years of dedicated, never-late, never-call-in-sick service mean anything? What else can I prove? Still, I can't look a gift horse in the mouth. I need to grasp onto whatever I get.

"Yes," I nod my head. "Yes, I want the job. I will keep doing what I'm doing." I stop myself from saying "doink," even though my brain and my mouth really want me to. It's hard not to pick up on the accent when I'm around her . . . or imitating her. I do it well, so I've been told.

She dismisses me with a wave of her hand, and I go back to helping everyone clean up so we can go home.

"What did she want?" Ashley asks, worry in her face.

I grab her by the arm and bring her over to Justin, so I can tell them both at the same time.

"She told me that if I keep—" I look around to make sure she's not in the room, "'doink vat I am doink,' that I might get promoted to catering manager." I try to keep my voice low so no one else hears. I don't want anyone else to overhear in case they are also vying for the position. I don't need competition. Plus, this is my job. Not a temporary step on the way to not-probable stardom. It's what I've wanted to do, and hopefully I'm finally going to do it.

"That's great!" Ashley says, holding her hand up for a high five, which I happily oblige.

"Nice going, Reynolds." Justin pats me on the back impersonally. Wow, his emotional intelligence doesn't even stretch to good things.

"Let's go celebrate," I say, looking between them.

"What are we celebrating?" Justin looks at me strangely.

Ashley whacks him on the arm. "That she might get the job she's been wanting for years? You're such an idiot sometimes."

"Oh, right. Well, I just figured we would celebrate when she actually got the job. Not the possibility of it." He shrugs his shoulders.

Men.

Ashley rolls her eyes. I'm so glad that she, at least, gets me.

"Anyway, I can't help celebrate. I have a callback in the morning." Ashley looks disappointed.

"Well, I can," Justin says, his tone showing that he still doesn't understanding why we are celebrating.

I'll take it, though. I don't want to go home. Gram will be asleep. I want to go out and bask in the new possibilities in my life. A possible new job.

And Ian wants to talk about his freak out. Who knows if that could lead to anything, but it's a possibility. And I like possibilities way more than finalities.

~*~

"So, what will you do if you get the job?" Justin asks as we sit at Ray's Candy Store, drinking chocolate shakes and sharing french fries.

"Well, my first order of business will be to fire you." I smirk at him.

"Ha ha. Ursula would never have that. She wants me, you know."

I nearly spit out my shake at his declaration. "Oh, really? What makes you think that?"

"It's just the way she looks at me. I can tell." He winks, and I instantly remember what Carla said at lunch today about how Justin looked at me.

Suddenly I have a pit in my stomach, thinking maybe Ashley and Carla were right after all. Maybe Justin does like me, as more than a friend. Oh, why though? Why does this have to happen to a great friendship? It will totally be ruined when I don't reciprocate. And I don't reciprocate those feelings. I adore Justin, but not in that way.

"What's wrong?" He scrunches his face, checking out whatever expression is on mine. It's probably not a pretty one, since I was contemplating. No one has a pretty contemplating face. I've seen mine in the mirror. There were double chins involved.

"Oh nothing." I try to brush it off, hoping I can kick the pit out of my stomach and go back to la-la land, where I believed Justin never liked me as more than a friend. It was only thirty seconds ago that I first had the thought, and now going back seems like an impossibility. Funny how things can change in the blink of an eye.

My hands feel sweaty, and suddenly I don't want to celebrate anymore. I just want to go home. Me and Justin. Justin and me. It doesn't make sense. It feels wrong. Doesn't he feel that?

I suck down my chocolate shake as fast as I can, and of course I get a piercing pain in my head right above my left eye. Ice cream headaches are of the devil.

"Owwww," I squint my eyes and pinch my forehead together, trying to get it to stop. I rub my forehead vigorously.

"Ice cream headache?" Justin asks, and all I can do is nod my head. He reaches over and starts rubbing my forehead, too. I suppose he's trying to help, but now I have a bunch of hands all over my face, with both of us trying to do the same thing. I push his hand away as the headache subsides.

Normally, I would be shocked that any gesture of the touching variety came from Justin. But now it seems to speak volumes. *I'm touching you because I like you.* Oh gosh, I need to get out of here. Quickly.

"Well, I guess I better get home," I say as I wipe my mouth and start to grab my purse.

"Wait, Bridge, I want to talk to you about something. Something that I've been thinking about for a while now." He grabs my arm lightly in an attempt to keep me in my seat.

No, we are not doing this now. I don't want things to get weird, and they are going to. I shake his arm off and stand up.

"Can we talk about it later? I'm really tired, and I have a lot going on tomorrow." I sling my purse over my shoulder.

"But—"

"Please? I'm so tired. It just hit me all at once." I fake a yawn. It's a horrible acting job.

"Fine," he says, shoulders slumping, looking defeated. Poor guy. He must have been working up to this for a while, and now I've gone and crushed it. I'm not backing down. If I avoid letting him tell me, maybe he will get the idea and move on. If nothing is out in the open, we can go on as we were. Yes, that's a great plan. Or a terrible one. But I'm doing it, regardless.

"Sure. See you tomorrow," he mutters, as I walk out of Ray's and into the perfect-June-night air.

The fresh air (as fresh as it can be in the East Village) feels good as I walk quickly to the subway. That was a close one. Crisis averted.

Now, how to avoid the topic further. That is the challenge.

CHAPTER 20

University of Connecticut, senior year, fall

I sat down next to Ian, who was outside the school of business building, reading a textbook about something that didn't really interest me.

"Well, it's done," I said, wiping my hands together as if to show I'm finished.

"You broke his heart?" he asked, eyebrows raised.

"Yes. He was devastated," I deadpanned. "Nah, it was mutual. We fizzled out over the summer. There was no saving it."

"Well, it's probably for the best. It's our last year after all," he said, keeping his eyes on his textbook.

"Yeah, I guess," I said. But I didn't have to guess. I knew. Matt was just a summer fling. He and I both knew that. We never said it officially at the end of the summer, and although I knew the feeling was mutual, I needed to actually say it to him. A clean break.

"Look at us." Ian put an arm around me. "I think this is the first time since we met freshman year that we are both single."

"Hmm, yes." I leaned my head against his shoulder. "Single and ready to mingle."

"Did you really just say that?" he teased, nudging my head with his shoulder. "Well, I'm not planning on any mingling. We're seniors. Time to buckle down."

I yawn. "Sounds boring."

"Yes, it probably will be. But you'll have me, and aren't I enough?" he asked, resting the side of his head on the top of mine.

"For sure," I said, smiling to myself. I had Ian. I supposed for now I didn't need anyone else.

CHAPTER 21

Another Saturday night and I'm working a party. An engagement party, no less. Way to rub salt in the wound. I feel like stomping my feet on the ground, saying, "I wanna be engaged!" But I'm not. Adam is, though. That still doesn't seem real.

I have to be on my best behavior tonight. Since Ursula singled me out to tell me about the catering manager opening, I need her to see I'm serious about this job and this opportunity.

Justin, somehow, got the night off (which is kind of helpful with the whole him-liking-me thing), but Ashley and I—and most of the other servers on staff—get the privilege of working tonight. And by privilege, I mean horrible luck. It's a full-service meal, so there's a lot to do.

Ashley and I stand in the back of the room, waiting for salad service to begin. Drinks have been poured. Champagne has been distributed. Now we sit and wait for the DJ to introduce the family and the engaged couple. Apparently, there's been a slight delay. I overheard someone tell Ursula it's because of the future bride. I don't really care, but it's fun to think of reasons why she would be late to her own engagement party.

Maybe she's drunk and not even able to walk, and someone—maybe a sister—is trying to sober her back up. Maybe there was a horrible car accident and she's in the hospital, only no one knows, and we are mistakenly waiting on her to get this party started. Maybe she's having an affair with the future groom's brother.

The most boring reason, and probably the most realistic: traffic. It's everyone's excuse in the city, because it's always true. And even if it weren't, no one would question you.

"What're you thinking about?" Ashley asks, in low tones, standing close to me so I can hear her. Background music is allowing us to have actual conversations without Ursula noticing, as long as we stand with our faces forward, looking like we're poised to work.

"Just the possible demise of the bride." I scrunch my face up, realizing what a bitter twit I sound like.

"Thinking about Adam, huh?" she asks, not bothered by my cynicism.

"Well no, not really," I shrug.

"What's up with Ian?"

"What do you mean?"

"Have you talked to him at all?"

"No. Just texting. We're supposed to get coffee on Monday so he can explain." I look down at the black work shoes—the hideous non-slick kind— adorning my feet. They're very unattractive, especially added to the knee-length, black skirt and white, button-up shirt topped with a black vest. If I get the job of catering manager, the first order of business will be to change up these horrid outfits we have to wear.

"So, what do you think about Ian?" Ashley asks, not giving up on the topic.

"I don't know. Being with Ian is so easy, you know? At least until he kissed me and ran off. We just fit so well together. I—"

The music gets louder, and the DJ starts announcing the wedding party of the future bride and groom. The bride-to-be must have finally shown up.

"Ladies and gentlemen, let's get this party started! And now, without further ado, let's begin the introductions. First off, I'd like to introduce the father of the bride," the DJ says. Applause fills the room as a man, possibly in his mid-fifties, with dyed-blond, poufy hair enters waving. He shows stark-white teeth when he smiles.

Ashley leans into me, "So, you think maybe Ian and you fit better than you and Adam did?" She raises her eyebrows in a know-it-all way.

"Yeah, I do," I say, feeling a little annoyed that I have to admit Ashley was right. "I guess I know now that Adam and I weren't right for each other. I know I once thought we were. It's just that—"

"And now the mother of the bride . . ."

"It's just what?" Ashley coaxes me.

"It's just that Adam was always so particular about everything. I was always trying to change things for him, to fit his needs. But with Ian, I don't have to change anything. And that kiss—"

"And now the mother and father of the groom . . ."

"Uh-huh, the kiss. Go on," she says, keeping her head forward in case Ursula glances over at us.

"The kiss brought back so many memories of the past. Good memories . . ."

"And now, ladies and gentlemen, may I introduce you to the future bride and groom . . ." The attendees get up out of their seats and start clapping and whistling.

I lean in closer to Ashley so she can hear me over the crowd. "I remembered all the good things I had with Ian. He's just so . . . so . . ."

"Bridgette?" Ashley nudges me with her arm, interrupting me. I momentarily freak out, thinking Ursula has caught us. But Ashley usually nudges me when that happens, letting me know I should move quickly away from her. This time, she grabs a fist full of my shirt, bringing me into her and turning me away from the front. This is not very Ashley-like.

"What's Ian's last name?" she asks, almost frantically.

"Davies," I tell her.

Her big, blue eyes go wide as she turns and points to the front of the room. My eyes follow to where she is pointing.

It can't be. My heart sinks far down into my stomach, and my mouth goes dry.

Somehow, either Ian or his doppelganger is standing at the head table, holding hands with someone I've never seen. He's smiling brightly, waving, while everyone claps loudly, and random whistling and whooping noises sound off from around the room.

"But . . ." I trail off, my eyes glued to Ian. What the hell is going on?

"Come on, you two," says Derek, one of the other servers, as he walks over to where we are, carrying a tray of salads for delivery to the tables. "Ursula is eyeing you." He nods his head toward the entrance to the staging area where Ursula is shooting us daggers, with her eyes.

"Come on, Bridgette." Ashley grabs my arm and drags me to the trays.

I'm in complete shock and so confused. I go into autopilot, grabbing a tray and balancing it on my shoulder. I follow behind Ashley, hoping and praying Ian doesn't see me.

"Vat are you doink?" I hear Ursula from behind me. "Get up to zee front, vhere I told you to go."

Oh geez, the front? I don't even remember her telling me that. I nod my head and walk toward the head table, hoping against hope that I can remain unseen. Maybe they'll be so caught up in conversation that they won't pay any attention to me.

I'm so confused. I still don't understand what's going on. Ian's engaged? This is *his* party? Why do I know nothing of this?

I place the tray on a stand that was set up prior to the party. It's at the end of the long, rectangular head table. With my head down, I start setting salads in front of guests. I serve the women first. Fortunately, Ian doesn't see me when I get to the mysterious woman sitting on his right.

I start to serve the men, hoping and praying my luck will hold, and Ian will be too busy talking to the people around him to even notice me.

But when it's time for me to serve him a salad plate, instead of keeping my head down, I find myself looking up — and right into Ian's face.

His eyes widen with disbelief and color drains from his face as we make eye contact. And then, clearly visible, another expression registers: caught.

I want to throw water in his face, or do something equally dramatic, but I can't. Not if I want to keep my job and get promoted. So, I do the next best thing. I paste a bright (though completely fake) smile on my face and place the salad in front of him.

I will kill him with kindness.

"Ian, are you okay?" mysterious bride-to-be says, looking concerned.

I don't really care if Ian is okay at this point, so I walk over to the tray, grab the salad dressing, and start ladling. Women first and then the men.

When I reach the bride-to-be, I can hear Ian and her discussing intently.

"I found it in your suit pocket," she says, not noticing me as I put dressing on her salad. "I thought you grabbed it for me after we found out the other caterers fell through."

"No, I didn't. I totally forgot about the catering thing," Ian says, anger tones in his voice.

I start dressing the men's salads, and when I get to Ian's, they are still arguing.

"I don't understand what the big deal is?" mysterious woman says to Ian.

"It's not. Sorry. Don't worry about it." I feel his eyes on me, but I don't make eye contact. I just keep doing my job.

I grab the pepper grinder from the tray and make my way down the head table, asking if anyone wants fresh-cracked pepper. Only poufy-blond-haired father-of-the-bride and Ian's mom say yes.

Ian's parents. I only met them once when they came to visit Ian at college. It was a brief meeting, and I barely recognize them.

I never look at Ian. I'm not a genius, but it's pretty easy to figure out what's going on here: Ian is a scumbag.

That pretty much sums it up. But it's also quite confusing at the same time. I never thought Ian could be a scumbag. Not to me, at least. I guess he's changed, and not for the better.

I put the pepper grinder on the tray next to the remaining salad dressing, and balancing the tray on my shoulder, I start working my way back to the kitchen. I'll have to switch places with Ashley. I won't be able to go back up there again.

From behind me, I hear someone ask Ian where he's going, and I know where he's going—to hell.

Well, that's where he'll end up going, because that's where liars go.

"Bridgette," I hear him say, as he tries to catch up with me. Fortunately, more than once someone stopped him to say congratulations, so I'm able to maneuver my way back.

I walk in the kitchen, put the tray down, and look around for Ashley. I have to find her before main courses go out. She has to take over the front for me.

Ashley walks in the kitchen, holding her tray on her shoulder. When she sees me, her eyes get huge. She has so many questions.

That makes two of us.

The door swings open and in walks Ian.

"Bridgette." He comes up to me, and my eyes dart around looking for Ursula. If she catches him in here, talking to me . . . I'm toast, and so is my hope of a promotion. I don't see her; however, everyone in the kitchen now has their eyes on me. Luckily, the chef, assistants, and servers all have an unspoken rule among us. We don't tattle on each other.

I turn my back to him, avoiding everyone's stares. Grabbing a box of cocktail napkins, I start making piles of them, unnecessarily.

"Bridgette." He touches my shoulder with his hand, and I shove my shoulder back trying to get it off. "Please, can I just explain?"

I close my eyes, willing him to go away. Maybe, if I say nothing, he'll get the idea and leave. But that's not me, and he knows that's not me, so I turn around.

"There's really nothing to explain," I say in harsh tones.

"Yes, there is. I —"

"You're engaged. I see that." I gesture to the door that goes out to the ballroom.

"Yes, but I wanted to tell you, I did . . ." he trails off, putting his hand to his head, rubbing his temples.

"But you didn't." I finish the sentence for him. "Why? Why wouldn't you tell me something this important?"

"No, it wasn't like that. It just never came up. I felt awkward that I didn't tell you the first time, when we had lunch, and I didn't know how to bring it up the other night —"

"So, you thought kissing me would be a better idea. That makes perfect sense." I nod my head, giving him a sarcastic look. An audible gasp comes from the onlookers. I'm a spectacle.

He looks around the room quickly, probably scanning to make sure no one besides the catering staff is here.

He looks back at me. "No, I didn't mean for that to happen, I just . . ." he trails off, looking for words.

"And how did this all happen?" I gesture around the room with my hands. "I mean, there are like, what, a gazillion caterers in this city? Why this one?" The coincidence is too ridiculous.

"Maureen found a flyer in my pocket. You gave it to me that day I saw you outside in that Heidi getup." He gestures with his hands toward my outfit. "I guess we had a last-minute issue with the caterer, and so she thought I had grabbed the flyer for her. I had no idea. Had I known—"

"What? You would have found another caterer and continued with the façade?"

"Bridgette, it's not like that," he says, his tone getting louder. I know that tone well. It's the one he uses when he's not getting his point across. The last time I heard it was when I refused to go to London with him.

I see Ashley peeking from behind the swinging kitchen door. She's been standing guard for me, looking for Ursula. She waves to get my attention. "She's coming."

"Ian, you have to go." I nudge him toward the door with my hands.

"I need to talk to you," he says, searching my face for any chance that I might hear him out.

"There's nothing to say." I point him to the door. "You need to go before you get me fired."

Without any words, Ian turns and walks out the door and back into the ballroom.

CHAPTER 22

"How did the rest of the night go, then?" Gram asks me as I sit on the couch telling her everything that happened with Ian last night. She is in her favorite chair, feet propped up, Kindle resting in her lap.

"It was terrible. I mean, nothing terrible happened. I switched sections with Ashley so I didn't have to face him again. Maybe I should have kept his section. I could have made him uncomfortable the rest of the night." I sniff, slouching on the couch, feeling despondent.

"I'm sure you made him uncomfortable enough."

"I know *I* was uncomfortable. It was hard, seeing them together, you know? It was almost, I don't know . . . kind of heartbreaking? That's stupid, isn't it? I mean, he barely just came back into my life. But spending time with Ian, it got my mind whirling again. Feelings I thought were gone were not truly gone, only buried." I look down at my hands, resting in my lap.

"Well, of course they were. You have a history, after all." I look up at Gram who is watching me intently.

"True. And it was good, you know? To feel something again after Adam . . . I wasn't so sure I could do it. At least not that quickly."

158

"Do you want me to tell you about *The Young and the Restless* to get your mind off of it?" she asks, head tilted to the side with concern.

"Sure," I say, not really wanting to hear about it but needing to think about something besides Ian.

"Well, there's a major love triangle going on between Heather, Tiffany, and Ian," she says. "Sorry about saying Ian," she adds, remorsefully.

"No worries, Gram," I say. But the sound of his name does do something to my heart, that's for sure.

"Anyway, so Heather and Ian just got engaged, but Tiffany is still in love with him." Her face starts to sag as she tells me the details.

We sit in silence for a minute. "You know," Gram says, "why don't I tell you about it later."

"Sounds good," I say, thinking the last things I need to hear about are engagements and unrequited love.

The doorbell rings, and I get up to see who it is.

Standing there as I open the door, looking red-faced, is Ashley.

"I didn't get the part," she says, sniffing back tears and snot. She holds up a large bag of miniature-sized candy bars. "Wanna help me eat my feelings?"

"Oh Ash—"

"Don't say it." She cuts me off. "I know you're sad for me, but I need to laugh right now. No pitying glances and words of comfort, got it?"

"Gotcha," I say and open the door wider for her to come in.

We sit down on the couch and, without apology, dig into the chocolate. Gram even joins in. I wish the candy would actually help my feelings, but instead it just leaves a waxy coating on the roof of my mouth. Not comforting at all. I hope it's working better for Ashley.

Gram excuses herself from the pity party to take a phone call from Margie, one of the ladies in her bridge club.

"So, last night was weird, eh?" Ashley says after Gram walks out of the room and we've spent way too much time avoiding topics neither of us wanted to talk about. Apparently, she has tired of the superficial conversation and wants to get into the nitty-gritty — so long as it's not about her.

I sigh. I've already discussed it with Gram, and I don't feel like going there again, but if it helps Ashley, I guess I can.

"Weird doesn't even describe it." I look down at the pile of wrappers sitting between us. Have we really eaten that much already?

"So, how are you feeling?" she questions, a concerned look on her face.

"I thought we weren't talking about feelings." I tilt my head to the side, giving her a mocking look.

"We aren't talking about my feelings. I didn't know yours were off limits." She grabs another mini chocolate bar from the bag.

"They're not." I smile slightly.

"So? How are you feeling?" she prods.

"I have no idea."

"What do you mean?"

"I mean that my mind is a big, muddled mess." I go to grab another piece of chocolate but decide the mounting pile of wrappers is starting to border on pathetic, and gluttonous.

"Explain," she demands.

I exhale loudly. "Well, I guess I feel sort of heartbroken. Not like Adam heartbroken. It's a different type of heartbreak. And it's kind of hard to feel heartbroken about someone who wasn't even mine. I mean, had he not kissed me, I probably would've still been annoyed that he didn't tell me before, but the kiss . . . it made everything different."

"Maybe he didn't mean it? Maybe he was caught up in the moment?"

"No." I shake my head. "I've kissed Ian before. It took me back to college. There were feelings behind that kiss. Feelings that were deeper than being caught up in the moment."

"So, now what?" Ashley grabs another piece of chocolate but then throws it back in the bag.

"You giving up?" I nod down at the bag of chocolate.

"Yep. It's not working. I now feel sorry for myself, and fat. Not the best combo. Stop trying to change the subject to me." She pushes me lightly on the arm.

I smile. Thank goodness for Ashley. Seeing as my ex-boyfriend is newly engaged and my ex-ex-boyfriend has been engaged all along . . . well, I'm just glad she's here for me.

"There's no 'now what.' He's getting married. That's the end of the story." I shrug my shoulders.

"Have you heard from him?"

"Nope. Don't expect to, either." I shake my head.

Gram comes back into the room. "Sorry girls, I had to take that call," she says, unnecessarily apologetic. "What did I miss?"

"Ashley here was just asking about my 'feelings,'" I say, using air quotes. "Tell me Grams, in your experience, when a guy kisses you, is it because he just feels like it, or is there some deep-seeded meaning to it?"

"Well, I'm no expert, but I did just run across a quote from a book I read recently that I thought was right on the money." She picks up her Kindle, and turning it on, starts swiping through the screens, searching.

"Aha, here it is." She pushes her glasses up on her nose. "'*Men aren't really complicated. They are very simple, literal creatures. They usually mean what they say. And we spend hours trying to analyze what they've said – when really it's obvious.*'" She looks up from her Kindle.

"But what's obvious with Ian?" I say, confused.

"Well, obviously, he meant to kiss you," Gram says, matter-of-factly.

"That quote sounds familiar," Ashley says, peering at Gram's Kindle. "What book is it from?"

"Oh, just that *50 Shades of Grey* book." She closes her Kindle cover, placing it in her lap.

Both Ashley and I go slack-jawed.

"Gram, you read *50 Shades of Grey*?" I ask, once I'm able to pick my jaw up off the floor.

"Oh yes. Wanted to see what the hubbub was all about. It was awful. All three of them."

"You read all *three*?" My eyes practically jump out of my face.

"Yes. There was so much cussing. Just awful. Terrible. They were ridiculous. It was my first time venturing over to *those* kinds of books, and I don't think I'll be doing it again. So unrealistic. I mean, no one actually has sex like that." She clicks her tongue, making a disapproving face.

Ashley and I look at each other. We don't have the heart to tell her that, yes, some people actually do.

A smile plays on the corner of Ashley's mouth. I can tell she's trying to hold back laughter. Seeing her try to hold it in makes me start to giggle, and then, before we can stop ourselves, we are laughing hysterically.

"Oh, go on, you two." Gram bats a hand at us but then smiles and laughs a little to herself.

"Oh my gosh, I am *so* glad I came over today." Ashley grabs at her stomach, looking pained from laughing so hard.

"Me, too. I'd never have been able to repeat that story so it was anywhere near as good as hearing it first hand," I say through stunted giggles.

"Well, I'm glad I can be here to help you both laugh through your difficult times." Gram taps her fingers on her Kindle cover, giving us a sarcastic look.

Oh, the things that woman says and does. I could write a book.

CHAPTER 23

University of Connecticut, senior year, winter

"Ha! I won!" Ian exclaimed after a quick game of laughing chicken.

"You cheated," I declared.

"No, I didn't," he denied. He didn't cheat, per se, but he did get me with that goofy, cross-eyed grin that he does. Hard as I tried, I could not keep from laughing when he did that.

I sighed, leaning back. "I don't think I can study one more page," I said, exhaustion in my voice. Ian and I were on the floor, sitting up against my bed, studying for finals.

"Yeah, I'm over it," Ian agreed, leaning his head back as well.

"I'm seriously starting to wonder if this is all worth it."

"This?" he asked, turning his head to look at me.

"This. College. I'm so tired of studying. I just want to be done." I closed my eyes, drained.

He grabbed my hand in his. It felt good, comforting. "Bridge, we're almost done. We can do this."

"No need for the pep talk. I'm only venting."

He sits up. "Let's do something mindless," he said and then stood up, dragging me with him.

"Like what?" I wasn't feeling like doing anything but crawling into a ball and sleeping.

"Let's order pizza and watch a movie." He smiled like this was the best idea in the world.

It sort of was. "Okay," I agreed with a brief lift of my shoulders.

We ordered a pizza to be delivered—no need to go out in the snow—and found what looked like a decent movie to watch after looking through my roommate, Amy's, questionable collection. She was studying at her boyfriend's place, so we had the apartment to ourselves.

After pizza, Ian grabbed a bunch of pillows and made a cozy place on the floor for us to snuggle up to watch the movie. This had become a sort of tradition for Ian and me, snuggling up and watching a movie, so it was nothing new or special.

"This is a stupid movie," I declared, halfway through it. We were lying close together, our heads touching, our bellies full of meat-lovers pizza.

"Spoilsport." Ian nudged me lightly with his head.

"No, but really, relationships don't work that way." I rolled my eyes. "Guys don't pine over girls for months without telling them, do they?" I turned my head to the side so I could see his face.

"Well . . ." he trailed off.

"Wait, you?" I rolled my body over to my side and propped myself up on my arm, searching his face. He kept his eyes on the ceiling. "How? I mean, how do I not know this about you? I know everything about you."

"You don't know everything." He smiled slightly.

"Okay, then tell me." I tugged on his shirt, willing him to confess.

"Nah, it's probably a boring story," he said, still looking up at the ceiling.

"Well, I'd rather hear it than watch this drivel." I pointed at the TV screen.

He propped himself up on his side so we were both looking at each other.

He shook his head, thinking better of it. "No. Never mind." He rolled to his back, face to the ceiling again.

"Oh no, you're not getting off that easy." I grabbed him by the arm, trying to pull him toward me so we were looking face-to-face again. He wouldn't budge, though.

He let out a long exhale, still looking at the ceiling and not at me.

"Okay, there was this one girl. We had been friends for a while, actually." He paused, sniffling lightly.

"Go on," I encouraged him.

"Anyway, I thought we were just meant to be friends, but then she started dating someone else, and instead of being happy for her, I found myself feeling . . . jealous." He went quiet for a moment, the movie filled in the background noise.

I laid my head down on the pillow and started to make loud snoring sounds. He grabbed a small throw pillow and smacked me lightly on the head with it.

"Never mind. Sorry to bore you." He turned his head toward me, annoyance played on his face.

"No, no, keep going. Just speed it up. Your dramatic pauses are almost as bad as this movie." I looked at him and smiled.

"Anyway, so then one night," he continued, looking up at the ceiling, "a long time after I'd started having these feelings—I found myself lying on the floor with this girl, watching a cheesy movie she didn't like, and somehow telling her this story and hoping it didn't ruin things." He closed his eyes briefly as if to wish away what he just said. But it was too late.

My eyes bugged out of my head. *Me.* He was talking about *me.* But . . . but . . . this was Ian. Ian didn't like me like that. He never gave off a vibe that he liked me like that.

"But . . . but . . ." I trailed off. "Why didn't you ever tell me?"

"Because I didn't want to hurt what we have. Relationships are complicated. What we have is simple and good. Why ruin that?" He stared upward again.

"Oh, wow," is all I could say.

He shook his head. "I shouldn't have told you. I don't want to ruin anything. Just . . . just forget it." He sat up, not making eye contact with me. He moved around awkwardly, looking slightly flustered, almost as if he was ready to bolt at any second.

"I should go," he said, starting to lift himself up from the pile of pillows we were lying on.

"Would you just wait?" I grabbed his arm, pulling him down next to me. "Would you give me a second to . . . to . . . think?" I laid my head back, putting my palm on my forehead, trying to ground myself.

Ian liked me. I had no idea. I needed to wrap my brain around it all. Did I like him? Since I first met him, he had always been the person I wanted to spend my time with. Even when I was dating someone, I would pick Ian over him. So, did I? There was only one way to find out for sure.

I rolled over onto my side, toward him, and then a little more so I was lying half on top of him.

"What are you doing?" He gave me a muddled look.

"I'm going to kiss you," I said matter-of-factly. I pulled myself up so I was looking him in the eyes. I brought my hand to his face, caressing it slightly. Then, not being able to help myself, I started to giggle. This was weird, looking at Ian this way. Then the giggles started to turn into laughs.

Ian at first seemed a little pissed that I was laughing, but then he started laughing too. Slightly at first, but then the laughter started getting harder until we were both laughing so hard, we couldn't breathe. We both rolled around on the ground, holding our stomachs, trying to catch our breath, but to no avail.

Finally, as we were able to steady our breathing, as the laughter died down, I heard him say, "Sorry."

"What are you sorry for?" I asked, a giggle still slipping out every now and then.

"For changing things. It was stupid." He laid his head back, running his fingers through his hair, looking slightly downtrodden.

"What's changed?" I gave him a serious look; the laughter was gone. The feeling in the room was suddenly too intense for laughter.

"Everything," he said.

"Why? Why does it have to change?" I asked, pulling myself toward him, half on top of him again, our faces close. "The way I see it, is we spend every moment we can together. In fact, I don't know if I could go a day without seeing you. What would be so different?" I reached up a hand to caress his face, not feeling like I wanted to laugh this time.

"Ian," I said, looking into his eyes, "I'm going to kiss you—"

"Would you stop telling me you're going to kiss me? You're totally ruining the moment." With that said, he pushed me off him and onto my back. He rolled himself half on top of me so our faces were close together again, but with his above. His hand came up to caress my face. He looked from my eyes to my mouth, and suddenly, his lips were on mine.

It was slow and soft and tender. There was a feeling there, one that I hadn't ever experienced. A feeling like this was right. It felt right to kiss Ian. I suddenly wondered why we had never done this before. And I wanted more. I wanted so much more of this. Of Ian.

He started kissing me with more passion, the temperature getting hotter between us. I wrapped my arms around his back, pulling him into me, tightly. His lips were hot on mine.

He let go of my lips briefly to kiss me down the side of my face, to my neck, kissing me right behind my earlobe. Mmmmmm, my favorite spot. How did he know that? Because he knew me. He always knew me. How did I not see it all before? How was I so clueless?

His lips found their way back up to mine, and he kissed me vigorously, cupping my face with is hand.

Suddenly, the front door slammed and we quickly pulled away, looking up to see my roommate, Amy, staring down at us.

"Finally," is all she said, and then she stalked off to her bedroom, shutting the door behind her.

And then we started laughing again.

CHAPTER 24

I have a feeling in the pit of my stomach that tells me I'm making a bad decision. Also known as the icky butterflies.

It's been a week since I found out that Ian is engaged. Two days later he texted me, and he hasn't stopped. He's even tried calling a few times, asking if I'll let him explain everything. In my defense, I did ignore his calls and texts at first. I even changed his name in my phone to "Don't Answer This," but I finally gave in and texted him back.

Right now, I'm standing outside a coffee shop Ian picked near his work, debating whether or not to go in. On one hand, I don't want to waste this outfit. A light blue, knee-length sundress with a chunky brown belt. But it's not so much about the dress as it is about the *shoes*. The most amazing brown cork platform sandals. I found them at a sample sale, and the price tag still made me gasp. Totally worth it, though.

I also know I will go inside to face Ian, because I'm curious. Curiosity has bested me once again. Well, curiosity and not wanting to waste an incredible pair of Jimmy Choos.

"Thanks for meeting me," Ian says as I sit down across from him at the little two-person table in the corner of the tiny café. He eyes my outfit but doesn't say anything. He's wearing a suit. He looks smart. I really wish he wasn't engaged.

No, Bridgette, don't go there. He lied to you. You obviously don't know him like you used to.

"Okay, you said you wanted to talk, so talk," I say, still fighting myself about making a run for it, still curious as to why he wanted to meet me, still taking note of how very handsome he is. I'm kind of a mess in my head right now.

"Yeah . . . I mean, yes. I wanted to apologize." He gives me a half smile—the one where the right corner of his mouth moves up just slightly. The one that, some time ago, would melt me. Not today, though. Okay, fine. It does a little. But very, *very* little.

"Okay, great. You've apologized. I don't forgive you. Are we done then?" I grab my purse as if to get up from my seat.

"Bridgette, don't do that." He gives me a knowing look. And he does know me. I mean, I've definitely changed over the past years, but deep down, I am still the Bridgette he knew from college. Especially stubborn, indignant, Bridgette. That part of my personality has always been the same (and I suspect always will be).

"Ian, there really isn't much to say, is there?" I leave my hands on my purse so that I can get up and walk out at any moment.

"I should have told you." He looks down at his hands. "I didn't mean to *not* tell you. It just happened."

173

"Yes, you've said that already." I roll my eyes.

"Yeah, I did. Sorry." He shakes his head.

"Do you want to know what's most embarrassing about this whole thing?" My mouth takes over for my brain. This was not what I had wanted to say when I rehearsed it. "I actually thought you were upset about the kiss because of what happened between us back at school. But really you were engaged. I've been beating myself up all of these years . . ." I trail off as it dawns on me how much time I've wasted on men. Two wasted years with Adam and four wasted years of worrying about Ian and his feelings.

What a waste, indeed. Maybe I was meant for so much more over the past four years, but because of men taking over my brain, I didn't accomplish anything of worth. I mean, what have I done these past four years that would be considered anything but ordinary? Nothing. It's men that have kept me from my dreams. I blame them.

"I don't know what else to say, Bridgette. I'm sorry."

"Well, you could start by telling me why, then?"

"Why what? Why am I engaged? Well, I met Maureen not long after I moved to New York—"

"No, I mean, why did you kiss me in the first place?"

He's silent for a bit, looking around the room, almost awkwardly.

"It's hard to explain," he finally says.

"Try me."

"Well, the truth is . . . the *truth* is, seeing you has brought back some old feelings," he says with a thin smile.

I nod my head. I can understand that. Old feelings have definitely come back for me as well.

"And I got sort of caught up in the moment, you know? We have history, you and I." His smile broadens a touch.

"We do, yes. Which is why 'I'm engaged' should have been the first thing out of your mouth when you saw me that night at your work party. Or at least the third or fourth thing out of your mouth."

"Bridgette, I cannot apologize enough."

I sit back in my seat. "I know. You really can't," I say and grin slightly. He smiles back. "Look, Ian, feelings came back for me, too—"

"They did?" He interrupts me. I'm surprised he's taken aback by this piece of information, but he is.

"Yes, of course. I mean, like you said, we have a history. Seeing you has made me realize how much I missed it." I look down at my hands. This is probably completely inappropriate for me to be saying to an engaged man. It's not like I'm trying to steal him away, now that I know. I just feel like it needs to be said.

"Bridge . . ."

"Anyway," I hold up a hand to cut him off, "under different circumstances, maybe . . . who knows . . ." I trail off. The possibilities are not important anymore. It doesn't matter now.

"So," I say, shaking off the seriousness of this conversation, "when's the big day?"

"Oh . . . um . . ." he shakes his head as if to bring himself back. He looked a little lost in thought there for a few seconds. "The wedding is set for September twenty-first."

"September twenty-first, huh? So, you still have a ways to go." I play with my purse straps, a little at a loss for words now. I'm not sure I want to know all the details. Funny though, that's the same date as Adam's. Only Adam's wedding is this year.

"Well, three months doesn't seem like that far away." He sits back, putting a hand on each leg.

My mouth drops, as does my stomach. "Wait, you're getting married September twenty-first? As in, *this* September twenty-first?" He's kidding, right? He has to be joking. "But . . . but . . . you just had your engagement party." Who has an engagement party three months before their wedding?

"Yeah, that was for Maureen's dad. He's been out of the country, working, and wasn't able to get back until last month. He wanted us to wait for him. We were supposed to do it over Christmas, but he ended up not making it back. So we postponed it but left the wedding date set for the twenty-first."

This can't possibly be happening. Two men in my life, *the* two men that I've loved possibly the most in my life thus far, are getting married on the exact same day — and not to me?

I'm being punk'd, right? Where are the cameras?

"Anyway, you'll come, right?" I barely register what he's asking. My head is spinning with this information.

"Um, no." I shake my head, finally realizing what he's just asked me. I don't want to go to Ian's wedding, and it's not because I am planning on attending Adam's wedding either. I see now that weddings are obviously designed by evil people to slap me in the face, and so I may boycott them altogether.

"Why?" Ian asks, his face upset.

"*Why?*"

"Yeah, why won't you come?"

"Seriously, Ian? Why would I want to come?" I don't even understand why he's inviting me. Wouldn't it be awkward? With my luck, I would do something foolish like drink too much and then tell everyone that I've recently kissed the groom.

"I don't know. I just thought you would want to be there. I thought we were friends again?"

"Well, yeah . . . I mean, that was before I knew you were engaged."

"So, my being engaged means we can't be friends?" he asks, getting heated.

"Yeah, of course. Would that be fair to Maureen? Does she even know about me?" His face answers that question.

"I mentioned you once or twice." He looks down, obviously not wanting to see the expression on my face, which I'm sure is not pretty right now.

That's weird, right? I mean, I told Adam about Ian. Maybe not a ton of detail, but Adam knew who he was. He probably wouldn't remember if asked. But remembering small details is not a guy thing to do, anyway. Especially for Adam.

"So, how did you even talk about college?" I had to ask. How did he get around telling her anything about college without bringing me up? We spent practically every waking minute together.

"Of course I told her about college. I just left you out of most of it."

Ouch.

"Well, thanks." I look down at my hands, now playing furiously with my purse strap.

"Why would I tell her about you, Bridgette?" His face goes slightly red. I know that look. I've set him off. I was always good at doing that. I guess I still am.

"I don't know, maybe because I'm a part of your past?" I'm feeling unexpectedly defensive right now. How dare he just brush me to the side like that.

He leans in toward me, his face still red. His eyes are on me, piercing me with his stare. "Why would I want her to know that in my heart she will always be second best?" He curses under his breath and puts his head in his hand.

"What?" I pick up my jaw, which has suddenly fallen to the floor.

He looks up at me. "You've ruined me, Bridgette. I've compared everyone I've ever been with to you. Maureen was the first person who came close."

"I . . ." My heart is racing, and I'm feeling like I can't take a deep breath. "Ian . . ." I start to say but then stop. What can I say right now? This might possibly be the most romantic thing that anyone has ever said to me in my entire life. But it's a romantic thing that can lead nowhere. Ian is getting married.

What I want to do right now is tell him what I should have told him years ago before he left for London. Why couldn't I just say it back then? How different would my life be right now? But it wouldn't be fair to say it now.

"I just wish," he starts to say, but then stops himself.

"You wish what?" Maybe he wishes he wasn't engaged? Maybe he wishes we could go back to the old days?

"I wish I never ran into you." He looks down at his hands, now resting in his lap.

"Oh," is all I can say. Ouch. That one hurt worse than telling me he left me out of his college stories.

"No, sorry." He shakes his head, "I don't mean that. It just made things harder for me, that's all."

"Sorry, Ian," I say, feeling incredibly sad.

"Don't be sorry, I shouldn't have said that. I'm glad I saw you. I'm glad you look good and healthy and that you are the same Bridgette that I lo –," he shakes his head, "that I knew."

We sit in silence. A million thoughts are going through my head. I wish, in circumstances like this, that we were in some sort of boxing ring, and I could go back to my corner and have Gram and Ashley help me break everything down and tell me what to say. Then I could come back into the conversation ready. But I don't have them here. I'm on my own.

"Do you love her?"

"Maureen? Yeah . . . yeah, I love her." He nods his head.

"Yes, I mean, of course you do." I look to the side, awkwardly. That was a stupid question. I don't even know why I asked. Being on my own is obviously not going well.

"She's pretty perfect for me." He runs a hand through his hair. "She just has one fault, really."

"Oh?" I look up, intrigued.

"She's not you." He gives me a small sad smile.

Oh gosh, what can I even say to that? That's like something from a movie. This was not exactly what I anticipated when I said I would meet him. I mean, of course, in my head, one of the imagined scenarios was him saying he still loves me and wants to be with me. And, essentially, he has told me he still has feelings for me, but it's not the same, is it? Knowing all of this is almost worse than not knowing. Especially when there's nothing I can do about it.

"Ian, I don't think we can be friends," I finally say, tears prickling behind my eyes. It kind of feels like we're breaking up all over again. But like a real breakup this time. Last time was all about words left unsaid and doors slamming.

"I think you're right, Bridge." He reaches across the table and grabs my hand. The touch of his hand makes me even sadder, and then the tears start to spill out.

"Bridgette, don't cry," he says, rubbing the side of my hand with his thumb.

I feel dumb for crying, but I can't help myself.

We stand up from the table without words and walk out of the café together. He puts his hand on the small of my back to guide me out. I'm still trying to gather myself. The tears keep escaping.

"Well," he says matter-of-factly as we exit.

"Well." I echo his tone.

We stand there looking at each other. "I guess this is it then?" I say, wiping my eyes with my hand. What a scene this must be for onlookers.

"Yeah, I guess so." He pulls me in for a hug, and I resist the urge to start blubbering, and also the desire to smell him.

"Take care, Ian," I say as I pull away from the hug.

"You too, Bridge." He gives me a small smile.

I turn around and start walking away without another word. I do look back and catch him doing the same thing. It's a heartbreaking look. He just stands there.

That's it then. Four years of wondering about Ian and how he is. Now I know, and now he's out of my life once again. This time, for good.

CHAPTER 25

"I swear it was her, Bridgette," Justin says as we spend another Monday doing more humiliating marketing for Edelweiss Catering. My dirndl is cutting off my breathing. I can only take short, quick breaths.

It's been nearly a week since I said good-bye to Ian once again. Well, at least this time it was definite. Last time, there was no official good-bye. I can't honestly say which one was worse. At least this one had closure.

Justin wiggles around in his lederhosen.

"What's wrong with you?" I ask as he practically starts to dance.

"I've got a wedgie." He hands me the sign he's supposed to be spinning. "Guard me."

I stand in front of him and wiggle the sign around while he takes care of the problem.

Once everything is back to normal, we start up again, Justin with the sign spinning and me handing out flyers.

"How could you know it was her?" I ask, getting us back to the pre-wedgie conversation.

"Who would forget her?" he responds, giving me a you-must-be-stupid look.

He does have a point. Serene isn't someone you forget easily. I would like to forget her, but I sense that will not be happening anytime soon.

"And where were you again?" I ask, trying to piece the details together in my head.

"At the café with Ash."

"When did you guys go there?" I ask because usually I'm with them at the café. It's our place.

"After we caught a play the other night," he says, looking out into the city.

Heavens, poor Ashley. I can only imagine what she was stuck watching for two (or more) hours. Justin's movie-picking skills are horrid, but his theater-picking skills border tortuous. For me they are, at least. One time, he made me and Ashley sit through a two-hour, one-act, one-person play about a woman experiencing post-traumatic stress disorder. I'm pretty sure *I* had PTSD by the end of it.

"Anyway, it was her, I know it was. And she was not with Adam," he says, spinning his sign around. Someone honks a car horn while driving by.

"So what? It could have been her brother or something."

"Does Serene make out with her brother?"

"What? She was making out with this guy?" My eyes bug out of my head. I pull a flyer back from a man who was just about to grab it. Oops.

"Yep, it was an all-out snogging."

"They were having *sex* in the café?" The pictures going through my head right now are not pretty.

How would that even be possible? With everyone around?

"No, that's what the Brits call making out." He shakes his head like that's something I should know.

"Oh . . . well, that makes so much more sense . . ." I trail off in thought.

When Gram watches the BBC, she is always appalled at how everyone is snogging each other. Well, she'll feel much better about that when I tell her what it actually means. Not that her concern ever stopped her from watching the BBC, mind you.

"You don't seem that shocked," he says, looking confused, sign twirling furiously.

"I don't know. I guess because I didn't see it with my own eyes, it's hard to believe, you know? It's dark in that café at night. Maybe you were mistaken?" This is not that farfetched. Once Justin swore he saw Gwyneth Paltrow walking down 5th. He even took a picture to prove it. He showed the picture to Ashley and me, but it wasn't her. So I'm not sure I can totally trust him on this one.

Justin shakes his head. "I don't think I was mistaken. It was her. It had to be. So, what are you going to do about it?"

I shrug my shoulders. "What can I do? I have no proof. I wasn't there to see it myself." I go back to handing out flyers and subsequently being rejected by the next person who walks by.

Silence lands on the conversation as Justin spins and dances around (he's a pretty terrible dancer, if you ask me), and I continue to get rejected as I try to pass out flyers.

"You wanna grab coffee after we're done with this torture?" Justin says, breaking the lull in the conversation.

"Can't," I say quickly. There can be no one-on-one with Justin until I know what I will say to him. Well, no intimate one-on-one time. We are alone, working. But obviously, he has not found this to be the appropriate place, or he would have said something.

Now I need an excuse for why I can't have coffee with him. *Think, Bridgette, think.*

"I still need to talk to you, you know." He doesn't make eye contact with me. He just keeps his eyes on the street in front of him.

"I, um, have to help Gram with something," I lie. I don't even know if Gram is home.

"What does she need help with? Does she need you to read smut books to her? Are her eyes going bad?" He swings the sign at me and hits me lightly on the arm with it. I roll my eyes. "Come on, Bridge. Just come have coffee with me."

I exhale loudly. I can't put this off anymore, can I? I guess I'll just bite the bullet and hope everything turns out okay.

My heart sinks. I truly hope what we have isn't eventually ruined by all this.

~*~

"So," Justin says, tapping the side of his coffee cup with his hand.

"So," I echo, not sure what else to say. This is already awkward. Oh gosh, I hate this.

We look like a pair of idiots, still in our work uniforms. Thank goodness we are in New York City. They've seen weirder. Even still, we keep getting the odd glance every now and then.

He leans in, serious look on his face. "Listen, I need to talk to you about something, and it's been on my mind for a while now."

"Justin," I start talking, hoping to ward him off. Maybe I can make the blow easier. "I think before you say . . . uh . . . what you are going to say, I think you should really think about it. I mean, I'm pretty sure I know what you're going to tell me, and I just want you to think about it."

"You know what I'm going to tell you?" He looks shocked.

Honestly? Men are so dumb sometimes.

"Well, I'm pretty sure I do. And I don't want it to change everything, you know?"

"You think it will change everything?" He motions his hand between us. His gesture speaks volumes. No words needed.

Oh gosh, Ashley was right. I was hopeful that she wasn't, but she was right.

"Justin," I say and grab his hand. I mean it only in a friendly way. I hope he can understand that. "I'm pretty sure the feelings aren't reciprocated." I look down at the table, unable to meet his eyes.

"They're not?" He lets go of my hand and rakes it through his hair. His eyes dart around the room, a feeling of embarrassment settles on us.

I *so* hate this.

"No. They're not." I look up to meet his gaze. He looks dumbfounded, confused.

I start to think back at our relationship and wonder if I'm this horrible person who has led him on, led him to think there was more there. Sure, I held his hand when we were at Adam's dinner. But that was all fake. At least it was for me. I've always downplayed all other flirting, never engaging.

"Wow," he says after a brief pause. "I'm a total idiot." He looks so sad. "All this time I thought she liked me, too."

"I know. I'm sorry, Justin. I wish I could tell you otherwise — wait, did you say 'she?'"

"Yes . . . she. Ashley." He shakes his head, not understanding me.

I close my eyes. Now I'm the total idiot. I look up at Justin who still looks so confused.

"You like Ashley?"

"Yes, of course. Who else would I be talking about?"

I start to giggle a little at how ridiculous this all is. I mean, I have some ego, don't I? But if it weren't for Carla and Ashley putting thoughts in my head, I would have never . . . Wait, why did Ashley think he liked me?

"I'm glad you think this is so funny," Justin says, looked irritated.

"No, sorry." I try to stifle a giggle. "It's not funny."

"Then why are you laughing?"

"Because," I say through more giggles, "I thought you liked me."

"You? Why would I like you?" He looks totally appalled at the thought.

My giggling suddenly stops. "Well, geez, sorry I'm so unlikeable," I say sarcastically.

"It's not that. It's just . . . you and me?" He motions between us again, "I mean, it wouldn't make any sense."

"I know, right?" I nod my head, agreeing. "That's what I told Ashley."

"Wait, Ashley thinks I like you?" He leans back in his chair.

"Yes, she got it in my head, actually. I was sure she was wrong, but she kept saying how obvious it was. I mean, you do blatantly flirt with me, so I guess I can see why."

"I flirt with you because it's easy, and it means nothing."

"Yes, I get it. I'm unlikeable. You've said that already."

"Stop. You know what I mean." He rolls his eyes.

"Then why don't you flirt with Ashley?"

"It's too hard for me. It means more." He looks down at his hands in his lap.

"Wait, you flirt with me because you *don't* like me, but you don't flirt with Ashley because you *do* like her?" I squint my eyes at him, trying to make sense of this. "Geez Justin, this isn't fifth grade."

"I know," he says, dramatically laying his forehead on the edge of the table in defeat. "I'm an idiot. That's why I wanted to talk to you. I wanted to see if you would feel Ash out. See if she feels the same."

"Are you serious?" I give him a you-must-be-crazy look. "Wait, I've got an idea." He looks up at me, very attentive. "Why don't you write her a note, and I'll bring it to her during gym class."

"Bridgette, help me. Please? I'm inexperienced in this area. The last girl I liked—really liked—was years ago, and it would've never worked out anyway. I have no idea what I'm doing." He looks like a sad, little puppy dog. A puppy dog that I would like to slap some sense into.

"Please?" he pleads further.

I let a breath out through my lips. Long and dramatic. "Okay, fine. I'll 'feel her out' and see what I can find out."

"Really?" His eyes brighten up.

Wow, this conversation certainly has not gone the way I had thought it would. It's better, but somehow not better, at the same time.

"Yeah, sure. In the meantime, would you work on growing a pair? I mean, this whole thing is a little ridiculous." I smirk at him.

He smiles brightly. "Thank you, Bridge. I owe you one."

"Well, you did suffer through the Adam thing. So I suppose I can help you with this." I roll my eyes.

"Actually, that was more fun for me. So I still owe you," he says, the left side of his lip lifting up in a half smile. I respond with another roll of my eyes.

So now I get to play the role of matchmaker. Or at least matchmaker of the grammar school variety: "Do you like this boy? Check yes or no." And I thought I was done with this phase when I went to middle school. How silly of me.

~*~

I spend the subway ride home contemplating my life and where I'm heading. Making a mental checklist, and it's quite depressing. I am most definitely not where I thought I would be at this point. I'm not working at my dream job, and I'm not dating my dream guy. I'm an optimistic person, but I'm not seeing any of this change for a while. Well, hopefully the dream job will happen soon. Catering manager isn't exactly my dream job, but it's a step closer.

My phone beeps.

I don't want to not be friends.

Ian. Butterflies start twirling around immediately in my stomach. I let out a deep breath. I thought the last time we spoke was good-bye. I didn't want it to be, to be honest. I guess he didn't either. Anyway, it's not that I don't want to be friends; it's just that I don't think we actually can. It's one of those things like treading on thin ice. I can foresee it not ending well.

I finally text back, after deleting and rewriting about ten times.

Me too. But I don't think any other way will work.

I contemplate telling him that maybe we should delete each other's number, but truthfully, I don't want to. It's like having his number in my phone makes me feel connected to him still, as silly as that may sound.

I slump back in my seat, waiting for my phone to beep again. Staring at it, willing it to make a sound.

It beeps after what seems like an hour—but was most likely only thirty seconds.

I heard my mom told you we set a date.

Oh gosh . . . not Ian. Adam. I haven't heard from him in so long, it almost seems like a stranger is texting me. A stranger I once thought I loved.

I text back quickly.

Yes, congrats.

I nearly added an exclamation point to the end of my text but decided against it. I'm not really excited. Why should I pretend to be?

I hope you'll be there.

Not him, too? What is the deal with men? Why would they think their ex would want to see them get married? How is that fun for me? Men are all totally clueless. At least the ones in my life are.

I don't even know what to text back, so I just leave it. Maybe my silence will be his clue that I don't want to be there to see him marry the supermodel-witch.

My phone beeps.

We can be friends, can't we? We can figure it out.

Oh geez, now Adam is back to the friend thing? No wait—that was from Ian. This is complicated, on so many levels.

I text Ian back.

I really don't see how.

I tap on my phone, waiting for a response. He doesn't text back. I guess it's good. Maybe he realizes I'm right and is going to let it go, which is for the best.

My phone beeps. Guess I was wrong . . .

Please come, you're part of the family.

Back to Adam. Really? How do I gently say via text that I would rather eat chili peppers on the hottest day of the year, in the Sahara, with no water, than go to his wedding?

I'll try. I may have to work.

So, the solution to that problem is to lie. I mean, I don't know the schedule this far in advance, so it's not a total lie. But I'm not going to try to go to Adam's wedding. Not even a little. Actually, just now, I've declared September twenty-first a wedding-free day for Bridgette.

I think that's the best plan.

CHAPTER 26

University of Connecticut, senior year, spring

"Are you okay?" Ian asked as we snuggled on the couch after attempting to study. We were basically tangled up, legs intertwined, arms wrapped around each other, my head nestled into his neck.

"Sure," I said. "Why do you ask?"

"You just seem distant," he said, running his fingers through my hair. It was one of my favorite things ever.

"Sorry, just got a lot on my mind," I said, nuzzling my nose into his neck.

I really did have a lot on my mind. My stupid mind, running away with itself like it often did.

Ian and I had been together for a little over three months now. At first it was weird and new and exciting. But soon we settled into us, and it's been pretty smooth sailing. Well, it should have been at least.

For me, it felt like we were moving much too fast. I suppose that's what you do when you start dating your best friend. The getting-to-know-you portion was done long ago. But it wasn't just the moving fast part, it was also the feeling part. I had never felt like this before. Not with anyone I had ever dated, not even Brandon. Things had moved slowly and in a normal manner with Brandon and there was comfort there. Comfort in the slowness of it.

There was comfort with Ian, too. In the fact that he knew me so well and that I could always be myself. But it was the future that scared me. Sure, sometimes I envisioned a future with Brandon when I was dating him, but only because it was the natural progression of things, like logically that was where things were supposed to go. With Ian, the future was real, and it was feeling very near for some reason. Nearer than I was comfortable with. I wanted it, but I didn't want it, at the same time.

What I did know, as I was wrapped up in Ian's arms and his breath started to slow as he drifted off, was that I loved him (even though we'd yet to say it out loud). This was real love. Not love that came from a natural progression. Mad, passionate love. And it was freaking me out.

CHAPTER 27

"Oh Bridgette, darling," Carla takes a dramatic drink of her wine, "aren't you a sight for sore eyes." It's not just a saying in this case, her eyes actually do look sore.

"It's great to see you, too," I say. "How are you?"

"Not fabulous." She bats a hand at me and takes another drink. Here it comes. "I really think life, as I know it, is over." Her eyes instantly well up.

"Oh, Carla." I put my hand out and grab hers, squeezing it. "Does this have to do with Adam and his," I swallow hard, "fiancée?" I know I'm basically over Adam, but it still hurts a little to say it. I'm like a child who doesn't want a toy, but doesn't want anyone else to have it either.

"Do you want to know what that witch did now?" she asks. I don't answer, because she would tell me regardless. "She," Carla cuts off, her eyes welling even more with tears, "she got him to throw out the prenup."

"A prenup?" I don't know why this piece of information takes me by surprise. I guess I never thought of it as an option. Of course, the Carla and Frank would want to protect themselves and their business. I wonder if I would have had to sign a prenuptial agreement if it had been me. I'm guessing I would have. And I would have signed it,

197

without question. I would never do anything to hurt Adam or his family, but if they needed it in writing, I wouldn't have even batted an eye before signing.

"Yes, she refused to sign it—said their love was enough and something about how it's not 'true love' when there's a prenup." She spits out the words "true love."

"Oh wow," I say, having no other words to say to that. "What are you going to do?" I ask.

"What can I do?" She takes another gulp of wine. "She's out to take everything, I just know it."

I'm not about to challenge a mother's intuition, but it does seem a little farfetched. I mean, Serene could actually love Adam. Also, I was with Adam for two years, so I'm pretty sure he's smarter than that. Although, he is marrying someone he just met . . .

"Sorry, Carla," I say. It's the only appropriate response. Plus, essentially, this is none of my business. But I'm grateful she still makes it my business. I do miss being a part of the family and am thankful for what I still have. When I think about it, my biggest loss was really them, not Adam.

"So, do you think you can come?" she asks, shaking off the last part of the conversation with her tone.

"Come to what?" I ask, pulling my brows in toward each other.

"The wedding," she says flatly.

"Oh right, that. Adam told me he wanted me there, but I don't know," I say, shaking my head in quick little movements.

Actually, I do know. There's no way I'm going to any weddings that day.

"Please come, dear Bridgette. I need you there as moral support for me," she says, pleading with her tone.

"Well, I might have to work. I'll have to see if I can get the day off," I say, giving her the same excuse I gave Adam. But I already know, whether I have to work or not, it's not happening. That seems to suffice, at least from what I can tell by the hope in her face.

"Enough about the wedding," she says, changing her tone. "What's new with you? How are things with Justin?"

"Justin?" I question. She gives me a strange look. Oh right . . . Why haven't I resolved this whole thing yet? "Oh, that fizzled out." I give her a small shrug.

"Really? That's so surprising. He seemed so into you." Her look of concern is enough to make me feel dreadful. I know I should come clean, but I won't. It's gone on too long. I would have to explain why it happened, and I think Carla doesn't need all of that right now.

"Yeah, it turns out he likes someone else," I say. Well, at least that's the truth.

"Dear Bridgette, we need to find you a man. You deserve so much more than that." She points at me with her extra-long, fake nail. "What about F.J.?"

I nearly choke on the drink of water I just took. "You're kidding, right?"

"Yes, of course. F.J.'s a disaster." She purses her lips. "I wouldn't wish him on anyone." She says this in all seriousness, then suddenly her eyes widen. "You know, I bet one of my nephews is single." She nods her head like this is the perfect option.

The last thing I need is the mother of my ex setting me up with men that are related to said ex. That sounds like something from a soap opera. My life is already soap opera-y enough.

"Thanks, but I think I'm just going to be on my own for a while," I say and then give her a closed-mouth smile.

That's truly how I'm feeling right now. It will be good to stand on my own for a while. Although my mind—and I guess my heart—keeps bringing up Ian. I know that's a lost cause, but it's hard to push it away. After he told me that I've "ruined everyone else" for him, it's hard to stop thinking about him. I wish he hadn't told me that.

"You're a strong woman, Bridgette." Carla reaches over and puts her hand on top of mine. "You know, I have to tell you that I wanted so badly for you to be a part of the family, but the truth is, you already are."

I look up to see her eyes welling up, and I smile. I know she's often said that I'm the daughter she always wanted, and even though I fight the thought in my head, I also know that we'll eventually grow apart. Life will change and move on. Adam will start a family with Serene and that'll become Carla's life. My life will change, and I'll move on. Well, hopefully. The lunches will start to become fewer and further between. The contact will change to an odd email or a text, and then it'll gradually become the annual Christmas card. I know that's coming. So I must appreciate the time I have with her now.

CHAPTER 28

"I'm so glad you came over," I say to Ashley, as we simultaneously plop down on the couch in the living room. Gram is in her usual chair, reading a book on her Kindle.

"What's up?" Ashley says as she leans back against the couch.

"I just needed some girl time." I lean back as well. "You've been so busy lately."

This is all true, of course. But I also have an ulterior motive for having her come over. I'm playing matchmaker today to find out how she feels about Justin. I totally could have texted or called her about it, and wanted to—I've had to hold it in for five days, after all—but I felt like she could hide things if we weren't face-to-face. I need to see her reaction.

"I know; these auditions are killing me. I've made callbacks three times on this one. It's hard not to get my hopes up, but I think I just need to face the fact that it's probably not going to happen." She closes her eyes.

"Ashley Tucker, you stop right now. You are talented, and the right part will happen. This might even be the one." I punch her lightly on the arm.

"Yeah, sure. It's all a bunch of bullsh—"

"Ahem." Gram clears her throat.

"Sorry," Ashley says in *not*-sorry tones.

"Oh, go back to your smut, Gram," I say, giving her my best irritated look. Such a double standard there.

Gram picks up her book, and with a quick glare at me, she goes back to reading.

"Want some chocolate?" I ask. Chocolate always seems to be the cure around here.

"I'd rather something harder, honestly." She clasps her hands together and sets them in her lap.

"Well, I'd offer you wine, but Gram had to get rid of it all. Doctor's orders."

"Psh," Gram says, looking up from her Kindle. "First coffee, now alcohol. What's there to live for?" She rolls her eyes.

I shake my head at her. "At least you still have chocolate."

"How long before he takes that away too?" She exhales loudly and dramatically.

"I'll take some chocolate," Ashley declares.

I grab a bag of Lindt truffles from the stash in the kitchen and come back to the couch.

"What's new with the Ian drama?" Ashley asks as I plop down. I start to open the bag of chocolate, which is harder than I thought it would be.

"Oh," I shake my head, "not much is new. He's been texting me, trying to be friends."

I've received a text every day since that first text where he declared his desire to still be friends. I've yet to text him back.

"And?" She reaches over and grabs the bag out of my hand, opening it with ease, and hands it back to me after she takes out a truffle.

"Well, there's no 'and,' really. I mean, we can't be friends. It just won't work." I sniff, grabbing a truffle for myself.

"Yeah, I guess that's smart." Ashley has always been my more practical friend, and I'm grateful for that.

"So, I have something to tell you," I say to Ashley, giving her a little smirk.

"What's that look for?" she asks, pointing to my face. I offer her another truffle, and she grabs it.

"Well, remember how you thought Justin likes me?" I smirk again.

"Oh, yeah." She bats a hand at me, as if to blow it off.

"What? Did you change your mind?" I lift my eyebrows, questioning her.

"Not really. I don't know what to think of Justin," she says, rather blandly.

"Well, we talked," I say, knowing she will perk up with this bit of info, and she does.

"You did? What did you say to him?" Her body language changes immediately. She's interested now.

"Actually, he told me he had something to tell me, and I kept avoiding it because I was afraid of what he might say — since you and Carla had gotten it into my head that he liked me as more than a friend." I pull the corner of my mouth up in a conniving smile. I'm taking my time telling her this, and I can tell it's getting on her nerves.

"Carla?" She scrunches her face.

"Yeah, she said something about how she saw it in his eyes when she met him," I say, while rolling my own eyes.

"I knew it wasn't just me." She slumps back on the couch, not looking smug like I would expect her to at this point. "So, when did you talk to him? What did he say?" She turns her head to me, clearly wanting me to get to the punchline of this story.

I'm not stretching this story out to annoy her — although, I can't deny that it's fun. I'm also trying to figure out if Justin's feelings are reciprocated. Ashley has been so focused on her hopes of getting into theater that I'm not sure if she's ever mentioned liking anyone. So if there have been any clues that she likes Justin, I've probably missed them.

"He made me go to coffee with him after work on Monday. I tried to get out of it, but I figured, if it's true, we might as well get it out of the way now," I say.

"So, what did he say?" Ashley asks, as her hands start fidgeting in her lap.

"Yes, what did he say?" Gram pipes in, her full attention on me. I didn't realize she was listening. I thought she had gone back to reading her book.

"He doesn't like me, not like that. It was quite embarrassing — thanks to you." I slap Ashley lightly on the leg.

"He doesn't?" The relief in Ashley's face is obvious.

"You seem relieved," I say, tilting my head to the side.

"I do?" She looks away from me, a faint blush on her cheeks. "I guess I just didn't want it to mess anything up. We have a good thing, the three of us."

"Yeah, I know." I look down at my hands in my lap. Things are going to change, regardless. If Ashley doesn't reciprocate feelings, then I'll have made everything weird. Well, mostly Justin has. If she doesn't like Justin, then I have to tell him— actually, no. No more high school for me. She can tell him. But then our trio is probably over. Truthfully, if she doesn't like him, any scenario means the end of our trio. A pang of sadness rushes through me.

"I'm glad. I don't want things to get weird with us, you know?" She holds her hand out for another truffle, and I oblige. "So what did he have to tell you then?" she asks as she opens the tightly wrapped candy.

"Well, I think things are going to get weird, anyway," I say, raising an eyebrow. Ashley gives me a muddled look.

"What do you mean?" Gram asks, before Ashley can respond.

"Because," I pause to look at Gram derisively. She's such a buttinski. I should expect nothing less at this point.

I turn back to Ashley. "Because he likes *you*, Ash."

Wow, I actually do feel like I'm in high school.

"What?" Her eyes bug out of her head.

"You heard me." I'm having a hard time holding back a giggle because of the expression on her face.

"But he always flirts with you?" She looks as confused as I probably did when he told me.

"Yes, I know. But it's not because he likes me. He's a weird one, that Justin." I say, not wanting to tell her everything he said. My loyalty to Justin—although very small—is still there.

"So?" I ask, poking her in the arm with my finger. If we are going back to high school, I might as well act the part.

"So?" Grams also interjects.

"So . . ." Ashley trails off, her mind obviously spinning.

"Well, do you like him?" Gram asks, her impatience showing. I have no idea how she reads romance novels where the plot is drawn out chapter after chapter until there is some resolution, only for some conflict to pop up so it can be drawn out another ten chapters.

I look over to Ashley, who is sitting back against the couch. She's still quiet, but then her head falls into her hands and sounds of hysteria start.

I look over at Gram, who shrugs her shoulders. I wasn't sure how this would play out, but I didn't think Ashley would cry.

"Ash," I say after a few seconds of her blubbering. I grab her arm, trying to pry her hand away from her face. "Are you crying? I mean, I know it's weird, and things will be different, but it's okay if you don't like him. It won't ruin things. We can figure it out."

She takes her hands away and she's not crying. She's laughing.

"What's so funny?" I ask, wanting in on the joke.

She takes a few seconds to bring herself back from the laughter. "This," she finally declares. "This whole thing."

"I don't get it," I say.

"Oh, I do," Gram says.

"You do?" I ask her.

"I've read enough romance books. This is quintessential romance right here," Gram points to Ashley.

"Huh?" I regard Gram with confusion.

"She likes him." She winks at me.

I turn back to Ashley, "Do you?"

Ashley is quiet and won't look at me.

"Do you?" I poke her in the arm again with my finger.

She turns to me, a smile spreads, quickly growing until it fills her small face as full as it can.

"You do!" I exclaim, grabbing her by the arm and shaking her slightly. "How long? Why didn't you tell me?"

She ponders her hands in her lap, twiddling furiously. "For a while now," she says, and then looks up at me. "I thought he liked you, so I never said anything. I didn't want to ruin things."

"You need to tell him," I say, once again grabbing her by the arm and shaking her briefly.

"Why do I feel like a teenager right now?" Ashley asks. "I mean, we're all adults here—why hasn't he told me?"

I shrug my shoulders. "I think Justin is rusty when it comes to stuff like this. Plus, you know— the whole rejection thing." I glance downward as Ian pops in my head. It isn't bizarre for him to be there, because he's been popping in a lot lately. I look up at Ash. "I guess I could say the same thing to you? Why haven't you told him?"

"Same reasons, I guess. Plus, I need to keep my head into my auditions. Unrequited love doesn't help in that area," she says.

"You love him?" My eyes widen.

"No." She pushes me and rolls her eyes. "You know what I mean."

"So, what are you going to do?" Gram asks.

"I don't know?" She looks to me for answers.

"Don't look at me," I say, shaking my head. "My high school work is done here."

"This is all so weird," she declares. "I mean, how awkward will it be now?"

"Why does it have to be awkward? You like him. He likes you," I say.

"I know, but do I just walk up to him and say, 'hey' and hope he understands?" She gives me a confused look.

"Well, however you do it, I want you to make sure I get to be maid of honor at the wedding." I grin brightly.

"Oh geez." She purses her lips and rolls her eyes. "Don't get ahead of yourself, Bridgette. First, I think we need to get it all out in the open."

"I think you just need to go out for coffee or something. See where things go." I smile at her but then feel my smile falter, as suddenly a new feeling starts to sink in: jealousy. Actually, jealousy is a strong word. More like envy. I'm not envious she and Justin like each other, quite the opposite. What I *am* feeling is a little envious of the pending relationship. New relationships are so fun. I don't have any of that right now. Only old drama-filled ones. I need to remember my decision to stand on my own for a while. I really do need it.

After concocting the perfect text, which ended up saying, "Hey Justin, wanna meet for coffee?" (It took fifteen minutes to compile that—we are such girls), Ashley was off to meet up with him. I would only let her leave when she had promised repeatedly that she would call me as soon as she could to tell me every detail. She seemed pretty nervous when she left.

"So, how are you feeling about all of that?" Gram asks as I come back into the room from walking Ashley to the door.

"Ashley and Justin?" I say, scrunching my face in confusion. "Why would you ask that?" I go back to my usual place on the couch.

"I don't know," Gram says, looking down at her Kindle. "I guess it's not as much fun to be excited for a friend in a new relationship when you don't have one of your own." Geez, that woman can read me like a book. Which, I guess, makes sense.

"Nah." I dismiss the thought with my hand. "Sure, there's a little envy there. I'd like something new and exciting like that. But I'm happy for them." I give her a thin smile.

"Well, you know what I'm going to say," Gram nods once, eyebrows raised.

"Yes, I know. Someone will come along, better than the last one," I say, acknowledging with my face I knew that was coming. "You read too many romance novels, Gram," I say as I stand up and start to walk to my room.

She clicks her tongue. "I don't read romance. I read historical," she states, shoulders raised proudly. Then she gives me a little smirk, and we both giggle.

I sure do adore that crazy lady.

CHAPTER 29

Friends.

We can totally to do this. I'm an adult and Ian's an adult. Why should I push him away when I just got him back? I mean, why not? There are pretty much a million reasons why not, but I'll push those aside.

I don't know what's gotten into me. I was sticking to my guns, not agreeing to try this whole friendship thing with Ian. But then he caught me in a moment when my guard was down. Maybe it was the whole Ashley and Justin thing. I was feeling lonely. Lonely and full of ridiculous self-pity. And then Ian texted me, and on a whim, I told him we could try being friends.

Oh gosh, this is a truly dumb idea. I've made some dumb choices in my past, but this one might be right up there at the top. Probably next to the time I dyed my hair red. Essentially, it was orange. My sister called me "traffic cone head" for weeks. I'm thinking this will end up ranking near that debacle.

I stand up from my seat in the café where I asked Ian to meet me. It's the café that Justin, Ashley, and I frequent. I wanted to meet up on my turf this time. I'm not sure why. It's not to give myself a one-up or something; it just felt safe. It doesn't matter now because I'm going to leave. It feels like the best thing to do. I grab my gold clutch purse and head for the door. It's better to nip this bad idea in the bud before it gets any worse.

"Leaving so soon?" Ian's voice croons to my left. I look over at him, which was a bad idea, because looking at him in his sharp black suit only makes me hate this friend idea even more. I don't want Ian as a friend. I want more than friends.

"Um, yeah," I say nervously, as I pull on the ends of my loose side braid and avert eye contact. "I need to be somewhere."

"You do?" he asks, confusion on his face as he looks down at my outfit, which is quite casual for me—a pair of cropped distressed jeans, a sleeveless cream top with an asymmetric hem, and gold, flat T-strap sandals. I was trying to dumb it down. Make my outfit more friend-like.

"Yes, I forgot." I pull on my braid again and start biting my lower lip.

"You liar," he says, a sly smile spreading on his face.

"Excuse me?" I crunch my face up, disdainfully. How dare he.

"You still bite your lower lip when you lie," he says, the grin remaining.

Crap.

"Oh, okay. Fine." I roll my eyes. I start walking back to the table, and he follows me. We sit down.

"I guess I was thinking this was a bad idea," I say, placing my purse in my lap.

"Why does it have to be a bad idea?" Ian questions.

"Because it just feels like a bad idea. With our history and all. I keep thinking that if the tables were turned and I was marrying you," I pause and swallow hard at the notion, "and there was someone from your past whom you were striking up a friendship with . . . well, I think it feels a little shady." I look down at my lap and stare at the buckle on my clutch. I nervously start rubbing my fingers over the cool metal.

"I thought the same thing," Ian says.

My head shoots up. "Huh?"

"I thought the same thing, which is why I'm having Maureen meet us here." He looks at his watch. "In five minutes."

"Say what?" I think I've been hoodwinked.

"Look," Ian says, leaning in toward me, "I want you in my life, Bridge. But if we're going to do this friend thing, then Maureen needs to meet you and get to know you, so everything is on the up-and-up."

"Okay," I nod my head slowly. "I guess that makes sense."

Yes, the up-and-up. If I know Maureen and she is okay with Ian and I being friends, then we might actually pull this whole friend thing off. There's still one small problem with that. I've been having fantasies about them breaking up and Ian marrying me.

This could be awkward.

I don't have time to think too much about it because Ian's eyes move toward the door as Maureen walks in. She's tall — very tall, and blonde, and pretty. And she's carrying a sort of briefcase. It's expensive looking and matches her outfit — a slim skirt and matching blazer with a white button-down blouse underneath. She looks smart. Oh no, she's probably a lawyer. She'll grill me and ask me questions, and Ian and I didn't have time to discuss what was on or off limits. I feel the sweat pooling in my underarms.

Ian stands up as she walks over to the table, and I follow suit and stand up as well.

Wait, why am I standing? I look like a complete idiot. Ian looks over at me, confirming with his face that my choice was dopey. I want to sit back down, but it's too late. I'm already standing.

"Hello," Maureen says in a throaty, take-me-to-bed voice. "You must be Bridgette." She smiles as she holds out her hand to shake mine. I reach out and shake her hand vigorously. A little over-vigorously, unfortunately. She gives me a strange look.

"It's nice to meet you," I say, a little breathless. Nervousness attacks me from all angles. She tries to remove her hand, and I relinquish after realizing I have it in a death grip.

I'm so freaking nervous. I hate it when I'm nervous. "Sorry for the standing thing," I say as I sit in my chair. Maureen gives me an odd look, possibly questioning my sanity. I don't blame her.

"So, I finally get to meet someone from college." She looks at Ian and smiles. "I swear, Ian was so vague about college that I wondered if he even had friends." She laughs, and then Ian laughs, and then I laugh because everyone else is laughing.

Oh hell. This is awkward.

"Yes, well, I was pretty much his only friend," I say, trying to calm myself so I can act like a normal human. I don't think it's working. I shrug, uncomfortably.

"I had more friends than just you," Ian says, trying to defend himself, not taking notice of my ungainliness.

"Well let's see, there was me," I say, ticking off a finger as I start to count Ian's friends, "a string of other woman," Ian rolls his eyes at that, "and Brandon." My eyes go wide after I say that name. Oops. I didn't want to bring up the whole Brandon situation.

"Whatever happened to Brandon?" Maureen asks, completely ignoring my comment about the string of other woman, which I now realize was totally inappropriate. I suck at this.

"Um," Ian scratches his five-o'clock shadow, which looks as if it came in way before five o'clock. "I haven't spoken to or seen Brandon since I graduated."

I could kick myself for even saying that name. Brandon's the huge elephant in the room. The huge, regrettable elephant.

"Why didn't you keep in contact with him?" Maureen pries. I silently pray she will drop it.

"I didn't feel like it," he says plainly. "Brandon was not a good part of my life."

My stomach sinks big time. He still hates me for that, obviously. Heck, I still hate me for that.

"So, Bridgette, where do you work?" Maureen asks as she settles back in her seat.

"I work in catering," I say simply. No need to elaborate.

"Oh right, you work for the company that catered our engagement party," she states as she recalls that bit of information. I was never officially introduced to her that night, so I suppose Ian gave her that bit of info.

"And you?" I ask, not wanting any more questions from that night. I definitely didn't act normally and neither did Ian.

"Lawyer," she says simply and looks to Ian. Right. Of course she's a lawyer. The grilling could happen at any second. I feel sick.

"Yes," Ian says, smoothing out his gray chambray tie with a couple strokes of his hand. "Maureen is a very talented contracts lawyer." He reaches his arm around the back of her chair, a look of pride on his face.

He's proud of her. Of course he is. Why does that make my heart hurt a little?

"That's great," I interject.

We sit in silence. This was such a bad idea, all around.

"So, Bridgette, why don't you tell me some stories about Ian at college? I feel like I know so little about that time in his life." She smiles brightly at me.

Little does she know *I'm* the reason he hasn't told her that many stories. This could not get more uncomfortable. I look over to Ian, and he doesn't look like he's feeling awkward. Rather, he looks happy to be here. Has he lost his mind?

"Well, let's see." I shift uneasily in my seat. This is ridiculous. It's not like I don't have a million stories to tell. We met as freshman, became friends instantly, but never dated until our senior year. So there are plenty of stories to tell without any of the dating drama added. "Well, there was one time when he made me set him up with my roommate, and it was a disaster," I finally say. Yes, this is safe. Allude to the fact that Ian and I never dated or felt anything for each other. That is what I should do.

"Really? That's the story you are going to lead with?" Ian looks over at me, questioning me with one raised eyebrow.

"What? It's the first one that came to mind," I say, reflecting back with eyebrows high.

"No," Maureen puts a hand on Ian's arm, "I want to hear it." She dips her chin once, giving me the go-ahead.

Ian rolls his eyes. "It's not that great of a story," he says blandly.

"Would you shut up and let me tell the story?" I ask, slapping his arm with my hand.

"Yea, Ian, shut up and let her tell the story," Maureen echoes.

"Fine." He leans back in his chair, folding his arms.

My nervousness starts to lessen as I go into the story about Ian and my freshman roommate, who turned out to be a nut job. That one seemed to go over well. Maureen was laughing. Ian wasn't even trying to shut me up with his facial expressions like I kept expecting him to. On the contrary, he was actually interjecting comments and trying to make the story sound better than it was. Before I know it, I'm telling all kinds of Ian stories. There were fun ones that I had forgotten about, and sometimes I let him tell his part of the story, and we banter back and forth. Maureen takes it all in, laughing and asking questions. I almost feel okay with it all. Almost.

"What was the chick's name who was a vegetarian?" I ask Ian after we finish telling Maureen about the time we got kicked out of the library.

Ian's eyes do a little nervous dance that I'm unable to read.

"A vegetarian, huh?" Maureen looks to me to finish the story.

"Yeah, she was a vegan, actually. It was unintentional. Ian had no idea, but once he found out, it was over. He said he could never be serious with a vegetarian," I say. I feel something in the air change as soon as the words are out of my mouth.

"Maureen's a vegetarian," Ian says, gesturing with his hand toward her.

Oh, holy crap.

"Oh my gosh," I say, feeling incredibly stupid. "I mean," I fidget with the buckle on my clutch, nervously trying to think of a way out of this, "obviously Ian is no longer the ignorant fool from college." I'm trying desperately not to convey the feeling of total idiocy that has taken over me. I so blame Ian for this. He should have warned me.

"Yes." Maureen turns her head to look at Ian. "He's definitely grown up." She looks at him, amusement in her eyes. She's clearly not offended by this whole exchange, thank goodness.

"Well, this has been enlightening," Maureen says, weaving her arm through his. She pulls herself close to him. They look at each other, and it's not the kind of look you expect between two people who plan to spend their lives together. There's no look of cheesy, goofy-eyed love, but something more like a mutual respect. Which I suppose is good. But now that I think of it, there hasn't been a look of love exchanged between the two of them this entire time. Maybe that's just what their relationship has settled into. Or maybe I'm reading too much into it.

"Sorry," I say, giving Ian a sheepish grin.

"No, really, thank you for sharing." She winks at me and I know it's meant to be a kind gesture, but it makes me feel kind of small . . . and very young, even though we are most likely the same age.

"Anyway, I've got to get going," Maureen says, standing up from her seat. "Gotta get back to the office. It's going to be an all-nighter again, I'm afraid," she says, looking at Ian for his response. He doesn't say anything. He simply gives her a thin smile. "Bridgette, it was wonderful to meet you." She holds out her hand again for me to shake, which I do, this time with less nervous gusto.

"Nice to meet you, too," I say as I start to get up from my chair to leave as well.

"Oh, don't go because I'm leaving," she says as she sees me start to stand up. "Stay here and keep my fiancé company. I fear with all the hours I work, he might get a wandering eye. You'll watch out for him, won't you, Bridgette?" She winks at me again.

I let out a nervous laugh. I'm probably the worst person to babysit her future husband.

I try to look away as she leans down and kisses Ian on the lips, but I catch a glimpse in my peripheral vision. *Curses.* That was not something I wanted to see.

I watch as Maureen saunters off, turning around to give us one last wave as she goes out the door.

"So, that was Maureen," Ian says, after a small bought of silence.

"You could have warned me she was a vegetarian, you know." I scrunch my face in annoyance.

"Sorry about that," he chuckles.

"Whatever," I mutter. "Anyway, she seems like good people," I say, trying to remember if she even said much during the entire conversation. It was mostly Ian and me relaying old college stories and skirting around the ones we shouldn't tell.

"She is." He nods his head a few times. "So now that you've met her, do you think you can put this whole 'we can't be friends' thing to bed?"

"I guess," I say with a little shrug. Honestly, even after meeting Maureen officially, I still don't think it's appropriate. Maybe saying that we *can* be friends will be enough for Ian to let it go. Like maybe the fact that I'm fighting it so much is truly what's bothering him.

"How did you meet?" I ask, picking at a tiny string that's hanging from the hem of my shirt.

"Mutual friends introduced us," he says, thumbs twiddling in his lap.

"How long have you been together?" I'm not sure why I'm prodding into a relationship I don't really want to know about.

"About two years," he says, looking down at his fidgeting hand.

That was about the same time I met Adam. Ian and I were both in the same city, doing nearly the same thing, neither of us knowing we were both here. Funny where life can take us. If I had run into Ian before I met Adam, how different would our lives be now? Would it be me marrying him? It's probably best not to entertain such thoughts. They won't lead anywhere good.

We're silent for a bit, Ian staring off into the café, looking lost in thought, and me toying with the same string from the hem of my shirt.

"Does she make you laugh?" I say without thinking. Where did that come from?

"Huh?" Ian says, caught off guard by the question. I know the feeling. I too, was caught off guard.

He bobs his head a few times as he realizes what I've asked. "Yeah, she does. I mean, we don't have the same exact humor. We have fun together, but not as much fun as you and —" he stops himself. He doesn't need to finish the thought.

"Good, I'm glad you have fun together," I say, completely ignoring his faux pas.

We smile at each other. There's a nostalgic look on his face that I'm sure is mirroring my own.

"Sorry for bringing up Brandon," I say. I don't want to bring his name up again, but I feel like it needs to be said.

He waves a hand, dismissing it. "It was a while ago, Bridge," he says, giving me a small smile.

"Yes, I know it was, but I feel like you deserve an explanation." I shrug my shoulders. I'm not even sure it would help anything, except maybe my own conscience.

"I don't," he says. "All is forgiven. Let's not waste any more time on that guy," he adds, his lips pulling up to the side in a half smile.

"Okay," I say, letting it go, but not really wanting to.

"Thanks for meeting me," Ian says.

"I'm glad I did. It was good to meet Maureen, too. She's pretty. You're clearly marrying out of your league," I tease.

"Nice," he says, giving me a smirk.

"Hey, I just tell it like it is." I start to punch him in the arm, but he grabs my hand to block it. His hand lingers on mine.

"Um," I swallow hard, removing my hand quickly. "I guess I better go." I stand up, grabbing my purse with my left hand, as I steady myself with my right hand on the table. I turn to head toward the door, only I pivot the wrong way entirely, and as I try to right myself, I spot something in the back corner of the café. Actually, I spot *someone*.

"Oh my gosh," I say in a near whisper.

"Bridge?" Ian asks, and then looks over in the direction I'm looking.

"No," I say in a stage whisper, quickly pulling Ian so our backs are turned to the offending corner. "Don't look." My eyes dart around the room, probably very crazy-person like. Did I really see what I think I saw?

"What's going on?" Ian asks.

"Do me a favor," I say, my lips to his ear. "Turn around slowly, and tell me what you see in that back booth in the corner."

"What?"

"Just do it," I demand, still using my stage whisper.

"Okay," he says reluctantly. Slowly he moves his body so he is standing slightly to the side, toward me, his torso leaning on my arm.

I will not pay attention to the hard stomach muscles I can feel through his dress shirt. I. Will. Not.

"What do you see?" I whisper.

"Um, which table?" he asks, his head moving around.

"Could you please try to look a little less obvious?" I say, my eyes widening at him with disapproval. "You are a horrible stalker."

"Yes, that's usually your job," he say, leaning in even closer.

"Shut up," I say, getting impatient. I need to get confirmation, and then Ian and I need to hightail it out of here so we don't get caught. "It's the very back corner."

"The girl with the long, dark hair?" Ian asks, and I wait for him to make a typical comment that I've come to expect when anyone of the male species first lays eyes on Serene.

"Yes, tell me what she's doing," I demand. Ian's torso is still up against my arm. I can feel his chest move up and down as he breathes. *Stop it, Bridgette.* I need to concentrate.

"She's snuggling up to some guy, it looks like," he says, keeping his face on me, but moving ever-so-slightly so he can spy effectively.

"Oh screw it," I say. Grabbing Ian by the waist, I turn him slightly and then, standing in front of him,

I pull him into a hug. He nuzzles his chin into my neck just like old times and for a split second I forget my real purpose in hugging him.

"Now get a good look," I say, once I've taken a deep breath to shake off the fact that we are so close, chest to chest. A not-so-genius move on my part.

"Um, okay," I feel his chin shift as he moves his head to get a good look. "She's definitely snuggling with some guy. Oh and —"

"What," I say into his ear, interrupting him.

"Well, they're no longer just snuggling," he says, pulling out of the hug and gesturing for me look. I take a quick glance and then turn my head back. There's no room for misunderstanding here. That's definitely Serene, who's now in a full-on make out session with someone that is definitely not Adam.

"Hurry," I say, as I grab Ian's hand and head out the door of the café.

"What was that all about?" Ian asks, as the door shuts behind us. We're still holding hands.

I look down at our adjoining hands and quickly let go. How easy it is to step back into old habits with Ian.

"That was Serene. The current fiancée of my ex-boyfriend. But that was not my ex-boyfriend."

"Oh," is all Ian says. "When did you break up?"

"Um," I say, feeling like my head is jumbled up, "like over four months ago."

"Oh," he repeats. I catch a look of hurt, or maybe annoyance, on his face. But it's gone too quickly for me to be sure.

"What's wrong?" I ask.

"Nothing." He shakes his head, putting a hand up to rub his forehead. "I just . . . I . . . never mind."

I should explore this further, obviously, but I can't. Not when my brain is moving around in circles, trying to figure out what course of action I need to take with this whole Serene-the-cheater thing. Obviously, I need to tell Adam. Or maybe I should tell Carla and have her tell him. No, I need to go directly to him.

"Ian, I need to go," I say.

"Okay, sure. I get it." He looks down at the pavement.

"Um, I'll text you?" I say, a sheepish grin on my face, as I start to walk backwards from him.

"Yeah." He nods his head, and the left corner of his lip pulls up.

I give him a quick wave and I'm off.

~*~

As I suspected, when I called Adam, he was home alone, since clearly Serene is not with him. I was slightly hopeful she would be, and then I wouldn't have to be the bearer of bad news. But I knew it was her in the café, and the fact that she is not with Adam only confirms it more.

I'm on the subway heading to the Lower East Side to go to Adam's apartment. He was really excited that I wanted to come over. He probably thinks I'm rethinking our friend status. I'm not. I think I'm at my capacity of ex-boyfriend-turned-friends.

Right now, my heart wants to think about Ian and meeting Maureen, but that will have to be saved for another time because my brain can only keep pondering how I'm going give this news to Adam.

How will he take it? Will he be sad? Angry? Relieved? Will he say he made a mistake and want me back? Would I want to go back to Adam?

I already know the answer to that. Adam and I were never truly right for each other. I mean, I thought we were, but I think I convinced myself he was the one I was meant to be with. It was a lot like my relationship with Brandon, actually. Very easy, very convenient. And with Adam I had the bonus of loving his family. But I was never really myself with either Adam or Brandon. I wasn't enough for either of them. Truthfully, neither of them were enough for me.

What does it say about me that I'm so willing to give my heart to the wrong guy? But when the guy who was probably the right one came along, I couldn't even say those three stinking words. And now it's too late.

The smell of the hallway as I walk to Adam's apartment brings back so many memories. So many good memories. We did have fun, Adam and I. The odd thing is I don't miss it.

"Well, hello stranger," Adam says as he opens the door. He immediately pulls me into a hug.

"Hey," I say, as we pull apart, and he ushers me into his apartment. His place looks pretty much the same as it did a few months ago. I guess I thought Serene would have done some decorating. From the looks of things, she's not a cleaner either.

"How's work?" he asks as we walk into the apartment. He's making small talk, which is so strange after our history. It doesn't feel natural at all. It feels forced.

"Um, good," I say, intertwining my fingers, rocking back and forth on my feet. "It looks like I will be promoted to assistant caterer soon." I go to nibble my bottom lip, but I stop myself. It's not entirely a lie. I just don't know when "soon" is.

"You?" I ask.

"Busy," is all he offers, which is fine by me. I don't need him to go into detail like he used to when we were dating, which could be quite agonizingly boring. But, of course, I acted like it was so very interesting.

"Have a seat," he says, gesturing to the couch. He sits down in a plain, brown armchair, leaning forward, elbows on thighs, hands intertwined.

"Thanks," I say, pushing an article of clothing to the side as I sit down. It's the sweater — the ratty old sweater I attempted so many times to get rid of.

"You still have this?" I hold it up, pinched between my pointer finger and thumb, handling it as if it has cooties. It just might.

"Yeah." He nods his head and smiles, looking down at his intertwining hands. He knows how much I hated that sweater.

"It doesn't bother Serene?" I ask out of complete curiosity. I drop the offending sweater on the floor.

"Nah," he shakes his head, "she's never said anything, at least."

I want to tell him that's a red flag because any girl who truly loved him would tell him to burn it (like I had tried so many times). But that's moot since I have an even bigger red flag to tell him about, like the reddest flag you can possibly have.

"So, what did you need to talk to me about? You seemed a little frantic on the phone," he says, looking up at me with a pleasant smile.

"Well," I swallow hard. This is not going to roll off the tongue easily. "It's about Serene."

"Oh yeah? Sorry she's not here, by the way. She had to go run some errands." He leans back in his seat.

"Um, yeah, that's what I want to talk to you about. I saw her," I say, and then start rubbing my suddenly-sweaty hands on my jeans.

"You did?" He smiles, most likely picturing her. I'm picturing her too, sucking on some other guy's face.

We sit there in silence because I'm not sure how to just come out and say it.

"Is that what you wanted to tell me?" he asks, clearly confused how that could be the only thing.

"No," I say and take a deep breath. "I saw her with someone else."

"Yeah." He nods his head quickly. "She said she had to meet up with her brother."

"Um, I don't think who I saw her with was her brother," I say. I raise my eyebrows, hoping he will get my insinuation.

He shakes his head briefly. "I don't understand."

Ah yes, Adam was never good at picking up on insinuations. There was one time that I wanted to leave a boring party, and I kept raising my eyebrows and nodding my head toward the door and . . . nothing. He didn't get it. After we left, I asked him why he didn't respond to any of my gestures, which were clearly stating my desire to depart, and he said, "Oh, is that what you were doing? I thought you had a crick in your neck or something." I learned then that I just needed to say "let's leave" so there was no room for misinterpretation.

"Well, I saw her at a café with a guy," I look down at my lap, not wanting to see his face when I tell him the next part, "and she was kissing him."

"What?" I look up to see Adam's face all scrunched up. He's leaning forward in his chair as if ready to pounce. "What do you mean?" he asks, clearly confused and rightfully so. This has to be so hard for him to wrap his brain around.

"I mean, I saw her and some guy . . . um . . . making out in a booth." I keep a steady eye on him to make sure he's accepting what I'm trying to tell him.

"That's not possible," Adam says. A hand goes to the back of his neck and he rubs it briefly.

"I'm so sorry, Adam," I say. I truly am sorry. I know Carla hates Serene, but I've never had any reason to hate her, besides the fact that she snatched Adam away. I've made my peace with all of that now. I never wanted to see Adam hurt, though. And here he is, hurt.

"Wow," he says, sitting back in his chair. His rubs his forehead. "Wow," he says again, but more under his breath.

And then the craziest thing happens. He starts to laugh. It's not a belly laugh—it's more of a maniacal, crazy laugh. The laugh of someone about to lose it. I don't think I've ever seen Adam react like this.

"Adam?" I want to go over to him and comfort him, but I don't. I stay rooted in my seat.

"Did my mom put you up to this?" he says, after the crazy laugh has subsided. It's now replaced by a crazy, red face.

"Carla?" I shake my head, "No? Why would you think that?"

"Because it's the only thing that makes sense." His hand goes through his dark, thick hair, leaving it messy and furthering this lunatic look he's going with.

"I'm sorry, Adam. I don't know what to tell you. I'm only telling you what I saw," I say, my hands out, palms up, pleading my case.

He sits there, staring at me. I stare back. Don't people look away or around the room when they're lying? Or, in my case, nibble on their bottom lip? Well, I'm not doing any of that because I'm telling the truth.

"You know," he says after a few seconds of our staring contest, "I've heard stories of crazy ex-girlfriends going to extremes to get their exes back, but I thought it was folklore or something. But wow, I guess it does happen." He leans forward in his chair and stands up.

"What are you talking about, Adam? I'm not trying to get you back," I say and stand up. I can feel the heat in my face; I've joined him in the red face of anger. "I'm telling you what I saw, that's all," I say, my volume elevating.

He rolls his eyes, "I know Serene, and that's not her." He tilts his head to the side, "I thought I knew you, but I guess I didn't because I really didn't think you would pull a stunt like this."

"Are you serious?" I grab my gold clutch from the couch. "This is not a stunt, it's the truth. I'm telling you what I saw. If you don't believe me, then that's your problem. But don't try and turn it on me." I walk toward the door and swing it open.

I'm not going to stay here and try to convince him of what I saw. In fact, I hope he marries her, and she cheats on him and steals all his money, and he lives the rest of his life in misery.

I walk out the door and turn back. "This goes without saying, but that is a big, fat no for coming to your wedding," I yell and turn around and walk out. As I slam the door, I can hear him start his crazy laugh again. I need to work on my final remarks when I leave in a huff. I could have said something much more profound than that.

I race-walk down the hall to the elevators and press the down button as many times as I can, trying to hurry up the elevator. Once inside the elevator with the door shut, I allow the full weight of the situation that just happened to hit me. I had a lot of scenarios running around in my head about how it was going to go down, but that was not one of them.

The ego of that man. How dare he think I would go as far as to make up a huge lie to get him back. Okay, so I did make Justin be my pretend boyfriend and go to his family's dinner in hopes Adam would see what he was missing. But, this is different. This is the truth.

What am I going to do now? I guess there's nothing I can do. Adam will just have to learn the hard way. Unfortunately, he's not the only one that will suffer. So will his family.

That thought makes my heart sink. Adam's family shouldn't have to suffer from his love-obsessed brain. But what can I do? I can tell his mom, but he'll only say the same things to her that he said to me. He won't believe her either.

The only thing I can do is hope Adam will see the truth. Maybe if he sees it with his own eyes, he'll believe me. And then he better apologize to me. I mean, after he's had enough time to grieve. I'm not that coldhearted.

CHAPTER 30

University of Connecticut, senior year, end of term

"Ian, I wish there was a way, but there's just isn't." I sat on his bed, my arms folded, my mind made up.

"Bridge, why are you getting so caught up in the details? Take a chance." He sat down next to me, taking my hand in his.

"I can't go to London with you." I shook my head. I knew it was impossible, but Ian was not giving up easily.

"What are you going to do in Goshen this summer? There's nothing there for you," he said, frustration in his tone. He let go of my hand.

"I need to find a job, Ian. I need to start making money. There's nothing for me in London." I fold my arms again.

Hurt spread across his face. "*I'm* going to be in London."

I shook my head. "I'm sorry, yes, you'll be in London. You are the only thing for me there. But it's just not . . ." I stopped myself before I said what I was thinking because I know I didn't mean it, but it was suddenly there on the tip of my tongue.

". . . enough?" Ian finished the sentence for me.

"No, you know what I mean," I said, heat rising in my face. Ian had already been red-faced for a while.

"I really don't know what you mean, Bridgette." He stood up from the bed.

I hated it when he called me Bridgette. It was too serious. It wasn't in Ian's nature to be so serious. It felt all wrong.

He cursed under his breath. "I'm a fool." He put a hand through his hair.

"What are you talking about?"

"I should have known this wouldn't work out." He pointed between him and me.

"What do you mean, 'this wouldn't work out?' Just because I can't go to London doesn't mean I want us to break up." I stared at him, my eyebrows pulled in tightly.

He ran a hand through his hair. "I can't believe what an idiot I've been."

"What are you talking about? Why does me not going to London make you an idiot?" My voice started to get louder.

"Bridgette," he turned to me, "it's not about you not wanting to go to London. It's about this. It's about us."

"I'm seriously confused. Maybe you need to calm down. Maybe I should leave." I stood up from the bed and walked toward the door.

He grabbed my arm, pulling me back to him. "Bridgette, look me in the eyes."

I rolled my eyes and then looked at him.

"I love you." He said it sternly, not romantically, which was odd as this was the first time he had said those words to me. "The question is: do you love me?" He searched my face, looking for an answer.

I didn't answer. I don't know why, but nothing would come out.

"Your silence is your answer." He dropped my hands and turned away from me.

I couldn't say anything. I didn't know what was wrong with me, but I couldn't bring myself to say the words he wanted to hear. I wanted to, I did. But nothing would come out of my mouth.

"You should go." He shook his head, not willing to make eye contact with me again.

I grabbed my purse as I walked out of his room, holding back the strong desire to slam the door as I left.

"Everything okay?" Brandon asked from the couch in the living room. As I walked past him, a single tear dripped down my face.

"Um, yeah," I said flatly. "Yeah." I repeated myself. Obviously everything was not okay, but I wasn't in any place to talk about it with Brandon, of all people.

But despite the fact that it was Brandon, I couldn't help but break down completely before I could walk out the door. I felt like a fool on many levels.

"Let me take you back to your apartment, Bridge," Brandon said. Walking over to the door, he tucked his cellphone into his back pocket. He opened the door and ushered me out, blubbering idiot that I was.

Whatever just happened between Ian and me was, by far, more heartbreaking than anything I had ever experienced. I didn't even know what was going on. Did we break up?

I felt numb as Brandon drove me back to my apartment. He didn't talk, which was good, because all I could do was cry.

He kindly walked me into my apartment, his hand on my lower back as he escorted me in. His hand felt foreign, but comforting at the same time.

"Thanks," I said as we walked into the apartment. Amy was nowhere to be found, which was probably for the best. A cry of epic proportions was about to happen.

We stood in the doorway for a moment, and then unexpectedly, Brandon slid between me and the door and walked into the apartment. He walked over to the couch and sat down.

"You don't look like you should be alone right now, Bridge," he said, a small smile on his face.

This caught me off guard for many reasons. This was not a Brandon thing to do. To be empathic in any way, shape, or form was possibly against his genetic makeup. At least that had been my experience in the past. He never took interest in me or my feelings. Only Ian did that. But Ian was different than most guys.

Of course, the thought of Ian made the tears start moving again. Only intermittent ones had been falling by this point.

Brandon patted the seat next to him. Blindly, without thinking about it too much, I walked over and took a seat. He pulled me into him, again surprising me with the gesture. He rubbed my back and kissed the top of my head, as I buried my face into his shoulder and just let it all go.

After some time of blubbering, I came to, pulling my face away from his shoulder. I looked up into his eyes. They were full of something I hadn't seen before from him. Compassion? Understanding? Again, I was baffled by this unexpected set of reactions from him.

He reached up and wiped a lone tear from my eye. It made me feel vulnerable and a little lost. My mind was a fog of heartbreak and confusion. This was not helping. I decided my best move would be to get some distance from him. He must have meant well, but truthfully, he was making my mind spin even more.

I tried to pull away, but he held me close.

"I'm so sorry, Bridge," he said, looking at me. "He's an idiot."

I was having major déjà vu. I'd been on this couch before, crying over a relationship, except it was Ian holding me while I cried about Brandon. But Ian was right about Brandon, and now Brandon was making assumptions he had no idea about. I was the idiot. Me. I did the damage.

"No." I shook my head trying to get the words straight.

"He is. Me, too. I was an idiot to let you go," he said, his expression softening.

"What?" That was not what I was expecting.

"I wish I could go back and change things," he said, looking me in the eyes.

My eyes searched his. What was he talking about? I've been to his apartment with Ian many times after the breakup. There was never any sign of remorse. I was finding this admission hard to believe.

I didn't have a response to that. My brain was swimming. Too many things all at once. I couldn't handle it. I tried to pull out of his lock, but he kept holding me. I made the single mistake of looking up, and he locked eyes with me. Before I could even comprehend what was happening, his lips were on mine.

My mind instantly went blank. I could hear something screaming in the back of my brain, but I was so confused and caught up in everything that was happening in the present moment that I couldn't make heads or tails of it.

Ignoring the screaming, and only for a moment, I gave in to the kiss. I didn't want it, but I didn't push it away either.

"You've got to be kidding me," a voice said from somewhere. It wasn't a loud voice, and I was so lost in what was happening with Brandon, that I had actually thought I'd imagined it.

But it was enough to snap me out of whatever spell Brandon had put me under, and I pulled away from him instantly. I turned slowly around and locked eyes with Ian.

"Ian," I said breathlessly, my hand going up to my lips, trying to cover up what had just transpired. But there was no hiding it.

He didn't say anything. He simply turned around and walked out the door, slamming it shut as he left.

I ran to the door, swinging it open so fast it banged against the wall. I ran out, looking in all directions for Ian. I found him getting into his car, and I took off as fast as I could, but even if I had the speed of a superhero, there was no catching up with him. His wheels made a peeling sound as he got away from me as fast as he could.

CHAPTER 31

"How do you feel?" Ashley asks, as she sits across the booth from me at our regular café. We stopped in after work.

"Pretty dang good," I say and smile.

I did it. I got the job. I'm now officially the assistant catering manager at Edelweiss Catering. I can't believe it. It all happened so fast. Well, not *so* fast . . . it did take nearly four years.

It was sort of a whirlwind thing. I came in to work this afternoon, Ursula pulled me aside, told me I had the job, announced it to the staff, and that was that. Then I walked around the rest of the afternoon with a silly grin pasted on my face. All of the relationships in my life may be completely in the crapper, but my career is off to a new start. I see big things in my future. I'm not exactly sure what those big things are, because it's not like Edelweiss Catering is going to take me to new, crazy heights, but I can feel it anyway. Big things are happening for Bridgette Reynolds.

"Justin told me he was going to have to a find a new job," I say, looking at Ashley with apprehension. I'm not sure how she'll respond. I've been trying not to bring up his name, but this pretending-he-doesn't-exist thing has to end.

"Did he?" she asks, looking at her nail beds as if I said nothing of importance.

"Yes. He said having me as a boss might be worse than Ursula."

Not even a smile. She just nods her head a few times.

"Ash, how long is this going to go on?" I can't keep being in the middle of all of this. Even though they have both tried to keep me out of it, it's pretty much impossible.

Apparently, when they met for coffee and declared their feelings for each other, the "relationship" lasted for all of thirty minutes before they got in a big fight about who-knows-what, and that was the end. Ever since, I've been bouncing back and forth between the two, no one asking me to pick sides. Which is good, because I don't think I could. It's only been a couple of weeks, though. That could change. So now my trio is gone, my ex-boyfriend hates me, and my ex-ex-boyfriend is . . . well, I don't know what he is. There's way too much drama in my life right now.

"So," Ashley says, her countenance clearly stating that she'll be changing the subject. "What is your first order of business as the new assistant catering manager?"

"Well, I do plan on cashing my check and rolling around in all of my new funds," I say, and giggle. I did get a substantial raise but not enough to do anything too crazy.

She laughs at that. It's good to hear Ashley laugh. She hasn't done much of it this past week. Justin either. Why don't they both get over themselves and realize they're perfect for each other?

"Really, I'm just going to be running my own events. So it's more work, but less grunt work," I say, thinking about how I will never have to wear that stupid dirndl again. I smile to myself. I'm finally getting somewhere in my career. It feels good.

"Gosh, that sounds nice," she says, pensively. "Maybe someday I'll be done with the grunt work myself." She gives me a dull smile.

"Ash, it's gonna happen," I say.

She sighs. "We shall see."

She's gone through the wringer, yet again, over this last audition. Back and forth with callback after callback. I'm sure it's probably overwhelming. Especially since there's still no answer either way. The waiting has to be the hardest part, I would think.

"Heard anything about the whole Adam thing?" she asks.

"Oh." I purse my lips and shake my head. It's been two weeks since that all went down. "It is what it is. Nothing I can do about it. He's just going to marry a cheater, I guess."

"Did you ever call Carla?"

"Yep. She told me Adam has forbidden anyone in the family to talk to me." I purse my lips together again.

"No way," Ashley says, disbelieving.

I'm having a hard time believing it myself. Hearing Carla tell me over the phone that no one in the family can talk to me until after things have settled—when all the wedding stuff is done—broke my already-damaged heart. And even after the wedding, there are no guarantees. I was only trying to help, and look where it got me. I guess I've learned my lesson there.

"Yep. It's like he's brainwashed or something." I ponder that for a few seconds. Maybe Serene really is a witch . . .

"It's so weird that he didn't believe you at all," she says, grabbing the last french fry from the basket we were sharing. She shoves the whole thing in her mouth.

"I know, right? Like I would make that big of a production to try to get him back." I slouch in my seat. Men are so dumb.

Ashley giggles.

"Okay, fine. I did make Justin be my fake boyfriend so I could try to get Adam back. I guess that was quite the production. But he had no idea that's what I was doing, so it can't be used against me." I give her snooty duck lips.

"Anyway, they can have each other. I'm officially done butting in," I say, wiping my hands together to add emphasis.

"And what about Ian? Are you washing your hands clean of that?" she asks, leaning back in her seat.

"I probably should," I say and look out into the café. I look back at her, "but I don't know if I'm ready yet."

I haven't seen Ian since I met up with him and Maureen, but we have been texting on a regular basis. I hate it that I can't stop my heart from pounding when I see his name on my phone screen. I need to learn how to control my freaking heart.

"Have you ever told him the truth?" Ashley asks, looking me in the eyes.

"I tried to tell him, remember? He said it was 'water under the bridge' or something," I say, using air quotes.

"I don't mean that," she says, shaking her head briefly.

"What do you mean, then?"

"Have you ever told him that you should have said you loved him that day?" She tilts her head to the side.

"No," I say, looking down at my hands. "I don't think I should. It feels wrong."

"Don't you think he deserves to know?" she asks.

"Not really. What good will it do?" I look up at her. "I keep putting myself in Maureen's—his fiancée's—shoes." I interject the fiancée part when Ashley gives me a confused look. "What if it were me? What if I was marrying someone and some girl crept in and made everything different. I can't be *that* girl," I say, looking down at the empty french fry basket on the table. I wish there were more. I suddenly have a hankering for eating my feelings.

"Even if it would make you happy?" she prods further.

"Yes," I say after a moment. "Even if it makes me happy."

"So loyal," Ashley declares. "It's one of the things I admire about you, you know."

That gives me pause. I've never thought of myself as loyal, but I guess that does describe me. How else would you explain my attachment to Adam's family even after the breakup, or the fact that I've stayed at a job longer than I probably should have? It also explains why I refuse to pick sides between Ashley and Justin.

"Thanks," I say.

"So, are you going to continue this friend charade with him, then?" Ashley asks in her normal non-sugarcoated way.

"Probably. Maybe. I don't know," I say, babbling.

"Which one is it, then?"

"I don't know," I say flatly. And that's the truth. I don't know.

Of course, thinking about Ian makes my heart pound in my chest, per usual. But my heart is going to have to get over it. It's too late.

CHAPTER 32

I think I romanticized the whole assistant catering manager job a little too much in my head.

It's not that I thought it would be easier than serving, but I did think I would enjoy it more. There are some parts I like, but overall, it has felt a little joyless. It's only been a week, so I suppose I haven't had enough time to fully judge.

I knew I would have to manage the staff and supervise the events, but what I didn't realize was that there were so many things behind the scenes that I would have to do. Like all of the administrative duties. Ursula has put me in charge of scheduling shifts and managing inventory. I have no idea what the other assistant managers have to do, but I feel like I've been given the hardest jobs. The scheduling is in a word: torturous. All of these future Broadway stars needing time off for auditions and trying to make it all work so there is enough staff for every event . . . well, it's mind-numbing.

Currently, I'm sitting on the floor of Gram's apartment, going over the schedule on my new company laptop (I feel so snazzy!), trying to find someone to fill a spot, and there is literally no one. I've even debated putting on a uniform and doing double duty. But I doubt Ursula would approve of that. Plus, I just got out of that horrid uniform. Why would I want to put it back on?

"Figured it out?" Gram asks as she walks back into the living room, carrying two freshly made turkey sandwiches.

"No," I mutter, staring at the laptop screen. Maybe I've bitten off more than I can chew with this job.

Gram hands me a plate with the sandwich on it, and I set it down next to me. With one hand, I grab a half and take a huge bite. I'm starving. All of this brain usage is making me ravenous.

"So take a break," Gram says, as she plops down in her favorite chair. "*The Young and the Restless* is on." I look up to see her giving me a little eyebrow wiggle.

I know I should say no, but I also know that if I don't take a break, I might . . . well, break.

I set my laptop down on the floor next to me and then pick up my plated turkey sandwich and place it in my lap. I grab the sandwich and take another bite.

"Fill me in on what's been happening," I say through the turkey sandwich bite.

Gram gawks at me, disapprovingly. She thinks it's unladylike to talk with your mouth full, as do most humans. But when I'm at home I feel like I should be allowed to do such things. Gram, apparently, does not. Of course, reading smut and giving advice from *50 Shades of Grey* is totally acceptable behavior.

"Well," she says, after finishing a bite of her sandwich, "I think Ian is going to propose to Jessica." She puts her sandwich on her plate and grabs a napkin to wipe her mouth.

"But I thought he was in love with Heather?" I ask, totally puzzled. I swear, you cannot miss one episode.

"He is, but Heather keeps making it seem like she's in love with that other guy, when it's totally clear she's in love with Ian. But she won't tell him. It's so frustrating."

Ugh. Ian. Love. I really wish they'd picked a different name for this character.

"Well, then please turn it on so we can see what happens," I say, gesturing with my hand toward the television.

Gram fiddles with the remote until the opening song for our favorite soap opera fills the room. Honestly, a soap opera is a poor excuse for an escape, but at this point, I'll take it.

CHAPTER 33

I know Ashley said I was loyal, but honestly, I just think I'm stupid. I'm totally a glutton for punishment. I deserve what's coming to me.

"Here you go," Ian says, handing me a wrapped sandwich he grabbed for us from a nearby deli.

We're sitting on a bench in Central Park. The park is full of tourists and midday joggers. I have no idea why anyone would want to run in this heat. I'm regretting sitting in it. My light-blue eyelet lace shorts and matching sleeveless peplum top were chosen to keep me cool, but they're not helping at all.

"Thanks," I say, taking the sandwich from him.

We both unwrap the top portion of our sandwiches. Mine is a Cuban minus the pickles and his looks like some sort of Italian sandwich.

He taps his sandwich to mine. "To old friends," he says, and smiles.

"To old friends," I say, and ignore the sinking feeling in my stomach.

This is totally going to work. We will make this work.

"So, how are wedding plans going?" I ask, after finishing my first bite of sandwich. I can play the role of a friend. I can do this. Even though I truly don't want to discuss any of it, I can pretend.

It's silent for a few seconds while he chews. "Um, it's good, I think." He wipes his mouth with a napkin. "Everything's pretty much done. Maureen's stepmom basically planned the whole thing."

"And you're okay with that?" I ask. Ian always seemed like the type of guy who would want to be part of all the planning.

"Yeah, sure," he nods. "It's not like I have a lot of time anyway."

"How's Maureen?" I ask.

"Good," he says simply. "Working a lot of hours. I guess she needs to since she'll be taking time off when we do all the wedding stuff and go on our honeymoon. It's just that—" He cuts himself off from finishing the thought.

"It's just what?" I ask.

"It's just that . . . nah, never mind." He shakes his head to himself.

"Ian," I say, pivoting myself more toward him on the bench, "if we're going to be friends, then you have to actually treat me like one." I tilt my head to the side, slightly.

"Right," he says, using the napkin to sop up the beads of sweat on his forehead. It's so freaking hot outside today. Who thought lunch in the park was a good idea? Oh right, it was me.

"Go on," I coax.

"Okay. She's gone a lot. I mean, I don't see her for more than twenty-four hours sometimes." He looks out into the park. "I keep thinking it'll change once we're married, but then I realize that doesn't even make sense. This is how it'll be. At least until we have kids. But who knows when that's going to happen."

I nod my head. I'm being a good friend. I'm listening. In truth, I'm sick to my stomach with the thought of Ian having kids with Maureen. It makes it all so real. He's thinking of a family with her. This should have been obvious but catches me off guard nonetheless. And it just feels so wrong. So completely wrong.

"See? You don't even care," he says and then takes a bite of his sandwich.

"What? I care," I exclaim. "I was thinking, that's all." Yes, I was thinking about how he should be with me and not Maureen.

This is *so* not going to work.

"It's nice to talk about it, even if you aren't offering any opinion." He nudges me with his elbow. "It's been on my mind for a while."

"Have you talked to her about it?" I ask, trying to sound like I want to talk more about this, even though I don't. But that's what good friends do. And we're friends. Stupid freaking friends.

"No, not really." He looks down at his half-eaten sandwich.

"See, Ian? That's your problem, right there," I say.

"What do you mean?" He scrunches his face.

"I mean, you never talk about stuff. You keep it all in." I look at him directly.

"I do not," he denies.

"You do. I think you just hope things will work themselves out, or maybe you can ignore it." I'm totally getting to the heart of his issues right now. I feel like Dr. Phil. It's also dawning on me that I'm like that as well. I recognize it in him because that's something I do, too.

"That's not true," he says, shaking his head. I can practically see the wheels in his brain churning. He's trying to defend himself, only he has no defense.

"It is true. You did it to me," I say, and he looks up at me. "You didn't even let me explain about Brandon."

"Bridge—"

"No," I say, a bolt of confidence hits me from out of the blue. I'm not going to hold back this time. "I need to say this." I take a deep breath. "I know what you must have thought when you saw me kissing Brandon that night after the fight about London, but it was not what it looked like."

"Bridgette." He looks at me as if he doesn't believe me.

"Just listen," I say. "It's not what you thought it was. I mean, yes, what you saw really did happen. But you have to understand, I wasn't in a good place. And Brandon, he . . . he, basically took advantage of that. He knew we had been fighting. He saw me crying as I walked out of your room. He offered to drive me home, and I thought it was just a kind gesture. He started saying things like what an idiot he had been to let me go. Before I could even wrap my brain around everything, he kissed me. It was so out of the blue and not expected, and I was so distraught over the fight we had. I don't know why I kissed him back, but I did. And of course, you walked in the door and saw it . . . saw us." I look down at the sandwich I'm holding in both hands, the shame and embarrassment of that evening swarming in my stomach. "Of course, it looked worse than it was. But then you took off, and I never saw you again. And you never got to tell me—wait, what were you going to tell me?" I've always wondered what he was going to say that night. Was he going to end it completely? Was he going to tell me that we could figure it out?

Ian breathes out slowly. He pauses for a few seconds, looking me in the eyes. My heart speeds up.

"I was going to tell you," he finally says, "that it didn't matter if you wouldn't come to London."

"Why? Because you were done with us?" Saying the word "us" makes me feel oodles of guilt. We shouldn't be talking about this. At the same time, I'm glad we are getting this out in the open.

"No, it didn't matter if you wouldn't come to London because I wasn't going to go. Not without you." He looks up at me, a sad smile on his face.

"That would have been dumb, Ian," I say, thinking how silly it was that he could throw away his future like that.

"Maybe. But I didn't want to be away from you. Not for that long." He closes his eyes and turns his head, a tortured expression on his face.

"So, instead, you went away. That makes so much sense," I say sarcastically because it makes no sense at all. "You know if you had asked me to wait for you, I would have," I say and then regret the words immediately. Even though they're the truth, what good do they do now? It's too late.

More silence. All of this out in the open isn't making me feel any better. I actually feel a hundred times worse. If only we had talked back then, we would be in a much different place right now. Maybe a much better place. Or maybe not. Maybe this was our destiny.

"Sorry," I say into the silence. He looks up at me.

"Me, too," he says back and looks down again.

"Maybe . . ." I start but then stop.

"Maybe what?" he asks.

"Maybe this was how it was supposed to be?" I say, but it feels like a lie when it comes out of my mouth. I keep going with it, even though. "I mean, had you stayed with me, you wouldn't have your career. Well, you might have, but it could have been a completely different path. And you wouldn't have Maureen . . . maybe this is just how it was supposed to be."

"Yeah," he says, his bobbing head, pseudo agreeing with me. I can see doubt in his eyes, though.

We sit in silence for a minute. It's awkward, and I'm not sure what to say or if anything should be said at this point. Not on the Ian-and-me subject, that is.

"Well," I finally say, setting my sandwich down next to me. I lean back in my seat, not realizing there is no back to the bench. So basically, I fall backwards. "Oomph," I say as I topple over into the grass behind me.

Crap.

"Bridge?" Ian says, leaning over the bench looking at me. He's trying to grab my hand, but I'm waving both around like an idiot, trying to get my bearings. He's finally able to grab a hand to help, but in my struggle to pull myself together, I end up pulling him down and right on top of me.

Double crap.

The nearness of him, his breath on my neck, my pulse—which was already up—moves to a rapid pace. I suddenly can't find my breath, and I feel Ian struggle for his as well.

We don't move. I know we should. My brain is practically screaming it. But I can't move. Mostly because I'm pinned under Ian and he isn't moving, but also because I don't want to. I look at his face, the face that used to be mine, that used to make me feel so safe. And I realize in that moment, I'm still in love with Ian. I knew I loved him, I always have. But this is more than that. I'm in love with him, and I think I've known all along. I just buried it deep down to protect myself.

Our faces are only inches away from each other, our lips perfectly aligned. Ian's eyes flash a darker color, and then his focus moves to my lips . . . He leans in closer. *Uh-oh.*

"Ian," I say breathlessly.

Saying his name must have snapped him out of the trance he was in because he shakes his head quickly, closing his eyes. He curses under his breath.

He rolls over, away from me, and quickly begins to stand up. My body instantly feels cold, even in the midday heat.

He rubs his temples. He looks frustrated, angry even. Looking away from me, he reaches out a hand and helps me to standing.

"Um, are you okay?" he asks, his voice struggling.

"Uh," I say, trying to adjust my shirt back to how it should be and also trying to catch my breath. "Yep, I think I'm okay."

"Good," he says flatly. We stand there trying not to look at each other. Ian's hand moves up to his forehead and he rubs it, wearily.

"I better go . . . back to work," he finally says.

"Yeah, sure," I say, my head bobbing quickly.

So, I guess the part where we forget that ever happened has begun.

"Thanks for lunch," he says, not making eye contact with me.

"Yeah," is all I say.

Then he turns and walks away, and once again I'm left standing there wondering what just happened.

CHAPTER 34

Later in the week, I find myself feeling very lonely in Gram's apartment. I haven't spoken to Ian since our bizarre predicament in the park. I pondered calling him to go out for coffee, but I still don't know what to do about that whole situation. On one hand, I want to see him because, well, I just want to. On the other hand, I know it would probably be for the best if I didn't. All this back and forth with him. Maybe my mind and my heart would do better with a clean break. I honestly don't know if I'm totally ready for that.

After some channel surfing, and a vain attempt to catch up with *The Young and the Restless* (I couldn't watch the Ian and Heather and Jessica drama—a bit too close to home), I decide to drag myself upstairs to Margie's place where Gram and the girls are playing bridge. I need something to get my mind off everything. I doubt it will work, but it's worth a try.

"Is Gram here?" I ask Margie when she answers the door.

"Sure is," she says, opening the door wide. She ushers me in with a sweep of her hand.

I walk into Margie's apartment, which is set up a lot like Gram's. And just as old-fashioned as well.

But, like Gram's place, it has a homey feel to it. I will say that there are doilies. Lots of doilies.

"Look who's here, ladies," Margie says as we walk into the living room.

Gram and two other ladies, Evelyn and Barbara, all turn to see who it is. Once they see me they all start talking in unison. Saying hello and asking me question after question. I try to field each query, but they keep talking over each other.

"Well, Bridgette, what brings you here?" Gram asks, after the chatter has settled. She looks slightly concerned. She wasn't expecting me. Likewise, I was not expecting to come up here, but here I am.

"I thought I would come and see what you ladies are doing." I knew they were playing cards, so that was kind of a dumb comment. "And also to check up on Gram," I say, pointing to the wine glass sitting to her left. That was not something I was expecting to find, but I'm glad I did.

She looks down at the glass and then back up at me, a sheepish just-been-caught look on her face.

"Oh, that's mine," Evelyn declares, and I roll my eyes. Evelyn isn't even sitting next to Gram.

"Gram, you've got to be kidding. Does she drink every time she's playing cards with you?" I ask, looking around the room.

"Not all the time," Barbara pipes in. "Just . . . most of the time."

Gram shoots Barbara a look, and Barbara immediately stares down at her cards.

"Stop looking at me like that." Gram stares me down with squinty eyes. "I can have a drink every now and then. It's good for the heart." She puts a hand up to her heart for emphasis.

I roll my eyes again. I'm going to let it slide in front of her friends, but we will be discussing it later when we get home. Why do I suddenly feel like a parent?

"So, what brings you up here?" Margie asks, holding out the wine and an empty glass, silently asking me if I would like some as well. I decline.

"I was lonely downstairs, so I thought I would come up and check out the fun going on here."

"We're playing hand and foot," Evelyn declares, nodding toward the table.

"I thought this was bridge night," I say confused.

"It is, but we like to mix it up every now and then, so tonight we're playing hand and foot," Margie says.

"Hmm. Sounds interesting," I say, not having the slightest clue what hand and foot is. It sounds like the name of a disease.

"Do you wanna play?" Margie asks. "It's a four-person game, but I can sit out. I'm sick of beating these ladies anyway."

"Oh please, you haven't won a game in over a year," Gram says.

"That's not true," Margie says, but then looks as if she's trying to remember when the last time she won.

"Um, I'm okay not to play," I say, looking at Margie. "I don't know the game anyway."

"You sure?" Margie asks.

"Yes, totally," I say. I grab an empty chair and pull it up to the table next to Gram. The ladies resume their card game.

"So, if you don't want to play, then what brings you here?" asks Evelyn.

"Evelyn, don't be rude," Barbara says and winks at me. "Can't you see the girl needs to talk?" She points the cards in her hand at me, but then, realizing everyone just saw her cards, she quickly pulls them back.

"What do you need to talk about?" Margie asks, keeping her eyes on the game.

"Um, well," I say. I didn't come up here to talk, but apparently, I'm giving off a need-to-talk vibe.

"So spill it, sister," Evelyn says, extra sass in her voice. She's definitely the snarky one of the group. Snarkier than Gram, even.

"Well, I . . ." I trail off.

"Gotcha some man trouble?" Margie prods.

Gram snorts and I nudge her with my elbow. "Does she ever," Gram says, ignoring my nudge. She looks at me. "May I?" she asks.

"By all means," I say, sarcastically giving her my permission to tell the ladies about my man drama.

So while they continue their game, Gram proceeds to tell the ladies about the past few months of my life, from breaking up with Adam, to running into Ian, and all of the drama that's gone along with it.

"Well, if you ask me, it sounds like you've been dealt quite a bit there, missy," Evelyn says, as she lays some cards on the table and gives a triumphant look.

"Did you win?" I ask, seeing the others' faces after she lays down the cards.

"Oh no," Barbara says. "Not even close. She just got us another red pile," she smiles.

"Oh," I say, not having a clue what she's talking about.

"So, what are you going to do?" Margie asks.

"Me?" I ask.

"No, Barbara," Evelyn says, pointing to Barbara. "Of course she means you; the rest of us ain't got nothing exciting to do. What you're seeing now is as exciting as it gets." She gives me a disdainful glance. "We're just trying to live out our days until we kick it."

"Well that sounds lovely," Gram states.

"It's the truth," Evelyn says. "So let us live through you, Bridgette. Tell us what you're going to do."

"What can I do?" I slouch back in my seat. "Adam doesn't believe me."

"Oh, who cares about Adam. He's a lost cause." Evelyn says. "Besides, your Gram never liked him."

I turn to look at Gram and catch her shooting daggers with her eyes at Evelyn.

"Gram?" I ask, confusion in my tone. "You didn't like Adam?"

"Oh." Gram bats a hand my way, trying to dismiss it as not that big of a deal.

"Gram," I say flatly.

"Okay fine. No, I never liked him. I thought he was smug, unfriendly, and he never treated you like you deserve." She reaches her hand to my back and rubs it slightly.

I sit there for a few seconds, contemplating.

"Why didn't you ever say anything?" I ask, feeling a little hurt.

"Would it have made a difference?" She gives me a thin smile, taking her hand away from my back. "Besides, it wasn't my decision to make."

"Yes, but . . ." I trail off not knowing what to say. She's right. It wasn't her decision to make, and even if she had said something, would it have made a difference? Probably not. It might have only proved to put a rift between us. She's a smart one, my Gram.

"So, what are you going to do about Ian?" Margie asks.

"There's nothing I can do. He's getting married," I say, with one shrug.

"Psh," Evelyn says, scrunching up her face, "he's not married yet."

"You should tell him," Barbara says.

"Tell him what?" I ask, looking at all the ladies as they give agreeing nods.

"Tell him you still love him." Margie says.

Wow. These ladies are good. I didn't even say I was still in love with him. I've never even admitted it to Gram. Am I that transparent? And if I am, why doesn't Ian see it? Of course he's a man, so that would explain it.

"I can't," I say after a tiny pause. "I can't be that girl."

"Well, hell, if I wasn't that girl, I'd be in a very different place right now," Gram says, and my eyes widen instantly.

"Gram, what are you talking about?" I ask, completely stunned by this declaration.

She turns to me. "Your grandfather was engaged to marry someone else before I snatched him away."

"What? How do I not know this?" I ask, looking at all the other ladies in the room, who apparently didn't know this story either. The game has completely stalled.

"Yep, Lorraine McCleary was her name, and she was a mean little thing. We were arch rivals in high school. She snatched your grandfather up so fast, he didn't even see it coming. And it wasn't long after graduation that they were engaged. But I had different plans." She looks at me, her pointer finger directed in my face. "I knew your grandfather and I were supposed to be together."

"So, what did you do?" Evelyn asks, impatience in her voice.

"One afternoon, I gathered all the courage I had, and I walked over to his house, down on Nantucket Street." She looks around the table as she tells the story. "I walked right up to the door and then . . . I completely chickened out and turned around to go."

"Oh geez," Barbara says. "How stupid could you be?"

"But," she says, pointer finger out again, "as I was leaving, guess who was driving up the road?" She turns to me, giving me one nod, "Your grandfather. He got out of the car, and I just stood there, totally tongue-tied."

"Then how did you tell him?" Evelyn asks, the frustration oozing from her tone. Evelyn apparently does not like stories. She only wants the punchline.

"After we stood there, looking at each other, I finally gathered myself together, and I told him. I told him he shouldn't marry Lorraine, that she was mean and rotten, and I caught her smoking behind her daddy's truck."

"The horror," Margie exclaims, and I stifle a giggle.

"Yep. I told him everything that was wrong with that girl, and then I said 'Leo, I can't let you marry her.' And he asked me why not. And then I said, 'because you should marry me.'" We were all silent at this point, waiting to find out what his answer was, which was silly because we already knew the answer. This was my Pops we were talking about.

"What did he say?" Evelyn asks.

"He didn't say anything. He took me in his arms, and he kissed me, and that was that. We were married five months later," Gram says, with a simple dip of her chin.

"Wow," I say, "how did I not know this story?" It feels weird that I wouldn't know any of this about my Gram and Pops.

"Well, you never asked," she says simply.

"So, what do you think?" Margie says, turning her attention back to me.

"Um . . . well . . . it's not that simple," I say, thinking of how different the times are. If I did something like that now, Maureen could have my face all over social media in an instant with a caption that says, "whore."

"Sure it is," Barbara says. "You're the one who's making it too hard."

"And isn't it not fair to him anyway?" Evelyn says. "He should know how you feel and make the decision himself."

I nod my head. Not to concede, but to make them think that I do. I don't know if I can bring myself to say it, to tell Ian that I should have told him I loved him that night, and that I still do. I just don't know if I have it in me. And even if I did, would he say it back? Would he want to leave what he has with Maureen, for me?

"Now, what I really want to know is," Evelyn says to me as she starts the game back up. The other ladies fall into place. "Which one of your two fellows has the nicest hiney?" She follows that up with a little double eyebrow lift.

Oh dear. This seems innocent enough—a little pervy perhaps—but I have a sinking suspicion answering that question would lead me down a road I most certainly don't want to travel.

"Well," Gram says, before I have a chance to talk. Thank goodness for Gram. She can get me out of this. "I don't really remember Ian, but I'll tell ya, even though I didn't like him all that much, that Adam had a nice one."

"Gram!" I say louder than I intended. So much for being saved by Gram. I really should have known better.

"What? You think just because I'm ancient, I don't notice a good butt when I see one?" She scrunches her face, pulling her eyebrows together.

"Don't hold back, tell us about it," Evelyn says. All eyes are off the game and now on Gram.

"Well, it was just nice and round, you know? One of those ones that looks like they'd be pretty firm. I often had to hold myself back from sneaking a pinch—"

"Okay, ladies," I say loudly and quickly, cutting Gram off. "This has been enlightening, but I better go. Early day tomorrow." Everyone mutters disappointment, and I catch a "so boring" from Evelyn.

I don't care if they think I'm boring. Is this how the conversation normally goes at these things? If so, I'm thinking I've been saved from many awkward moments by not joining in.

I stand up from my chair, wanting to exit this room as soon as possible.

They each say their good-byes, once again talking over each other as I leave.

I'm not sure any of that helped, except to confuse me further and make me realize that I won't be joining their bridge club anytime soon.

I wish I could flash forward to the future to see what's there. Then I could let all of this go and be done with it. But I hate thinking of a future without Ian in it, and that seems to be what my future holds.

CHAPTER 35

"I knew it," I yell loudly. "I knew it would happen!"

Ashley giggles and jumps up and down in her seat on Gram's couch.

"You'll remember me when you're big star, won't you?" I tease. Actually, I'm not teasing. She better remember me.

"It's only an understudy," she says, the huge smile on her face faltering slightly.

"Who cares," I exclaim. "This is just the beginning for you, Ash. I can feel it." I tap her on the knee.

"What's all the racket?" Gram says, coming out of her bedroom.

"You're looking at the next big Broadway star!" I say loudly and dramatically, presenting Ashley to Gram with arms outstretched, like she's already a superstar.

Gram gasps and then clasps her hands together and shakes them, yelling out some bravos.

"Well, isn't that exciting," she exclaims. "And I get to say I knew you when."

"Don't you two get ahead of yourselves," Ashley scolds. "I'm not a star, not yet at least."

"Well, this calls for a celebration," Gram says, walking toward the kitchen. We hear her rustling around, and then what sounds like a bunch of pans falling out of the cabinet.

"You okay in there, Gram?" I yell out.

"Yes, yes," she grumbles, "just trying to grab something. Aha! There it is." Her tone changes instantly.

I look at Ashley. The perplexity on her face probably mirrors mine.

Gram walks out of the kitchen holding three wine glasses and what looks like a bottle of champagne.

"Gram," I say, appalled at the sight. "You can't have that. Doctor's orders." I point at her. We've yet to have the discussion about bridge night as well.

"Oh, pish-posh. I can have a drink every now and then." She purses her lips, annoyed.

"Yes, I'm starting to wonder if it's more now than then," I say, giving her my best accusatory glare.

"Just stop it. You're ruining Ashley's fun," Gram says.

I decide to let it go for now, but she better know that the talk is coming soon. Along with a complete prohibition, if I can arrange it.

Gram sets the wine glasses down on the coffee table, and with ease, she takes the foil off of the bottle and the wire. She twists the bottle, and the cork releases with a muted thud. A mist travels out of the bottle, but there is no big spray like I had expected. Obviously, Gram's knows what she's doing. Which is no shock, really. She's had years of experience. She pours us each a glass.

"To Ashley," she says, holding up her glass. Ashley and I follow suit. We clink our glasses together, very fancy-like.

One and a half bottles later (Gram had another one in her stash), I'm feeling a little more than tipsy. I'm pretty sure Ashley is too because she keeps giggling at practically everything. We're not totally drunk, but there's just enough alcohol in us to make us do and say stupid things. Last time this happened we nearly ended up with matching tattoos. Thank goodness Justin was there to talk some sense into us.

Gram only drank a half glass, surprisingly. She excused herself and headed off to bed not long after the giggles started. I'm pretty sure she was sick of it.

"Hey," Ashley says with an added giggle. "Have you talked to Ian?" She's practically sprawled out on the couch, her feet nearly invading the square inch I'm squished into.

"No," I say, my buzz instantly tainted when I hear his name. He still hasn't tried to contact me since the Central Park incident.

"He never texted you after the last lunch?" she asks and then giggles. I'm not sure what there is to giggle over.

"Nope," I say. Leaning back on the couch, I close my eyes. The room spins a little less that way. "It's probably for the best." I mean it when I say it, even though I really, truly hate it.

"Why don't you text him?" she asks.

"Because. What's the point?"

"Because," she says, "he's not married yet." I look over at her. She gives me an insinuating eyebrow raise.

"Oh, gosh. Not you too? I've already gotten the third degree from Gram and her cohorts."

"Cohorts?" Ashley furrows her brow.

"The bridge club gals," I say.

"Oh right. Well, whatever. You should do it. You know you want to," she badgers.

"I don't," I say, even though it's a lie. "I'm not the kind of girl who goes after practically-married men." I hiccup, which does nothing for my defense. Ashley giggles.

"You're so boring," she says through the giggles.

Boring. Am I boring? Evelyn said the same thing. It was under her breath, but I heard it. I'm not boring. I'm realistic.

"What about you?" I say to Ashley, turning the tables on her so we don't have to talk about Ian anymore. "Have you talked to Justin?"

"Oh, no." She bats a hand at me. "I'm over that."

"I see you're still lying to yourself," I say, and go back to closing my eyes. The room is now tilting to the side.

"No, I'm not," she declares.

"Liar."

"I'm not lying!" She grabs a decorative pillow from behind her and throws it at me. She misses.

"Liar, liar, pants on fire." Wow, I haven't said that one in a while.

"Okay fine," she says, folding her arms, her lips pouting. "Maybe I'm not totally *over* it."

"I knew it!" I say loudly. My whole body turns toward her, eyes wide open. My head feels sloshy. "So, what are you going to do about it?" I ask, hiccupping again. Dang it.

"Nothing," she says and then burps loudly.

"Nice," I say flatly. It was actually quite gross. Especially coming from the mouth of a petite redhead.

"Anyway, if Justin wanted me, he would have told me by now. He's obviously just not that into me."

"Not that again." I roll my eyes.

"What? It's the truth."

"It's not the truth. And anyway, I don't think that's the case with Justin," I say, nudging her foot with my leg. "I mean, the guy had me tell you that he liked you. He's clueless. Besides, he's pretty miserable."

"He's miserable? How can you tell?" She sits up. A little too fast, from the looks of it. She wobbles slightly.

He's a bit more than miserable, truthfully. He tried to be okay the last time we hung out, but I could see it in his face.

"Yes. Miserable. How can you not see it?" I scrunch my face.

"Well, I haven't really been paying much attention to him, if you haven't noticed," she says and shrugs.

276

"That's true," I declare. That's slightly an understatement. She's been outright ignoring him. I see him try, even to say something just to say it, and she won't even give him a courtesy glance.

It's so depressing, the whole thing. My two best friends fighting, me in the middle. Well, I'm only figuratively in the middle. They have both been great about not talking about it with me, and both too prideful to talk to each other. I swear, I would do anything to help make it better, to get things back to the way they used to be.

"I think you should talk to him," I say.

"Yea, maybe." She doesn't sound convinced. I look over to her and she looks contemplative, or possibly completely zoned out.

"Hey," she says, after a few minutes. "I'll make you a deal." She juts her chin forward, a devious half smile on her face.

"What's the deal?" I ask, only slightly intrigued, but mostly scared.

"I'll text Justin, if you text Ian," she says.

"What?" She must be tipsier than I thought.

"I'll text Justin and tell him how I feel if you text Ian and tell him how you feel." She's got her deal-maker game face on. I've seen it a few times before.

"No way," I say, shaking my head. "I have principles, you know."

"Oh you and your principles." Her eyes roll to the ceiling briefly, then back to me. "What if —"

"No." I cut her off.

"Just hear me out. What if you don't tell Ian and then he goes on to marry Maureen and lives a life of misery?" Her mouth twists to the side, in true smart aleck form. "You could be saving him a life of sadness."

"I could say the same to you," I counter, my defense rather flimsy.

"Hey, I've already agreed to do this, so it's you who's going to potentially ruin things for Justin, if you don't text Ian." She gives me a big, smartass smirk.

"No," I say again.

"Come on, do it. Take a chance." She nudges me. "I'll do it, if you will."

Now peer pressure? I thought I was done with that in high school. She and Justin are perfect for each other. Are Ian and I? I know the answer to that. Yes. But I can't be the one to break up what he and Maureen have. If he really wanted to do that, he would. Or would he? He's not great at expressing himself. Would my telling him even change anything? It can't make anything worse. Our "friendship" is clearly in ruins, as evidenced by the last time we were together.

Oh, what the hell. I grab my glass, and I gulp down what's left. I'm going to need more liquid courage to do this.

"Okay, fine," I say, feeling regret swarm around in my stomach instantly. This has "bad idea" written all over it.

"Yes!" She sits up, grabbing our phones off the table. She hands me mine. I stare at it. What am I doing?

Ashley starts texting Justin immediately. I can tell by how fast she's working, she's already written this text a thousand times in her head.

I have nothing in my head. Absolutely nothing. I pull up his name in my messages and stare at the blank box.

"Are you ready to hit send?" she asks, peering over at my phone. "Hey, you haven't written anything," she says, annoyed.

"I don't know what to write," I say, still staring at my phone screen.

"Just tell him the truth," she says.

"Okay, the truth." I can totally do this.

I should have told you I loved you that night. Because I did.

I stare at the text I'm about to send. It's the truth, staring me in the face. I'm going to leave out the part about how I'm pretty sure I'm still in love with him, though. Don't want to give all my secrets away.

"Alright," Ashley says. "On the count of three. One . . . two . . . three."

We both press send.

CHAPTER 36

"BRIDGETTE!" Ursula yells as she walks in the kitchen door off the main ballroom of the hotel where we're currently working.

Oh crap.

"Bridgette," she says as she eyes me and starts to walk toward me. "Vat are you doink back here?"

"What do you mean? I'm helping," I say, showing her the napkins I'd been folding. The event is set to start in just under an hour.

"Vell, you are not supposed to be doink this, you are supposed to be in the front helpink," she says, her large head tilted to the side, her face oozing with aggravation.

"Sorry, yes . . . of course. I will go back to the front." I hand the napkins to Derek, and he puts them on the pile he was making. He shakes his head and laughs quietly to himself. I'm so glad I can be the entertainment tonight.

I walk out to the front and look around. The service staff is running around like chickens with their heads cut off. It's not entirely in disarray, but mostly.

"The chair covers are not here," Ashley says, as she walks toward me.

"What? Are you sure? I ordered them," I say, my eyes moving frantically around the room. Just as

I'm about to go into full panic-attack mode, a door to my left opens, and in walks someone with a box full of chair covers.

Thank you gods of event planning for covering my butt tonight.

I had hoped by now that I would have settled into this assistant manager thing. But I still haven't. It's so much harder than I thought it would be. And stressful. Oh, the stress. Apparently, you have to be assertive, and I'm not assertive unless I get tipsy, which would not be a good idea to do at work (although the thought did cross my mind).

A little chill pricks my spine when I recall the last time I was tipsy-assertive. It was only a week ago, but, oh, to go back and redo that night. Ian never texted me back, and it's just as well. He knows now (there was no room for interpretation on that one), so now I can let him go off to his new life with Maureen. The new life without me in it. I'm learning to be fine with it in my head, but my heart is more resistant to being convinced.

"Come on, Bridge," Justin says as he sees me standing there, mouth open. "Let's get these chair covers on."

"Hey, you're not the boss of me." I give him some snooty duck lips. "Last I checked, I was the boss of you. So get to work putting those chair covers on."

He rolls his eyes. Ashley walks by us, and he quickly reaches over and gooses her as she passes. She giggles.

"You guys," I say through gritted teeth, my eyes wide, "I told you, not at work."

Not that it matters. Ashley gave notice and only has a little over a week left before she starts her understudy role. And although I won't admit it to him, I now understand why Ursula keeps Justin around. He's actually quite useful.

Ashley's text to Justin went over far better than mine did. Apparently, he texted back right away and they met up for coffee. Justin did the unthinkable and apologized for the fight that ruined everything in the first place. (He never apologizes.) This must have been enough for Ashley's heart to melt completely. They both declared feelings and things moved beyond coffee. I didn't want to know all the details. They weren't taking things slow, in fact they both jumped in head first. But I guess this was a longtime coming.

I'm still having a hard time getting used to them being together. Although, anything beats having them apart. That was tough. We are once again the three amigos, only they constantly have their hands all over each other as I sit by myself. We may have to have a chat about keeping it to a minimum when I'm around. No one wants to see that.

"BRIDGETTE!" Ursula yells, and I jump.

I hope I will get used to that someday, but I doubt it.

~*~

"I think I want to cry. My feet are killing me," I say, sprawled out on my side of the booth. Across from me are Mr. and Mrs. PDA.

"Hmm? What did you say?" Ashley can barely peel her eyes away from Justin to acknowledge my existence.

"I said my feet—never mind." It was a stupid comment anyway.

It's so strange to see them like this. Especially Justin. He's so kind and doting and intuitive as a boyfriend. Yet, he is none of those things as a friend. Well, he's kind . . . sometimes.

"So, Bridge," Justin says, finally deciding to acknowledge that I'm here. He has his arm around Ashley, and she's nestled into him, her head leaning on his shoulder.

"Yeah?"

"How do you liking being the big boss?" he asks, and then he turns his head and gives Ashley a kiss on the forehead.

Gag. I have to be careful here because while it's annoying, it's mostly getting on my nerves because I'm envious. I can't let my two best friends—the missing pieces of my trio that I just got back—know or think that. So as much as I want to tell them to stop being so cheesy, I won't. I can get used to it. Hopefully.

"It's a little crazy," I say. "I'm not really sure if I'm 'management material.'" I use air quotes and then get annoyed with myself for doing so.

"Don't say that," Ashley commands. "It'll take some getting used to, that's all."

"You're so smart," Justin says in some sort of annoying baby talk I've never heard come out of his mouth. Ashley looks up at him and beams, and they kiss.

I am *so* not going to get used to this.

We sit in silence for a bit. Well, it's silent because Ashley and Justin are talking low and quietly to each other while I stare at my horrid nailbeds trying desperately not to be *that* girl. I can't be her. Yet, this whole Ashley and Justin thing is bringing out a side of me that hasn't come out in a while. In fact, the last time was when I had to endure one of Ian's conquests in college. I hate this feeling.

"Tell her," Ashley says to Justin, sort of under her breath, but definitely loud enough to hear.

"Tell me what?" I look back and forth between the two of them.

Justin eyes Ashley hesitantly. She nudges him with her shoulder and nods her head. Wow. They've already moved into the talking without talking mode in their relationship? That happened fast. Although, they were friends before, and I — of all people — should know the best relationships come from friendship. I just hope theirs ends better than mine did.

"Tell me," I prod.

Justin gives Ashley the go-ahead head bob.

"Justin's written a play," Ashley says, extra-enthusiastically.

"Huh?" I say, taken aback. Actually, that's an understatement for how I'm feeling. I'm utterly confused.

"Justin wrote a play," she says again. I still don't understand.

"You wrote a play?" I say, looking at him like I have no idea who Justin is at all.

"I did," he says, nodding his head, looking away. "I've written several, actually."

"But . . . how?" I'm so confused. I feel like I've been shoved into a dream sequence. I did not see that coming.

"But that's not the best part," Ashley says, her smile practically reaching her forehead. "He's a finalist for the *Samuel French Festival*." She wiggles around in her seat, too excited to sit still. Justin pulls her into him, holding her tightly. Her excitement about his accomplishments gives Justin a look of pride I've never seen on his face before.

I, on the other hand, am trying hard to stifle my what-the-hell face, because seriously. What the hell?

"Wow, really?" My brow furrows. I work to make an effort to wrap my brain around it, because it's getting enormously obvious that I can't bring myself to accept it. I shake my head, closing my eyes briefly.

"Is it that hard to believe, Bridge?" Justin scoffs, raising an eyebrow.

"Well, kind of," I say and he lets out a frustrated sigh. "I mean, it's kind of like me telling you I've been . . . uh . . . raising gerbils on the side and I've been doing it for years and you had no idea."

"But you don't like rodents of any kind," Ashley interjects.

"Exactly," I say, pointing at Ashley. "It's just so random. Although," my finger goes to my chin, contemplatively, "I guess you did make us go to those terrible artsy movies and plays all the time. But honestly, that was the only sign."

"My taste in movies and plays is not terrible," he says, looking appalled.

"Uh, yeah. It is." I say, unapologetically.

"Do you think so, babe?" He turns to Ashley.

"Of course not," she says sincerely, but I suspect she's lying. She has to be.

Justin. Mine and Ashley's Justin—well, more Ashley's now, but that's beside the point. *Our* Justin is a playwright?

I start to giggle.

"What's so funny?" Justin asks, clearly peeved.

"Sorry," I say through giggles that suddenly morph into near-hysterical laughter. Neither Ashley nor Justin is joining me. It's awkward.

Justin flagrantly gives me the middle finger and then adds a comment that would make Gram's toes curl.

"No, sorry," I say, trying to calm myself. I take a deep breath. "It's just . . . so not expected. I mean, I sincerely had no idea. How did you keep this to yourself for so long?"

"No one knows. Well, except for you two." He looks at Ashley and then me. "Besides, you're always caught up in some guy drama, and Ash was always auditioning."

"Hey, I'm not always caught up in some guy drama," I say defensively. Justin and Ashley both regard me with the same disbelieving face.

"Whatever, you guys. Hey, wait . . . oh my gosh." My eyes go wide with realization, as I focus them on Justin. "So *that's* what you've been doing with your time? We've always wondered." I point back and forth between Ashley and me.

"What did you think I was doing with my time?" Justin asks, slight suspicion in his tone.

"Well, we," I start, but then a wide-eyed you-better-shut-up glance from Ashley stops me. "We just never knew," I quickly recover.

"Well, now you do," he says.

"Yes, I guess we do. It's really amazing, though, Justin." I reach across the table and put my hand on his, my attempt at an olive branch. He gives me a small, thin smile.

"It really is," Ashley says, beaming up at him as he looks at her. He pulls his hand out from under mine, reaches up to her face, and caresses it lightly. Then his hand goes under her chin. Lifting it, he kisses her briefly. He looks sincere, thoughtful even. It's going to take me a bit to get used to this. Justin in love or lust or whatever is going on here, and Justin a playwright. My world feels completely turned upside down.

"So, what's it about?" I ask, looking down at my empty plate. I scarfed down my burger. I was so hungry. Also, it was a good place to keep my eyes to avoid the lovefest across from me.

Justin and Ashley look at each other, doing that talking without talking thing again.

"Justin, what's the play about?" I ask again, wondering why they both suddenly look a little shell-shocked.

"It's . . ." Justin trails off. A hand goes to the back of his neck, and he rubs it self-consciously.

What's their deal?

"It's just based on something from Justin's past," Ashley says, and Justin nods agreeing.

I eye them both suspiciously. I'm no mind reader, but I wouldn't even need one to tell me they're hiding something.

"I'll let you read it," Justin says. Ashley looks up at him with wide, skeptical eyes.

"What's going on?" I say, my eyes on Ashley.

"Look, Bridge, it's no big deal. I'll send it to you, okay?" he says and then gives Ashley a comforting look, as if to say everything will be fine.

At least, I thought it was a comforting look. Maybe it was a sensual look because they start kissing, and I go back to averting my eyes.

This is all going to take some serious time getting used to.

CHAPTER 37

"Hey, Bridge," Ian says as he spots me walking into the coffee shop he asked me to meet him at. He stands and gives me a quick hug. Try as I might, I am unable to hold myself back from sniffing him. He smells wonderful.

My heart is literally going into overdrive. I almost said no to meeting up with him, but then the fear of not knowing what he might say—what he might be thinking—seeped in.

"Hey," I say, feeling sheepish . . . and utterly girly.

"How are you?" he asks, smoothing his tie down. He looks amazing in his charcoal- gray pin-striped suit with a blue collared shirt that makes his eyes a more blue-green color. My heart speeds up a little more. I've got on a pink racer-back shift dress and espadrille wedge sandals. A little less of a friend-like outfit, but I didn't know what to expect today.

"So, what did you want to talk to me about?" my mouth says, not even answering his question like my brain was preparing to. Apparently, my mouth wants to forgo small talk and get right down to the nitty-gritty. I take a seat in the chair across from him.

"Um, yeah," he mutters. He seems nervous.

I look up at his face, and for a moment our eyes meet, and I feel my breathing start to sharpen. Ian is what I want. He is home for me.

"Bridgette," he says, breaking the trance. "I need to apologize to you."

"You do?" That was not exactly how I expected him to start the conversation. That's what I was going to say if he seemed sour when I saw him. I was prepared to apologize for my text and tell him I was tipsy. Anything to cover my butt. But maybe . . . no, I shouldn't let my mind go there. I need to hear him out first.

"Yes, I'm sorry." He looks down at his hands. "You were right." He looks back up at me.

"You're sorry I'm right," I say, confused.

"No." He shakes his head, a small smile appearing on his face. "I mean, you were right. About the friend thing."

"Oh," I say as my heart plummets rapidly. I know immediately this is not going to go as I had, in my heart of hearts, hoped it would. I'm a fool for even letting my mind wander there.

"It was really selfish of me, and I'm sorry," he says, not making eye contact with me. "I was just so glad to have you back in my life that I was holding on to whatever I could. But I see now it can't work."

"Right." I chew on my bottom lip, feeling a mixture of emotions right now. Without warning, tears sting my eyes.

"You and I weren't meant to be just friends, Bridge. And I need to commit to what I have with

Maureen. I can't do that with you around." He looks down at his hands twiddling in his lap.

"Okay," I say, the tears flowing now. I grab a napkin from the holder, which was conveniently on the table, and wipe my eyes and nose. "Sorry," I apologize for my tears.

"Me, too," he says, a closed-mouth, sorrow-filled smile on his lips.

"And now," I look downward as shameful feelings wash over me, "I'm really sorry for the text," I say.

"What text?" he questions, and my eyes go back to his. He isn't being facetious. He's serious.

"You never got the text I sent?" I ask, feeling a mixture of relief and sadness at the same time. Sadness because it means he doesn't know.

"No." He shakes his head. "What did it say?"

"What did it say?" Oh crap. I need a lie. I'm so not good at lying on a whim. I need preparation for my lies. I start to chew on my bottom lip but stop myself.

"Bridge?" He looks at me inquisitively.

But I can't tell him. Not after what he just said to me. It would be wrong.

"Oh," I say and bat a hand, "it was nothing." I can tell by the look on his face that he knows I'm lying. I really needed more prep.

"Bridge," he prods, tilting his head to the side.

"Really, it's nothing," I say, forcing a smile through the tears. "And I'm glad you realized I was right." I give him a little know-it-all smirk, trying to lighten the mood in any way possible so I don't start blubbering.

"Yes, you always did love being right." He smirks back.

"Still do."

"Well, I wish this time you weren't," he says, remorse in his voice.

"Me, too," I say, tears beginning to spill.

"For what it's worth, I'm glad that I got to see you again." His lips form into a small, very sad smile.

"Me, too," I say. It seems to be all I can say right now. But I need to keep my answers quick and precise. I'm literally on the verge of a blubbering-fest. Which I'll promptly be having as soon as I leave this coffee shop. I can guarantee it.

He stands up, and I follow suit. I'm having major déjà vu right now. It's not hard to remember why. Ian and I just had this conversation. I thought it was good-bye then, but here we are once more. This time, it has a definite finality to it.

We walk out of the café and stand together on the sidewalk. It feels wrong. It all feels wrong. I want to tell him. I want to tell him to pick me and then promise we would be happy together, because we would be. But the words don't come out of my mouth.

"I guess I'll see you when I see you," I say.

"Well, I'll see you at the rehearsal dinner," he says, matter-of-factly.

"Right, we're catering your rehearsal dinner," I say, a forced forgetful tone to my voice, even though I've known for some time. "Well, no worries there. I've requested to have it off." I smile, feebly.

"You don't have to do that, Bridge," he says, his head tilting slightly to the side. "We can be in the same room, can't we?"

"Yeah, maybe," I shrug and then let out an uncomfortable laugh.

"I'm gonna miss you, Bridge," Ian says, pulling me into a hug.

That nearly unnerves me, but I hold the sobbing in. Tears are streaming down my face, but I've managed to limit them to just a handful. Waterfalls threaten to fall at any moment.

"Me, too," is all I can get out.

We stand back and look at each other, and then without words, we turn and walk away. This time, I don't look back.

The crying, which had already started, now morphs into a full-on hysterical fit. I walk as far as I can go before I feel like my knees will buckle in a ridiculous, dramatic fashion. I know it's absurd. I know I'm being over-the-top, and yet, I don't care. I spot a bench and sit down, my face falls into my hands. And I blubber.

I'm probably a spectacle right now. I'm heartbroken in a way I've never been before. I know I thought I was this heartbroken with Adam, but this feels different. It feels like my heart is literally falling apart. With Adam, it felt like my heart had been crushed. This time, it feels like it's being ripped apart, and Ian is taking some of it with him.

I don't think I will recover from this, ever. Well, I know I will, because that's what I do, but I don't want to. I don't want to recover from Ian.

CHAPTER 38

I'm not sure how I got here. Well, I know exactly *how* I got here, but I'm not sure how I let myself get to this point.

Currently, I find myself hiding in a rather tall bush, Ashley squished next to me (there's not much room in this thing), and we are, well, we're spying. It's true. It's Ashley and Bridgette: super spies.

The only problem is, we kind of suck at it.

To onlookers, this might appear pretty bad. But luckily for me we are not in a touristy part of town, and the locals, if they see us, truly couldn't care less that Ashley and I are spying from a bush, and frankly, they've seen worse. This is Manhattan, after all.

In Manhattan — an island that is thirteen-ish miles long with a population of around 1.6 million people — it seems highly illogical one would randomly run into the same person twice in any amount of time, and yet, here we are.

Spying. On Serene, no less.

How did we get here? Well, it's pretty simple, actually. Ashley and I were eating ice cream at our normal café. I hadn't seen her in a couple of weeks, what with her new understudy gig, and her new . . . Justin. The girl barely has time to sleep. So I was thrilled when she called me to meet up. I had yet to fill her in on my last visit with Ian. I mean, of course I had told her bits and pieces through text, but I hadn't had the chance to give her every painstaking detail like I've so badly needed to. I tried to make Gram sit down and analyze it, but she was not having any.

I was just telling Ashley the part about my last gut-wrenching, heartbreaking, tear-streaming, hug with Ian, when I spotted Serene. She was sauntering past the café, dressed completely in black—black blouse, black leggings, black four-inch heels (no joke). She was wearing dark sunglasses, and tucked under her arm was a black clutch. Her long, black hair and her ensemble were doing nothing to negate the witch thing.

I stopped midsentence when I saw her, of course—as probably do most creatures when they see her.

"Oh my gosh," I said.

"What is it?" Ashley asked, following my eyes and looking out the window from the booth we were sitting in.

"It's her," I said, not taking my eyes off of Serene.

"Her, who?" Ashley asked, still confused.

"Serene," I said, turning back to Ashley.

Her eyes went wide. "You mean Serene-Serene? The model-witch? Where?" She maneuvered herself so she could see where I was looking.

"I don't see her," Ashley declared, after looking in vain in the direction I was.

"How can you not see it?" I said, feeling slightly pleased with myself for referring to Serene as an "it."

As chance would have it, Serene had stopped not far from us to answer a call, apparently the call was too important for her to continue walking (I guess Serene was not one to be able to walk and talk, go figure).

"Oh," Ashley said as she spotted her. "So that's Serene." Her face registered the same look most give when their eyes happen upon the model-witch. "I mean, I guess I saw her before—that time in the café with Justin—but I couldn't see her face, since she was making out with some guy."

We both stared at Serene, watching her as her conversation looked to get a little heated. Abruptly, she hung up her phone, and thrusting it back into her purse, she started walking again.

"I wonder where she's going?" I said, mostly thinking aloud.

"Well, there's only one way to find out," Ashley said, a mischievous look on her face.

"How's that?" I asked, feeling curiosity mixed with a bit of skepticism.

"We should follow her, of course," she said, sliding out of her booth in a hurry.

"What? Wait . . . no. We can't do that," I said, sliding out of my booth and chasing after a quickly moving Ashley.

"Ash, we can't follow her," I said, grabbing her by the arm to try to slow her down. It didn't work, though. The girl was on a mission.

"Why not?" she asked, pulling her arm away and picking up the pace. I scrambled to follow.

"Seriously, Ash, what's the point?" I questioned, pulling up alongside her. Meanwhile, I still had an eye on Serene. She was just about to cross 20th.

"The point," Ashley said, grabbing me by the arm and pulling me in the direction of Serene, "is for you to get some proof. You said yourself you wished you could show Adam some proof, right?"

I nodded. It was true. I didn't have Ian, and I didn't want Adam, but I'll be damned if I lost my Dubois family. They were . . . well, family, after all.

"Then, let's go." She kept her hand on my arm and we started across 20th, keeping a good distance from Serene, which was not hard because she did have a fairly good head start.

"Wait a second." I stopped us both after we crossed the street. "There's no guarantee we will even get proof," I said, realizing this was probably a lost cause.

"We won't know unless we try," she said, grabbing me by the arm yet again and guiding me down the street in the direction of the model-witch.

We followed her for about eight blocks (not long blocks, thank goodness), and then, ducking behind a trashcan, we saw her walk into a rather large-looking brownstone house. We found a tall bush across the street where we set up camp, camera-phones ready to catch her in the act.

And that is how we came to find ourselves hiding in a bush.

"This is ridiculous," I say for the fiftieth time, even though I've got my eyes trained on the door, ready at any moment to see her make her escape . . . or just leave. Whatever.

"Shhhh," Ashley scolds. It's probably the fiftieth time she's said that. I was not meant to be a spy. Too much quiet time. Not that anyone could hear us. We are in a bush for hell's sake.

"Here she comes," Ashley gets the camera ready on her phone.

Serene comes out of the door, long legs taking the stairs of the brownstone with the grace of a gazelle. I hate her stupid long legs.

Ashley curses. "She's alone," she stage whispers.

"See," I say, echoing the stage whisper. "I knew this would be a waste of time."

"Shhhh," she says, putting a hand over my mouth. She nods her head toward the door Serene just came out of. It opens again, and out comes a man dressed in a gray suit. His hair is black like Serene's and slicked back with what is most likely a lot of product.

"It's him," I whisper. It's the guy from the café that time I caught them sucking face. I'm sure of it. He's wearing a different suit today, but the greased back hair is the same.

He walks down the stairs to meet Serene, his arm going immediately around her. He kisses her lightly on the lips. It's not an overly romantic kiss, but it's clearly not a kiss between friends.

Kissing friends . . . that makes me miss Ian. And instantly, my heart feels like the life has been sucked out of it. It does that every time I think of him.

"Start taking pictures," Ashley demands, pulling me out of my quick jump into melancholy.

I start snapping pictures with my phone, grabbing whatever I can. I missed the kiss, but maybe Ashley got it.

Serene and mystery man start to walk arm in arm down the street.

"Are we going to follow them?" I say, feeling like I don't have enough evidence.

"Of course," Ashley says, still concentrating on taking pictures with her phone.

"Well, what are we waiting for?" I say, grabbing her arm.

"Bridgette, we need them to get a little ways away, don't you think?" She looks at me, eyebrows pinched, obviously frustrated by my lack of spying skills. I can't be blamed. This is my first time, after all.

"Right," I say, nodding my head quickly.

"Okay," she says when she's decided that they're a sufficient distance away.

We exit the bush, pulling leaves and twigs out of each other's hair, and start to trail Serene and the mystery man. Only as we start to follow, they stop abruptly, which makes Ashley stop short with her arm out to block me from going forward. Before we are able to assess the situation, like good spies, Serene's lover—I guess that's what he is, after all—whistles at a taxi, which pulls over and they get in.

"Well, I guess that's over," I say, feeling slightly relieved and slightly disappointed at the same time.

"Doesn't matter," Ashley declares. "We have proof." She holds up her phone, waggling her eyebrows, grin on her face. She's enjoying this.

"Let's go back to Gram's and assess," I say, tucking my phone in my pocket.

I feel adrenaline pumping through me because of what we just did, but also for the fact that I can now help Carla and Frank. I just hope it works.

~*~

"How is this possible?" Ashley asks, looking at her phone, infuriated.

"I don't know," I say, scanning and rescanning the pictures on my phone. All of them are complete crap. Apparently, phone cameras are not suitable for surveillance. Who knew? And since this was my first, and probably last, jaunt into a career as a spy, this piece of news is pretty useless.

There's only one picture that might possibly work, and even though it doesn't show Serene doing anything wrong, it might put questions in Adam's head. I attach it to a text and send it to Carla. No way am I sending it to Adam.

"Do you think it will work?" Ashley asks, after I hit send.

"Who knows," I shrug. "But at least I tried, right?"

"If you ask me, I think you're only confirming what Adam accused you of last time you tried to bring this up," Gram says.

No one asked her.

It's true; I stalked Serene and took pictures of her. That puts me well into the crazy category. But I had a good reason, didn't I? I thought Carla was a little over-the-top when it came to her concerns about Serene, but it's pretty obvious her motherly intuition was right on. I'm merely trying to confirm that. She's definitely not marrying Adam for love. If she is, she has a sick way of showing it.

"Well, I had to do something, didn't I?" I say to Gram, trying to defend myself. "Clearly, there's something going on. I can't sit back and let her get her talons into the Dubois family without some sort of fight."

Gram shrugs. I know she's only looking out for me. After all, the last time I tried to intrude, it didn't go so well. But my intentions are genuine. There was a time when I would have done just about anything to get Adam back, but not anymore. Now, more than anything, I want to protect his family.

After Ashley leaves, I sit down in my normal spot on the couch. Gram is watching *The Young and the Restless,* and I'm trying not to get sucked into it but having a hard time. On today's episode, Heather is telling Ian to pick her, that Jessica is all wrong for him, even though Ian is already officially engaged to Jessica. Holy hell, I've got to convince Gram to find another show to obsess over.

With Ashley gone and the remnants of adrenaline taking its last jaunt through my veins, I'm starting to come down from the high. And when I don't have anything else to keep my brain occupied, that's when Ian comes back into my mind. I'm better than I was two weeks ago, I think. Actually, I'm probably not. But I'm better at finding things to get my mind off him.

"Thinking about Ian?" Gram asks. The music that comes at the end of the show starts to play, and so she can now put her attention on me.

"How did you know?" I asked, pulling my eyebrows in.

"Because you sighed."

"I did?" I didn't even realize I did.

"Yes, you've been doing a lot of that lately," she says, her elbow perched on the armrest, her chin leaning into her hand.

"Sorry," I say, not truly sorry. I've been saying that a lot lately without really meaning it.

"What's the hardest part?" she asks.

"What do you mean?" I scrunch my face again.

"What's the hardest part of all of this?" she asks.

"I don't know," I say and sigh. She gives me a quick eyebrow raise, noting the sigh. "I guess the hardest part is that it all feels so wrong. Now that I've had Ian in my life, I can't be without him. I don't want to be without him."

"Did you ever tell him that?" Gram asks.

"No," I say flatly.

"Well, then how did you expect him to change his mind if he didn't even hear the truth from you?"

I slump back in the couch. I totally pulled an Ian. I kept my feelings to myself. Mostly because of fear. Fear of rejection. Fear of embarrassment. Fear that he wouldn't pick me. Fear that I would break him and Maureen up. Fear of being *that* girl. And now it's too late.

CHAPTER 39

"Carla, you need to relax. No one is going to see you fraternizing with the enemy," I say, trying for the fiftieth time to reassure Carla that she won't get caught with me. We are in the darkest restaurant I've ever been in, seated in the very back. I'm not so sure we'd be found even if there were some sort of catastrophic event and people were *actually* searching for us.

"Well, you can never be too sure," she says, looking around suspiciously, yet one more time. Funny how Serene never worries about being seen. She just prances around the town with her lover, not thinking anyone will see her. Or maybe not caring.

"Anyway, you have something you wanted to talk to me about?" I ask, trying to get her to relax, and honestly, her neuroses are starting to wear off on me. I'm starting to feel paranoid, although I will not be admitting that out loud.

"Yes, that picture you sent me," she pauses to gulp down some wine, "how did you get it?"

"Oh . . . well . . .," I stammer, "I . . . uh . . .," I gulp down some water to gather myself. "Uh, Justin sent it to me. He . . . uh . . . saw her." I stumble, or rather *lie*. I nibble my bottom lip, grateful Carla doesn't know that little tic of mine.

305

"Oh, well, that's good." She looks slightly relieved and even slightly relaxed. "Although it doesn't matter where you got it. Adam doesn't buy any of it. Doesn't think it was even her." She sniffs and shakes her head.

I almost tell her that I know it was Serene and why I know, but she seems relieved to know (or think) it wasn't me who took the picture. Telling her the truth might only prove Adam's theory that I'm crazy and still in love with him. Which is not the case. I have a flimsy defense, though, so best not to go there.

"Anyway," she goes on, "we had a huge argument, and for a while I was uninvited to the wedding, which is ridiculous because Frank and I are the ones paying for it. We worked it all out though." She looks off in the distance, contemplative.

Crap. I didn't think that would happen. That was not one of the scenarios I had envisioned. Him not believing was certainly one (the main one), but kicking his mom out of the wedding was not a possibility in my head. It seems more likely than not, these days. Adam is clearly under some sort of spell. Yet again, confirming Serene's witch status.

Carla sighs dramatically, her shoulders slumping.

"I'm sorry, Carla," I say, knowing where the sigh is coming from.

"Yes, me, too." She looks so tired, so drained. I hope we've been wrong about Serene. Maybe when they get married she'll realize she's happier with Adam and ditch the other guy. For Carla's sake, if nothing else. I would hate to see Serene be exactly who she appears to be. This family can't be ripped apart like that. They are good people. They don't deserve it.

"Well, it's not long until the wedding," I say. "Maybe the truth will come out somehow."

"Two and a half weeks. That's all we've got," she says, "and I hope so. Desperately."

I feel so awful and useless right now.

"One good thing has come of it, I guess," she says, her frown dissipating a bit.

"What's that?"

"Well, F.J. has really stepped up," she says, staring at her wine as she swirls it around in her glass.

"How so?" I ask, intrigued.

"He's just been very supportive of me and helpful with the business. It's been nice, actually." Her lips curl up into a closed-mouth smile. "He offered to hire a private investigator to look more into Serene. Says he knows people." Her eyes convey an emotion that I've never seen from Carla in regards to F.J.: pride.

"He did?" I say, wondering why this hadn't occurred to me. Of course. A P.I. could be the answer to it all.

"Yes. But after the whole picture thing blew up in my face, I think it would be best to not." The smile disappears as quickly as it had shown up. "I'm just going to have to hope now. That's all I've got."

"Sure. I understand." I bobble my head a few times, understanding. Or trying to, at least.

"Tell me about you," she says, still swirling her wine around in her cup. "I need to not think about all this right now."

"Well, I got a promotion at work," I say, shrugging. It seem so miniscule compared to the things Carla's going through. I highly doubt it can help her get her mind off her life right now.

"Isn't that wonderful," she says. Her voice has little inflection. "You've been working for that for a long time."

"I have," I nod. "It's been a little more stressful than I thought it would be, but I think I'm getting the hang of things."

That's actually true. The past few events have gone fairly smoothly. Smooth enough, in fact, that Ursula is letting me do my own event soon. The thought makes me feel all kinds of sick in my stomach, but I have to prove I can do it so I can keep this promotion. I also want to prove it to myself.

"I remember my first job. It was for a little boutique in Queens. I had the biggest crush on the owner . . ." and just like that, Carla's back. Well, sort of. It's more of a shadow of Carla, but I'll take it. At least she can tell me stories to get her mind off everything, and I'll be here for her, as long as she needs me to be.

That's what you do for family.

CHAPTER 40

I will kill him. Actually I will cut him first and watch him bleed out. That sounds fair enough. All I know is Justin must die.

He finally sent his play over. I had to pester him about it, and he still seemed unsure, as did Ashley. But he sent it. And now that I've read it, I can't honestly believe he sent it to me. If the roles were reversed, I wouldn't have the nerve. But he did. I'm not so sure it was his smartest move.

It's a one-act play, and under normal circumstances I would probably find it funny, but instead, I find it insulting and, well, basically rude. It starts out innocently enough. Scene opens with a family seated around a dinner table. Everything is calm, and they're making small talk while forks and knives clank on plates.

But when the dialogue truly begins, that's when I started to recognize this play for what it actually is: a complete reenactment of the dinner with the Dubois family, the one where Adam proposed to Serene.

I'm going to kill him.

He didn't word it verbatim, but it's close enough. Obviously, he was recording the whole scene with his mind. I thought I was taking lazy, old Justin with me to dinner. Gamer or comic book reader

Justin. Not playwright Justin. Had I known . . . but I couldn't have known, could I?

It would be one thing if I were written as this heroine who sweeps in and deals with what's being dealt to her in stride, but instead I'm written as a whiny, love-sick moron, who can't seem to grasp what's going on in front of her. And I'm not like that. Well, not like that anymore, at least.

And of course, it's getting rave reviews. How could it not? It's full of drama and ridiculousness, and I know because I lived it. I lived the whole damn thing.

I pick up my phone and text Justin.

You are dead to me.

I click send and wait for his response. If he's smart, he won't even try to stick up for himself.

My phone beeps.

Bridge, it's not personal.

I roll my eyes, even though I know he can't see me. What a guy thing to say.

I didn't need this today. It was a long morning already. I was over at the office with Ursula asking (actually begging) her to change the schedule. But Ursula was not having it, and why would she? She has no idea what's been transpiring the last few months of my life. Even if I tried to explain it to her, I doubt she would care. She's a practical woman.

Trivial things like managing the catering for your ex-boyfriend's rehearsal dinner wouldn't matter to someone like The Sea Witch.

My first event, by myself, is Ian's rehearsal dinner. I asked weeks ago to have it off because I wanted no part of it (call me shallow, I don't care). Apparently, other scheduling conflicts left me as the only option to run it.

I could cry. Actually, I have. And now I can add Justin's play to my list of reasons to cry.

"Do I warn him?" I ask from my normal perch on the couch. Gram is in her chair, Kindle in her lap. I've explained the whole Ian-rehearsal-dinner situation to her, but I've left out the Justin story. I'll save that for later. Knowing Gram, she'll most likely say it sounds fabulous and ask when she can go see it.

"I guess you probably should," Gram says.

"I told him last time I saw him that I would ask for it off," I say, closing my eyes, remembering his face the last time I saw it. It's not hard to recollect — he'll probably haunt my mind forever.

"What did he say?" she asks, closing her Kindle cover. She must have assumed that I'm not letting her get back to her stories quite yet.

"He said we were adults and we could be in the same room, or something like that." I lean my head back on the couch and move my forearm up and cover my eyes. Oh, woe is me.

"So then, can't you?" she asks, although her attention has moved back to her kindle.

"I guess," I say, semi-pouting. I don't want to be okay with it. I don't want to be an adult. But I guess I'm going to have to put my big girl pants on and do it. I have no choice.

~*~

"So, what did Carla say about the picture?" Ashley asks as we walk down Fifth Avenue a few days later. I needed some mindless shopping to help me stop thinking about, well, everything. Luckily, Ashley was available to join me in my shopping stupor.

"Nothing good," I say, and then let out a long, defeated exhale.

"Really?" Ashley asks, a need-more-information look on her face.

"She said Adam didn't believe it, and he temporarily uninvited her to the wedding," I say, feeling useless and downtrodden by the whole thing. I probably should let it go. It's going to happen. There's nothing I can do about it.

"Oh wow. I wasn't expecting that," Ashley says, looking down at the sidewalk as we continue walking through the crowds in the noonday sun.

"Yes," I say, "unexpected things will happen until you stop meddling. Well, I'm done with the meddling business."

"Yeah," Ashley concedes with her tone. "I guess you're right. He hasn't believed you so far. Probably nothing will make him believe you anyway. He's really whipped, isn't he?"

"You could say that," I say. "Can we talk about something else?" I'm sick of thinking about it.

"Have you heard from Ian?" she asks, a small smirk on her face.

"Seriously?" I eye her with irritation, and she laughs.

"Okay," she says, slowly. "What about Justin? Have you forgiven him?"

"No," I say indisputably.

"Really?" she asks, frustration in her voice.

I roll my eyes. "No, not really," I say. "I don't want to forgive him, but I guess I have to."

"Good," she says.

"Couldn't he at least change my fake name? Why did my character have to be named Buffy? There are other 'B' names out there, you know."

"I'm not sure he intended to have your name start with the same letter. It just worked out that way," she says.

"Yes, well, if you ask me, it worked out a little too well." I give her a frown.

I've made my peace with it and with Justin. Now I just have to hope he doesn't get accepted into the festival. With my luck, though, he'll get in, and it will be the featured play.

Ashley's phone beeps, and she pulls it out of her back pocket. She stares at the screen, and a huge smile spreads across her face.

"What is it," I ask, peering over at her phone, but I can't see anything.

She holds it out in front of me so I have a full view of the screen. Speak of the gangly devil . . .

Justin: *I love you.*

"Oh!" My eyes go wide as I realize the impact of those three words. I had no idea they'd moved to that.

"I know," Ashley squeaks in delight.

"I have many questions," I say, my voice taking on the tone of a school teacher.

"Shoot," she says, looking down at her phone, still smiling.

"How long has he been saying it, and have you said it back, and can I be your maid of honor?" I rattle off my queries.

"Shut up," she says, whacking me on the arm. "Stop going there."

"What?" I question. "Isn't the saying, 'Ashley and Justin, sitting in a tree. First comes love, then comes marriage—'"

"Shut up!" She cuts me off, swatting me once again.

"Well, I just want you to know that I expect a dress I can wear again. Not one of those frilly yellow things that make me look like a canary. Do we have a deal?"

"Shut up," she says flatly this time.

"Okay, fine." I hold up my hands, relenting. At least temporarily.

She's still staring at her phone. "Are you going to text him back?" I ask, questioning her with raised eyebrows.

"Yes." She rolls her eyes at me. "If you would shut your mouth for a second, I will."

I make a motion of zipping my lips and stay quiet as she texts.

"What did you say?" I ask after she's hit send. I know fully well I'm stepping over boundaries here, but Ashley is my best friend, after all. I mean, there really aren't boundaries.

"Just that I love him back," she smiles slyly.

"Awwwwww," I tease, and she gives me a dirty look.

My two best friends are now in love. I have to give myself a little pat on the back. Mostly because I made that happen . . . well, I mean they had to actually like each other, but I helped facilitate. But also because even though I don't have any love in my life right now — not the romantic kind, at least — I'm truly happy for them.

CHAPTER 41

This is it. I've got my big girl pants on. Well actually, I'm wearing a pair of black trousers, a sleeveless blush-colored silk top, and a black blazer. Not typical Ursula-wear (She tends to do more polyester pants with elastic waistbands and loose-fitting floral blouses that do nothing for her tall frame and large build). I'm sure she would approve, though. Well, of everything except the shoes. Patent leather black platform pumps. Totally Louboutin knockoffs, but I love them. They are slightly risky with the four-and-a-half-inch heal, but I can handle it.

This event, on the other hand, is not making me feel so confident. Not the work. I think I can do that. The fact that it's Ian's rehearsal dinner is what makes it all so daunting. I'm feeling a mixture of emotions right now. Excited, nervous, stressed, nauseous . . . and a splash of heartbroken thrown in there as well.

This night, even if the catering part goes without a hitch, is going to suck no matter what. Watching Ian happily celebrating with his soon-to-be wife? I honestly have no experience, but I'm thinking this could be what torture is like.

Per Gram's advice, I sent Ian a text to let him know that I would be working his rehearsal dinner and added a "sorry" at the end. He texted back something about how there is nothing for me to be sorry about, and he's glad to get to see me. I wish I felt the same. It would be better if I didn't see him ever again. That's how my heart feels. It's too hard.

I tear up a little at the thought, as I've been doing for the past week.

"Bridge, I need —"

Justin cuts off as he sees me wipe my eyes.

"Are you crying?" His brow creases as he studies my face. I avoid his eyes.

"No," I sniffle.

"Bridge, it's just a job. You'll survive, I promise," he says, putting an impersonal hand on my arm for an alarming three seconds (which might be a record). No warmth, no feeling. Only a hand.

"I'm not crying," I lie. "And even if I were, it certainly wouldn't be over a job." Though, I'm pretty sure I've shed tears over work before.

"What did you need?" I ask, trying to steer him away from this pointless conversation.

"I can't remember," he declares after a few seconds of trying to remember. He stands next to me and looks over the dining area with me.

Round tables with cream-colored tablecloths, formal place settings for each guest. Large arrangements of fall flowers displayed in the middle of each table. Since the first day of fall is only a couple of days away, I'm guessing Maureen wanted an autumn theme. This is my favorite time of year. I love the changing colors and the crispness in the air. I think if and when I get married, I would have wanted fall colors for my wedding. But not now Maureen has stolen it from me. So, it suddenly feels tainted.

I blink away tears. This should be my wedding. I should be marrying Ian. I thought I could handle managing this event, but I'm thinking this was a huge mistake. Not that I had any choice in the matter. I guess I better suck it up; there's no going back now.

"You ready?" Justin asks as he hip checks me.

"Nope," I declare, staring straight ahead, still blinking away tears. I hip check him back, so he doesn't look at me and ask me, yet again, if I'm crying.

"Well, you better be," he says, hip checking me again.

"Ouch!" I turn to him, the tears blinked all the way back at this point. "You have the boniest hips, ever," I say, rubbing my side.

"Well, Ashley likes my hips," he says, with a double eyebrow lift at his insinuation.

"Gross," I say flatly.

I take a deep breath in as I look around me. Everything looks great, even if I hate what it represents. It's a smaller space, for only about forty people or so. If forty people are coming to the rehearsal dinner, I can only imagine how many people are coming to the actual wedding tomorrow. I'm just grateful I won't have to be a part of any of it. Ian and Maureen are getting married at Gotham

Hall, which was probably a gazillion dollars, and — thank goodness — comes with its own catering.

"The food's here," Alyssa, one of the servers working tonight, tells me.

I go to the staging area and make sure everyone is getting things ready. Everything appears to be running smoothly, which can only mean one thing — something is about to explode, fall apart, or break. It's just the nature of the beast that is catering.

Of course, like clockwork, or because I just jinxed myself, an entire tray of salads is suddenly on the ground.

Derek curses. "Sorry, Bridgette," he says. He starts to clean it up and the others pitch in.

"Just trial by fire," I say as I walk over to assess the damage. Luckily, you never show up to a catering gig with the exact amount of food needed, or this would be a catastrophe. I ask one of the prep cooks to re-plate the tray.

As far as crises go, this was on the smaller scale. I can handle the small stuff. Here's to hoping things don't get any worse than that.

The rehearsal dinner attendees start to arrive promptly at seven. Butterflies take flight in my stomach every time someone comes through the door. I see Maureen's parents arrive. Her dad with his coifed hair and bleached teeth, and her stepmom looking more like a trophy wife. She's showing a lot of cleavage for the mother of the bride, I would say. If Gram were here, she'd offer a tsk in disdain.

319

Next to arrive are Ian's parents. I wish I had the kind of relationship with them where I could just walk up and give them a hug or something. They're an extension of Ian, and because of that, I feel drawn to them. But I've only met them once or twice back in college. Tonight, I'm only the catering manager, not the girl who used to date their son and is still in love with him.

Another person, who is not Ian, comes through the door. I feel like I need him to get here so we can get the awkwardness over with. I'm not sure what to expect. A smile from across the room? A handshake? A hug? Whatever it is, I need it to happen so I can go back to getting my job done and getting this night behind me. The anxiety I'm feeling about seeing him is making me crazy and slightly paralyzed, as if I can't do anything until that part is over.

There's not much that needs to be done at this point. The water poured, the wine bottles uncorked. Once everyone is seated, we will begin salad service, and then the rest of the evening should go as I carefully, painstakingly planned out. I wrote up an entire schedule and put it on a large cardboard poster and hung it near the door of the staging area. I don't know if we will stay totally on track, but it's my hope. I'm also hoping it will work, so I can present it to Ursula as an idea for all of our events. The current system involves her barking orders from a schedule known only to her. The other two assistant catering managers have taken her lead. I'm hoping to change things up a bit.

As soon as this weekend is over, all of the man drama will be out of my life, and I will be able to focus solely on my job. It's taken me a lot of work to get here, and I'm going to put all of my focus on doing the best job I can. I just need to make it to Sunday.

As I turn to check that everything is ready in the back, for the thousandth time (I'm not even sure that's an exaggeration), in walks Ian, followed by Maureen. I won't lie . . . there were scenarios (or fantasies) going through my head earlier in which Ian came through the door alone, devastated that Maureen dumped him. Or that she died on the way here. I'm ashamed of the latter fantasy. But I can't help my thoughts, even though I *did* entertain the notion for longer than I'd want to admit.

But here he is with Maureen, and they look happy and healthy and ready to get married tomorrow. Everyone applauds them as they enter, and my stomach plummets. The butterflies are replaced by hollowness. I feel empty.

I glance up to see Ian looking at me, and I give him a small half smile, and he gives me a tiny nod. I can see a touch of sadness in his eyes. Maybe it's melancholy. Regardless, it's a silent conversation, but the message is clear: this is awkward. Maureen gives me a little wave, and I wave back. With the initial encounter over, it's time for me to put on my manager hat and get this party started.

I go to the back, but before I open the door, I close my eyes and take a big breath. This is going to be a hard night for so many reasons. But I can do this. Hopefully.

I already gave everyone a little pep talk before we started. Something else I'd like to incorporate into how we run events. Ursula only talks when she needs to yell at us for something, so I'm thinking pep talks are not her forte. But if it makes a difference, maybe she can learn? Doubtful. But it seemed well received tonight, so I'm running with it.

Everyone is doing their jobs and I stand in the staging area as everyone works around me. I've delegated and managed to the point of near perfection, so I look for something else to supervise. I go over to the food case and monitor the temperatures to make sure nothing will get dry. I'm quite sure the prep cook is taking care of it, but seeing as I don't have much to do at this point, I'm feeling not very useful. Also, I have no idea what I'm even looking at. Note to self, I probably need to have the chefs and cooks explain all this stuff to me, so I don't get caught sans kitchen knowledge.

With everyone busy around me, and me fidgeting with a machine I know nothing about (I'm not changing any of the settings or anything, I'm just looking at it), I'm finding it hard to focus on anything but Ian. This was not the plan. I need to keep my mind on my job so I can make it through this night.

Since everything is going well in the kitchen, I decide to go out to the dining area and make sure everything is running smoothly there. I take another deep breath before I go out. Time to see the happy couple in all their wedding bliss.

The tables are full of people chatting with one another. Jazz is being played over the intercom at just the right volume. It's a beautiful scene, really. With the lighting and music and the décor. Everyone is happy and jovial and behaving as they should before a wedding.

Everyone but Maureen and Ian, that is.

I know Ian well enough to know the look on his face. He's not happy. I hide near the bar to make sure everything is okay. Which is just a nice way to say I'm spying.

They're trying to look happy, but Ian's smile is fake, and they keep turning to each other and making small comments. At one point, Ian says something that makes Maureen's eyes go wide, and then she looks away from him and exhales in frustration. A millisecond later, she's smiling and asking the grandmotherly woman to her left if she's enjoying her salad. Wow, great recovery. It must be the lawyer in her.

Ian gets up and excuses himself, saying he has to use the bathroom. He quickly glances over at me and gives me a weak smile.

Do I follow him? No, that's ridiculous. What am I going to do? Stand outside the bathroom and wait to ask him if everything's okay? A tingle of embarrassment shoots down my spine as I picture doing just that. I must be crazy. Anyway, I'm sure he's fine. Nerves are probably tense right now. I'm sure everyone fights the night before their wedding. I wouldn't know, of course, but it makes sense.

The salad plates are cleared, and we're getting ready to serve the main course. No sign of Ian. Someone stands up to make a toast, but Maureen quickly shakes her head then tilts it to the side, briefly acknowledging the empty seat next to her.

Maybe I should go after him. *No. Don't be ridiculous.*

I wonder if I should wait for Ian before I start the dinner service, but I try to think of this like any other event, not the rehearsal dinner of the person my heart belongs to. Under normal circumstances, I wouldn't even notice the groom was missing and would start serving. So I go to the back room and direct everyone to start taking out the plated dinners. Salmon, steak, and vegetarian plates are loaded on trays and go out the door.

I peek into the dining room, and Ian is back. I see him grab Maureen's hand and squeeze it just once. They look at each other, apologetic smiles all around. And just like that, whatever was wrong, is right again. Or at least they're able to put it away for the moment.

I don't want to admit that I was slightly happy when I saw them fighting, but I would be lying if I didn't. Happy isn't the best word. More like, hopeful. That's probably not the best word to use either. I'm a mixture of emotions right now. But none of it matters.

I will be glad when it's Sunday, and all of this is behind me. Adam will be married. Ian will be married. I will be . . . by myself. But standing on my own is going to be okay. I can do that. This feeling of helplessness with Adam and his family, and heartbreak with Ian—Sunday will be the first day that's all in my past. And even though it may take a while to get over the Ian part of it, I can at least begin to accept reality and start the process of moving on.

I suddenly feel small tingles of butterflies in my stomach at the possibilities. Of course, they are completely smashed when I hear someone making a toast to Ian and Maureen and how their love "knows no bounds" and is "everlasting." Gag.

I go into the back to hide from all the love and happiness. I putter around in the kitchen until the toasts are over and dinner has been cleared off the tables. All that's left are desserts and coffee. We're almost done, near the home stretch.

I walk out to the dining area to make sure everyone is doing their job right. So far tonight, I haven't had anything to complain about. Maybe it was my pep talk. Maybe it's due to the fact that it's a smaller event, and I have a smaller crew, so fewer worries. Whatever it is, I'm grateful my first experience as the event manager has gone better than I expected.

Deciding I should sneak out for a little bathroom break while I can, I walk toward the exit. But as I'm about to head out the big, wooden doors to the ballroom, the heel of my shoe catches on something, and in a flash, I'm down, my ankle twisted beneath me. Apparently, my fall was accompanied by a small scream because when I look up, all eyes are on me, and Ian is right there to help me up.

"Are you okay?" he asks, worry in his eyes.

"Yeah." I sit up and look at my ankle. I rub it with my hand. It feels a little tender, but definitely not broken.

"Let me help you up," he says. Reaching his hands down, he grabs mine and pulls me to standing.

Heat surges through my hands with his touch, and my heart goes pitter-patter. I try to steady my breath.

"Are you sure you're okay?" he asks.

"Yes," I say. My ankle will survive, but my heart may not. I put weight on the ankle, and a wince slips out.

"Come on," Ian says. He puts my arm around his neck, one of his arms around my waist, and guides me out the door to the couch in the lobby.

As we leave, I swear I hear a few "aws" and "isn't he terrific." If they only knew who he was helping. At least Maureen knows who I am, but she doesn't *really* know.

"Thanks," I say as Ian eases me onto the couch.

"I'm just going to run and get some ice," Ian says, standing.

"Ian," I say, my voice thick when I say his name. The tears linger, waiting to reappear.

"Yeah?" he asks, turning back from going to get the ice.

"Is everything okay?" I ask, feeling sheepish for even going there, but I do want to make sure he's okay.

"I saw you and Maureen, um, earlier." Oh yes, I sound like a stalker. "You didn't seem, uh, thrilled," I add, piling on the stalker evidence. I look down at my hands, feeling silly for even prying. But in my heart of hearts, I do want to know. I want him to be happy. Even if it's not with me.

"Yeah," he says, traces of a frown on his face. "Everything's great." His frown lifts to a hint of a smile. I know he's lying, but I don't say anything. "I'll be right back with the ice." He pats my ankle lightly.

"I should have told you," my mouth says, unexpectedly. Where did that come from? Crap.

"Huh?" he asks, turning around again and looking at me. "You should have told me what?" He furrows his brow.

"Um," I swallow hard. What am I doing?

"Bridge, tell me," he says, sitting down at the end of the couch by my feet.

I let out a long shaky exhale. "I should have told you," I close my eyes because I can't look at him. This is poor timing, I know. But I can't help myself.

"I should have told you I loved you that night," I say and then look up to see his face, which looks ashen, as if the life has been sucked out of it.

"What?" he says, his voice so quiet I barely heard it.

"I'm sorry, for so many things," I go on. "But one of my biggest regrets was that I never told you I loved you that night before you left me, before you left for London."

"Bridgette—"

"I know," I swallow hard, "this is total crap timing. But seeing you again, spending time with you, I realized that I never stopped loving you. And I know I'll probably never see you again after tonight, but I wanted you to know."

This is not at all how I envisioned this night going. My heart is pounding in my chest at the words I've just said to him—words that should have been said so long ago—and my mind is racing, trying to figure out why I chose right now to say this.

Ian looks at me. "Are you serious right now?" he asks. Fire burns in his eyes and I know immediately he's angry.

"I'm sorry," I plead with my voice, "I don't know why I'm telling you this now." I look down at my hands, trying to find feelings of shame, but I don't feel shame. I feel brave. Stupid, but brave.

"Bridgette, this is really terrible timing seeing that my fiancée is sitting in the next room." He spits out the word fiancée.

Without warning, tears come quickly and run down my face.

"I know," I say, sorrow in my voice. "I'm so sorry. I shouldn't have told you."

Ian curses. He stands up and starts pacing in front of me. "I'm getting married tomorrow, Bridgette. I'm going on my honeymoon to freaking St. Thomas on Sunday." He runs a hand through his dark hair, tousling it. I can't say this is how I expected him to react because I had no idea I was going to say what I said. But this seems about right.

"I know," I say again, my voice thick as the tears keep coming. "I'm sorry. I'm so sorry," I say in a whisper.

"Me, too." Ian nods his head. I can practically see the steam coming off his burning face. It's London all over again, but this time I'm actually telling him that I love him, but he's still going to leave.

"This was selfish of me," I say, wiping the tears away with the back of my hand.

"Bridge," he says, his voice different. I look up, and there's a smidgeon of kindness in his eyes. Maybe even some forgiveness for my ridiculous timing. He sits down at the end of the couch again. He looks at me. Our eyes meet, and something flashes in his.

He loves me, too. Ian still loves me.

"Ian." I sit up toward him and grab his hand, heat shooting through me when we touch. We keep staring at each other, our breathing heavy. I see on his face that his mind is working, thoughts swirling through his head. I want to know what they are.

"Ian?" Maureen says from the doorway of the ballroom, breaking the spell between us.

How long has she been standing there? What did she hear?

"Maureen," Ian says, dropping my hand and standing quickly from the couch. He looks guilty. We probably both do.

"Is everything okay?" She eyes us both suspiciously.

"Yes," Ian says, then rakes a hand through his hair. "Everything's fine."

"Are you okay?" She peers curiously at me, and I'm sure shame is written all over my face. I can only hope it's covered up by the tears falling in rapid succession.

"Sorry," I squeak out. "The pain has gotten worse," I say. The pain is definitely worse, but not in my ankle.

"Everyone is wondering what's taking you so long." She looks at Ian, suspicion still in her eyes.

"Right." Ian shakes his head quickly. "I was just helping. Let's go back inside. I'll send someone out with ice," he says without looking back at me.

He grabs her hand, and they walk back inside.

What was that? Something definitely happened. Like something profound. I saw it in Ian's eyes. Maybe it was horrible of me to tell him right now. Or maybe . . . maybe he knows now he's making a mistake.

330

My heart plummets into my stomach as I realize that sort of thing only happens in the movies. And this is most certainly not a movie. More like a nightmare. The man of my dreams is marrying someone else.

My brain will eventually accept it. I know this. My heart, though, may never.

CHAPTER 42

"Rise and shine, buttercup," Ashley says, waking me from a slumber that took a ridiculous amount of time to find.

"Go away," I say, words muffled from underneath a pillow.

"No can do," she says. I feel her sit down on the bed next to me. "I have plans for us today. Fun plans. Just-you-and-me plans," she adds, nudging me with her elbow.

I smell coffee. I pull the pillow away from my head to see that she has two large cups labeled "Starbucks." I sit up and, without words, grab one of the cups from her and take a sip. The hot liquid seeps down my throat, waking me up.

Waking up, though, comes with consequences. I'm now conscious on a day when I would rather be sleeping. September twenty-first is here. The day of the weddings.

I hate weddings.

I take a deep breath, blinking my eyes to bring them into focus.

"So, do you want to know what we're doing today?" she asks, and then takes a sip of her coffee.

"If it doesn't involve sedation of any kind, then I want no part of it." I push my two pillows up against the headboard and lean back.

"Nope, no sedation. Sorry. But I'm sure we could find some. This is New York, after all," she says.

"Don't you need to be at rehearsal?" I ask, pulling my eyebrows together.

"I'm off today, lucky for you," she says, a mock-condescending look on her face.

"Yes, lucky me," I say, with as much sarcasm as I can muster. "Fine, what's the plan?"

"Well, first, I thought we would get a mani-pedi," she says, ticking off the ideas on her fingers. "Then I thought we would catch a movie, not —" she cuts me off with her hand when she sees the objection on my face. Her gesture also stops the protest that was about to cross my lips. "Not a chick flick. Something with no love or romance in it at all. We'll call Justin and have him give us some options."

"Ugh," I declare. Justin's picks most definitely won't have romance, but I doubt I will leave the theater happy.

"Do you want to hear the rest or not?" she asks, her head tilted to the side.

"Fine." I roll my eyes. "Go ahead."

"Then, I thought we could do a little shopping," she says, with a double eyebrow raise.

"Now you're talking," I say, sitting up a little bit. I could do some major retail therapy damage today.

"And then we'll see where the day carries us. The future is bright." Her smile reaches her eyes, and I know she means more than today.

Unfortunately, my future looks bleak at the moment. Lonely and depressing, actually. I sink back into my pillows and wish once again that I could just sleep the day away.

"Get up." Ashley nudges me with her hand. "Come on, get dressed, and let's go."

I resolve to the fact that she will probably not take no for an answer, so I throw out a "fine" and get out of my bed.

Ashley goes out to the living room to sit with Gram while I get ready for the day. After a quick shower, I throw on a floral dress that lands slightly above my knees and grab a cropped jean jacket in case it gets a little cool. It's been unseasonably warm for this time of year, but the nights are starting to feel a little nippy.

I wrap my ankle for extra support, even though it's feeling a lot better this morning, and wear brown leather wedges that are surprisingly comfortable. I just hope Gram doesn't notice and makes me put on flats. I don't think I could survive the day in plain old flats.

"You look lovely," Gram lies as I come out the door.

My outfit might be cute, but I saw my face in the mirror. My eyes are puffy and red and look lovely against my lackluster skin tone. I sort of look like death. I also feel like it, so that makes sense.

"Well, thanks for the chat," Ashley says to Gram as she stands up from the couch.

"A pleasure, as always," Gram says from her favorite chair. "Have a fun day today, you two," she says, her eyes smiling.

"See you later, Gram." I walk over and plant a kiss on the top of her head.

"Oh wait," Gram says as I start to walk away.

"Yes," I turn around.

"Can you help me with the DRV thing?" she asks, a look of frustration on her face.

"You mean the DVR?" I ask, a small smirk on my lips. She can't even get the name right, much less use the darn thing.

"Yes. I want to watch *The Young and the Restless* from yesterday. I haven't had a chance to watch it yet." That's Gram for you. Can't even miss a day. I'm totally over that show. It's like watching my current life on television. No thank you.

"Sure," I say and she hands me the remote. I press a few buttons and within seconds the opening music for Gram's favorite soap opera fills the room.

"I'm so excited for this episode," she says, her face turned toward the TV. "I think Jessica's going to try to stop Ian's wedding."

Her eyes go wide as she turns to look at me and Ashley.

"Don't worry, Gram, I can handle it," I say before she can apologize. It was an honest mistake.

I can't lie, though. The words "Ian's wedding" did make my heart sink and my stomach drop. Whatever smidgeon of an appetite I did have is surely gone now.

My phone beeps, and I reach down into my purse and pull it out.

Sorry.

Ian. His ears must be burning.

My heart rate jumps. He's sorry? Why is he sorry? I'm the one who should be sorry. And why is he texting me? It's his wedding day.

I show the phone to Ashley and Gram. Ashley gasps. I take the phone back and type.

Me too, I text back.

"What did he write back?" Gram asks, now with full attention on me, the television muted.

"He hasn't had time to write back yet, Gram. Or maybe he won't." Just as I say it, my phone beeps.

We really messed things up, didn't we?

Messed things up? You could say that.

Yes. We did.

I hit send.

Gram, Ashley, and I are all crowded around my phone, waiting for another text from Ian. The phone beeps, and we all jump.

The text is not from Ian this time. It's from Justin.

Is this chick for real?

I look at Ashley, and the confusion on her face reflects mine.

"What chick is he talking about? What's Ian talking about?" Gram asks, looking back and forth between Ashley and me.

"Not Ian, Gram. Justin," I say, looking at my phone.

"You kids and all your texting, in my day we—"

The beep of my phone cuts her off, and we all gather around. This time it's a picture. A snapshot of Serene with that same guy, in the same back booth at our favorite café. She's wearing sunglasses and a canvas-colored fedora, but it's her alright.

Isn't she supposed to be getting married today?

Another text from Justin. I text him back, confirming that she does, indeed, have vows on her agenda—in just a few hours, in fact. The wedding is scheduled for two this afternoon.

"Wow, she's got a lot of nerve, going out on the day of her wedding," Gram says. She shakes her head, incredulous.

I wish you would have told me sooner.

"Ian," I say, showing the phone to Gram and Ashley. My heart practically leaps out of my chest at his text and tears instantly fill my eyes. Gram puts a hand on my back, a gentle rub to comfort me.

Me too, I text back.

I close my eyes, and tears roll down my cheeks.

Be happy.

Be happy? I don't want to be happy. Not without him. I don't care how dramatic that sounds.

I move over to the couch and sit down. Ashley sits next to me, and Gram goes back to her chair.

"Well, I think that's just a rotten thing to do, him texting you like that on the day he's going to get married. If you ask me, it sounds like he's having second thoughts," Gram declares, all indignant.

"What? No," I say, looking down at the screen on my phone. But my heart picks up pace at the thought, which may not be good. It was already racing.

The television unmutes, and Gram looks frantically around for the remote, only to find that she's sitting on it.

"If any person has reason to believe that this union should not happen, let them speak now, or forever hold their peace," a man's voice streams from the television.

"*I object!*" The camera pans to Jessica, who is standing up in the back, her hand raised.

Gram, Ashley, and I are immediately glued to the television.

"*Jessica,*" television Ian says. "*What are you doing here?*"

"*You love me,*" Jessica says, now walking up the aisle toward the bride and groom. "*Don't make this mistake and marry the wrong girl,*" she declares.

"*How dare you show up here and ruin my wedding!*" Heather screams, but she's too late. There's a jolt between Jessica and Ian. As they walk trancelike toward each other and he grabs her and dips her and kisses her in front of the congregation.

Gram turns the television off after that. I look at Gram and Ashley, my eyes frantic, my mind running wild with possibilities — thoughts that should not be going through my mind right now.

"Well . . ." Gram says, trailing off.

"Well," Ashley says, standing up. "Let's go get those mani-pedis." She grabs me by the arm and drags me up to standing. She can see the wildness in my eyes, and she knows where my brain has gone.

She says good-bye to Gram and pulls me out of the apartment.

"Let's get this day started, shall we?" she asks as we leave the apartment.

I haven't said anything because my heart and my mind are going someplace that's hard to come back from.

Ian. My Ian. Marrying the wrong girl.

I know it's a stupid soap opera, but what if it's like some crazy sign from the cosmos? I mean, that's too weird, right? Is the universe telling me something?

Ashley knows exactly what I'm thinking. She yammers on, trying to keep the focus away from weddings and men, and I'm barely listening to a word she's saying. I'm not even paying attention to where we're going. I'm on autopilot, just following her. When I finally take in where we are, I see we've somehow made it to the subway. I have no recollection of getting here.

We get on the train and both take open seats toward the back of the car.

My phone beeps just as I sit down. I look at the screen.

Gross.

Justin. A picture follows. Serene and the mystery dude making out. Gross, indeed. My stomach turns. Not just because of the picture, but because I know I need to do something.

There are two weddings today—two weddings that shouldn't happen.

I show the picture to Ashley, and she shakes her head and rolls her eyes.

"Ashley," I say, looking her in the eyes. "I have to do something."

She shakes her head because she knows me so well. She knows what I want to do without my having to say it. And even though she knows she should talk me out of it, she realizes she can't.

"I think we're gonna need reinforcements," she says, pulling out her phone. She sends a text, and four stops later, when we walk up the stairs from the subway, Justin is waiting there for us.

"What're you making me do now, Reynolds?" Justin asks, a smirk on his face.

"Bridgette needs to stop two weddings," Ashley says to him, answering for me. I didn't even tell her I was also thinking about Ian's wedding, too. She knows me well.

"What are we waiting for?" Justin asks, rubbing his hands together like this is something you do every day.

But this is not something you do every day, and I have no idea what I'm doing.

"Where is Adam getting married?" Ashley asks, her smart phone in hand.

"Um . . ." I rack my brain trying to remember where Carla said the reception was going to be. "It's in Jersey. Somewhere in Jersey."

"Well, that only narrows it down to a billion places," Justin says, rolling his eyes.

"Not helpful," Ashley says, squinting her eyes at him.

"Okay, hold on," I say, putting a hand to my forehead, "let me think."

We stand there in the middle of the sidewalk, Ashley with her phone ready to go once I remember the name. People walk around us, not even taking care to notice us. They just keep walking.

Think, Bridgette, think.

"I've got it," I yell, and get a few inquisitive glances from strangers. "Park Savoy," I say, fast and breathless.

"Really?" Justin says, looking confused. "I would have thought they'd do something big, like the Waldorf or something."

"Justin, have you ever been to the Park Savoy?" Ashley asks, an eyebrow raised in his direction.

"No," he says flatly.

"Trust me, it wasn't cheap."

While Ashley is looking up the address for Adam's wedding, I pull up the web on my phone and type in "Gotham Hall," hoping they post their events, so I can find out the time of Ian's wedding.

"I have an address," Ashley says, pulling it up on her phone's map app. "Now where is Ian's?" She looks to me.

I give her the address, and she puts it into the map.

"What time is Adam's wedding?" she asks, once she has the maps pulled up for both locations.

"Two o'clock," I say, looking down at the time on my phone. It's twelve thirty.

"And what time is Ian's?" she asks, looking at me.

I search Gotham Hall's site looking for a listing of events, but of course I can't find anything.

"I can't find any information," I say, my heart sinking.

"Never underestimate the power of the Internet," Ashley says, typing like a madwoman into her phone.

"Got it," she says loudly, after a few minutes of furious searching.

She looks up at me, sadness written all over her face. "Ian's wedding is at two o'clock."

My heart sinks. They're at the same time. Of course they are.

We all stand there in silence. My mind is doing the math. If I left right now and got to Adam's wedding in time to out Serene, I could rush back and hopefully catch Ian before he goes down the aisle. I look at the clock on my phone. It's now 12:45. I couldn't even make the round trip.

"What are you going to do?" Ashley asks, her eyes full of worry.

"I don't know. Maybe give up?" A small laugh escapes my lips. I must be crazy to think I could do something like this.

"The way I see it is you have to make a choice," Justin says. "And you have to make it fast." He looks at his phone.

Right. I can't intervene with both weddings, but I can try with one. "Which one?" I look between Ashley and Ian.

"That's for you to choose," Ashley says, a slight shake to her head because she can't help me do this.

"Okay, um." I try to get my brain to move quickly, and it's a scrambled mess up there. "Let me think." I pace around the small area of the sidewalk where we've been camped out.

"I think you need to think of the pros and cons to each situation and then decide," Ashley says.

"I don't have time to do that," I exclaim.

"Then don't think about it. Go with what your instincts are telling you."

"My instincts, right," I say, searching my instincts. But I don't have to search too hard. The answer has been there, and I know what I need to do.

"I know which one," I say, nodding my head fast.

Ashley looks at me. "Then let's go."

CHAPTER 43

Am I really going to do this? *Breathe, Bridgette, just breathe.* The butterflies in my stomach are making flying circles. I fidget in my seat, and the person to my left gives me a look that says, "Please stop."

The ceremony was already starting when we got here. Ashley and Justin are outside waiting for me. We couldn't all come in, and they had to create a diversion for me to even get inside. I obviously didn't have an invite, and I'm completely underdressed.

I rest my hands in my lap and try to keep calm and still my shaking legs, but it's difficult. *Get to the part, already.*

And then the preacher says it.

"If anyone knows of any reason why these two should not be married, speak now or forever hold your peace," he says, looking out the attendees. A formality that is said, but rarely acted upon, and here I am about to act. If I could just get out of the seat.

I have to do this now. Right now. If I don't, I will regret it. At least I think I will. Maybe I will regret doing this. But there's no way to know unless I try.

I stand up, clenching my fists to give me strength. "I object!" I say, feeling like I'm having an out-of-body experience. I can't believe I just did that.

Suddenly, two hundred heads turn toward me.

"What?" Adam says, looking out into the crowd. He spots me, and his shoulders slouch. "You've got to be kidding me. Bridgette, what the hell are you doing here?"

Both he and Serene look as if they could kill me. The officiant looks confused. I doubt he's ever had this happen to him.

I move from my seat and out to the aisle, apologizing profusely for stepping on toes and bumping knees as I go. Whispers and gasps run through the crowd. Camera phones start appearing everywhere. I walk slowly up to the front. I see Carla and Frank and F.J. seated on my left. They all are slack-jawed. Actually, that's the look I'm getting from pretty much everyone. I recognize many faces—extended family members I had met during the two years Adam and I were together.

I look over to my left, the bride's side, which is poorly populated to say the least. In the back I recognize a face. It's him. The guy from the café. Did she seriously bring her lover to her own wedding? That's sick. I mean, really sick. It makes my resolve stronger.

It's also helping that the slacked-jaw has now been replaced by something else on Carla. Now she has a more hopeful look on her face. She's silently cheering me on. Frank, too. F.J. even looks like he's hopeful.

"You can't marry Serene," I say, defiantly. I try to ignore that everyone's eyes are on me.

"Bridgette, this is ridiculous," Adam says. Dropping Serene's hands, which he was still holding, he steps off the podium and starts walking toward me. Venom is practically pouring from his face. He is pissed.

"It's over between us. Don't you get that? Get out of my wedding," he says loudly. He looks around the room. "Can someone please escort this woman out?" He looks toward the crowd. "She's obviously crazy."

"No!" I exclaim. "I'm not crazy. You can't marry Serene. She's been cheating on you," I say from the aisle where my legs are planted and can't seem to move anymore.

"You've already tried this tactic, Bridgette." He gives me a condescending look. "Please, you need to go." He pleads with me.

"Adam, I have proof," I say, holding up my phone. I look to Serene and her eyes are practically bugging out of her face. My feet finally unroot themselves, and I walk toward him with my phone in hand.

Adam looks at me, and for a second, I think he won't even look at the picture on my phone, that he'll escort me out himself. But something flashes in his eyes. It was quick, but I caught it. There's doubt there.

He grabs my phone and looks at it. His eyes go wide with disbelief. There's no mistaking the picture Justin got with his phone this time.

He pivots his body to Serene, holding my phone up. "Serene?" he questions. "And John?" I can't see his face right now, but I can see hers. She's searching her brain for an excuse.

"It's not what it looks like," she says, frantic tones in her voice.

"You said John was a family friend," he says, swiping a hand over his face angrily.

Adam turns back toward me and points out into the crowd, right to where the other person in the picture is sitting.

"You," he says, fire in his eyes. He throws my phone to the floor and tears after him. John tries to get up from his seat and move but is unable to do it fast enough.

Then all hell breaks loose.

Adam is on John, F.J. not far behind. Adam takes a punch, and F.J. joins in. Frank runs down the aisle and is trying to pry them all off each other. Other family members join in. There's yelling and screaming coming from all around the room. A teenage kid, probably a nephew, picks up the chair he was sitting in and carries it over to join in the fight.

"I knew it!" Carla yells, and I turn my attention to her. She's walked up to Serene, and Serene looks like she's about to try to make a run for it. "I knew you were a fake," Carla screams as she takes the bouquet from the maid of honor and starts hitting Serene with it. Serene tries to get away, but Carla's relentless.

Some family members see Carla and try to get her to stop. Others grab bouquets from the bridesmaids and join in. Serene is screaming and covering her face.

I'm standing in the middle of all the chaos. It's almost like it's going in slow motion. The entire crowd is on its feet. Those not involved in the fighting have their camera phones out, taping the entire thing.

I feel a hand on my arm, and I look up to see Justin.

"Irish good-bye?" He gives me a little half smile.

I look around and realize there's not much more I can do here. I'm pretty sure I've done enough. I look down and see my phone by my feet and reach down quickly to grab it.

"Yep," I say to him, with a quick nod of my head.

He grabs me by the hand and rushes me out of the ballroom and away from the madness.

We run to Ashley, and then we continue running until we are far away. I don't even know why we are running. It's Serene and John who should be running. But for some reason, we run.

Adrenaline courses through my veins. I can't believe I just did that. I truly can't believe it.

"Hold on," I say. I lean over, trying to catch my breath.

Justin curses loudly. "That was crazy," he yells.

"That was totally crazy," Ashley says, agreeing, a half smile on her face. I think she might be impressed that I did it. I'm kind of impressed with myself.

"I know," I say. I take a deep breath. "Let's get out of here."

~*~

"So then what happened," Gram asks, sitting in her chair. Ashley and I are on the couch relaying the whole story. Justin had to go to work, so he left us after we got back into the city.

"Everyone started fighting," I say. "I'm sure the cops had to show up." I look to Ashley, and she silently agrees with me with a few quick nods of her head.

"Wow," Gram says, sitting back in her chair. She had been leaning toward us, totally lost in the tale. "So, how do you feel?" she asks.

"Well, my heart is still moving at a rapid pace," I say. My veins are still full of adrenaline. I doubt I'd be able to sleep for a while, even if I wanted to.

"I think Gram wants to know how you feel about *everything*." Ashley eyes me with concern. I think she's afraid of the answer.

Right. So not what I'm physically feeling, but what I'm feeling emotionally.

"It was the right thing to do," I say, looking at Ashley and then back to Gram. They both nod in agreement.

"And Ian?" Gram asks. Hearing his name makes my stomach plummet.

"Married." I say simply. It was a long shot with Ian anyway. I knew I could make a difference for the Dubois family. Well, I hoped I could, anyway. Of course, the plan was for me to catch Adam *before* the wedding started, but apparently the universe had other ideas.

"That was really brave of you," Ashley says for probably the tenth time. I glance at her and smile. She has a look of admiration on her face.

I know I made the right choice. Even my heart can't deny it.

CHAPTER 44

A full week has come and gone since I crashed Adam's wedding. Since then I've received the largest bouquet of flowers ever from Carla (seriously, it barely fit through the door of Gram's apartment), and even an apologetic text from Adam. He actually asked me if I wanted to go out for coffee, but I declined. I'm not assuming he wanted to jump back into a relationship with me. I think he just wanted to talk. I think where Adam is concerned, I should probably keep my distance for a while.

I found out from Carla that F.J. had hired a private investigator after all. Only, the guy wasn't able to get him any info until after the wedding. So if I hadn't intervened, it would have been a huge disaster. Apparently, Serene and John have pulled this stunt a couple of times and made quite a nice hefty sum doing so.

"Where does Carla find this stuff?" Ashley asks, her mouth full of chocolate. A huge box of chocolates also came with the flowers. I'm like a superhero to Carla Dubois. I've "saved the day" as she's told me so many times.

"I have no idea, but I think it's the best chocolate I've ever had," I say as I grab another piece and shove it in my mouth. We're sitting on the couch in

Gram's apartment after a long day of work for me and rehearsals for Ashley. Justin is on his way over.

Life went right back to normal after I stopped Adam's wedding. Not that I expected it to be any different. But after you do something as huge as that, you do sort of feel like something should be different. But I'm still Bridgette, doing the same old things. I would love to say that when the name Ian is mentioned my heart doesn't still feel like it's being ripped from my chest, but I imagine it will get better with time. It's only been a week, after all.

A knock at the door stops Ashley and me from grabbing more chocolate. I reach for the lid to the box and put it on, and we quickly hide the evidence under the couch. No need for Justin to see us gorging. Actually, the truth is, I don't want to share.

"Don't get up," Gram yells as she walks out of her room toward the door. "I'll get it. I'm already up."

"You have some chocolate in the corner of your mouth," I say, eyeing Ashley. She quickly wipes it off, muttering a "thanks" for saving her the embarrassment of getting caught with chocolate on her face.

"It's for you, Bridgette," Gram says, as she walks back in the room.

"Huh?" I question.

"There's someone at the door for you," she declares, her eyebrows raised in speculation.

"Oh geez." I get up from the couch. What's Justin playing at? I'm sure he's got some joke he wants to pull on me or something. He's so annoying.

I walk up to the door, which Gram has left cracked and yank it open.

Not Justin.

Ian.

What?

"Ian?" I say, confusion in my voice and most definitely on my face.

"Hi," is all he says. He's in jeans and a fitted gray tee shirt. A look I haven't seen on him since college.

"What are you doing here?" I step out of the door, half closing it behind me.

"I needed to find you . . . I wanted to see you," he says, his green eyes intense.

"Why?" I say, still not making any sense of this. "Ian, you're married. This is wrong."

A small half smile appears on his face.

"See, that's the thing," he says. "I didn't get married."

My eyes practically jump out of my face. "You didn't? But . . . why?" I stammer. My mind races, and my heart starts beating at a rapid pace.

"Because," he says, "Maureen and I . . . we just weren't right. I didn't see it until I ran into you. But it was meant to be. It got me to wake up. Bridgette . . ." he trails off as he grabs my shaking hands in his. Part of me feels sort of reluctant, like my mind is playing tricks on me or something.

"It's always been you, Bridge," he says, looking into my eyes. "I thought I was over you, but I don't think I ever got over you. I don't think I can. It's always been you."

"Is this real?" I say, not believing what I'm hearing and seeing at this moment. My brain is mush. I can barely get a coherent thought out of it. I can't help myself. My mind cannot catch up with what he's telling me.

I look down at his left hand, and there's no ring.

Slowly, as my brain comes to accept the reality in front of me, my mouth breaks into a smile. And try as I might to stop them, tears form in the corner of my eyes.

"I . . . Ian . . ." I try to get the words out — the right words to say at a time like this. But with my mushy brain, I'm having a difficult time even making sense in my own head. "I'm an idiot," I finally say.

Ian questions my statement with one raised eyebrow.

"I mean, I *was* an idiot. I should have told you back then how I felt about you. You have no idea how many times I've changed our past in my mind. We've lost all this time because I was scared or stupid or whatever I was." He pulls me into him, reaching up to swipe a tear off my cheek with his thumb.

"I love you," I say, and smile because I've said those three words, and finally at the right time.

With that, Ian reaches up, and tenderly caressing my face, he kisses me. It's soft and loving. A kiss that speaks volumes and jumbles up my brain even more, but in a good way. He lets go of my face and wraps his arms around me. He pulls me tight to him, and the kiss deepens.

Finally, when I feel like I need to come up for air, I pull away slightly so I can see his face again. I need to see that it's all real. Something dawns on me as I take in the sight of him. The wonderful, amazing sight of Ian standing at Gram's doorstep. *Not* married.

"Wait, how did you find where I live?" I ask.

"I scoured the Internet," he says, smiling sheepishly.

"You stalked me?" I ask, surprised.

"Yeah," he says. Unwrapping one arm, he rubs his jaw with his hand. The other arm still has me pulled in tight, as if he will never let me go. "I guess I stalked you," he admits.

"Good," I say. "Now we're even."

I grab his face with my hands and bring it to mine, kissing him as passionately as I can.

This time no one is walking away or flying off to another country.

This time it's for good.

The End

Visit Becky's website and sign up for fun giveaways and e-newletters

www.beckymonson.com

Join Becky on Facebook
www.facebook.com/AuthorBeckyMonson

Twitter: @bmonsonauthor

ACKNOWLEDGMENTS

I've decided it takes a village to write a book. Therefore, I must thank the following people for helping make this happen:

To Lori Schleiffarth, my sister, bestie, and content editor. Without your help, this book may have been a big pile of poo.

To Robin Huling, also known as my BFF. Thanks for being my styling guru and for talking me down when I needed it.

To Kathryn Biel. Thank you for helping me work through the crazies. I know I owe you chocolate chip cookies. They are totally in the mail. I swear.

To Karen Pirozzi and Chrissy Wolfe for editing and making me sound smarter than I am (quite the task).

Huge, massive, thanks to Sue Traynor for drawing the perfect cover! Your talent amazes me!

Special thanks to my siblings and extended family for being the supportive and wonderful people that they are. I love you all!

And finally, my hubby and my babies. What would I ever do without you? I love you more and more each day. Thank you for making my life complete.

Made in the USA
Middletown, DE
12 April 2019